DEATH IN
THE SCILLIES

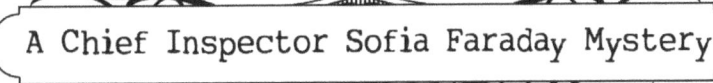

A Chief Inspector Sofia Faraday Mystery

PAULA WELCH

This edition published 2025
Copyright © Paula Welch 2025

Cover design: Donika Mishineva (www.artofdonika.com)
Typesetting and e-book design: Amit Dey (amitdey2528@gmail.com)

The right of Paula Welch to be identified as Author of the Work has been
asserted in accordance with the Copyright, Designs and Patents Act 1988.

ISBN number: 978-0-6459910-7-9 (paperback)

A catalogue record for this
book is available from the
NATIONAL
LIBRARY   National Library of Australia
OF AUSTRALIA

Other books by Paula Welch

PROLOGUE

'Stay the fuck away from her. Do you hear me, Hartnell?' Burrows gripped Hartnell by the collar and shoved him up against the brick wall.

'Yes! Now, if you're finished, remove yourself,' Hartnell demanded, not that he was in any position to do so.

Burrows let him go and walked off. He never turned around; he didn't need to. He knew the type of man Hartnell was. Airs and graces, but when you peeled off the pompous layers, there was nothing but shards of egotism. Burrows scoffed and sniffed in the sea air as he walked down the promenade. He'd missed the smell of home.

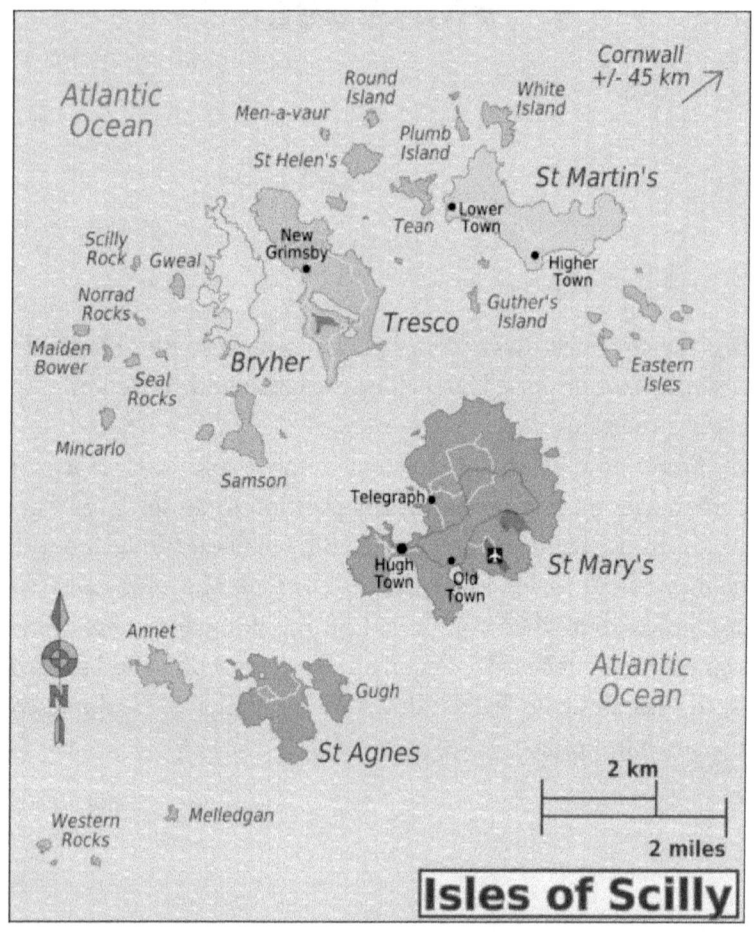

Atlantic
Ocean

Round
Island

Men-a-vaur

White
Island

Cornwall
+/- 45 km

Plumb
Island

St Helen's

St Martin's

Tean

Lower
Town

Scilly
Rock

Gweal

New
Grimsby

Higher
Town

Norrad
Rocks

Guther's
Island

Maiden
Bower

Bryher

Tresco

Eastern
Isles

Seal
Rocks

Mincarlo

Samson

Telegraph

Hugh
Town

Old
Town

St Mary's

N

Annet

Gugh

Atlantic
Ocean

St Agnes

2 km

Western
Rocks

Melledgan

2 miles

Isles of Scilly

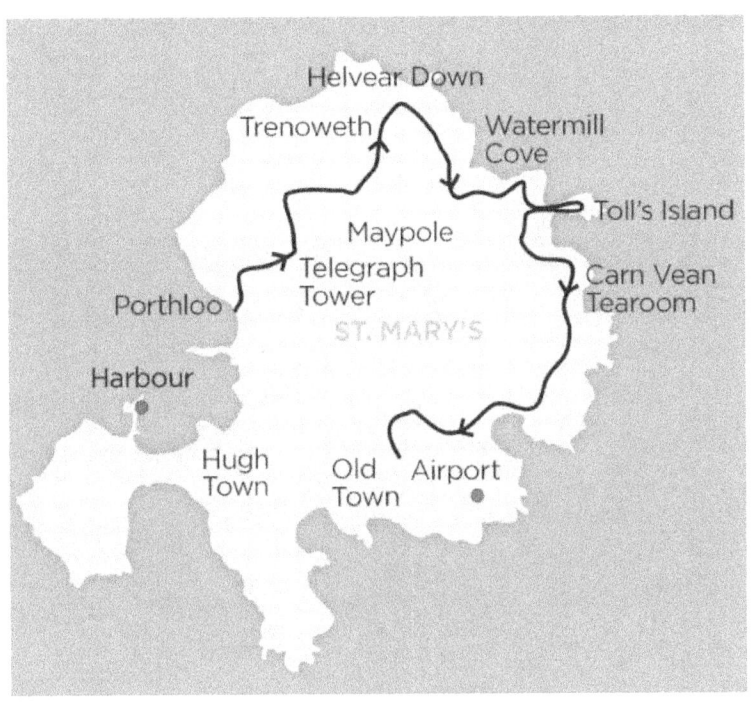

The Windermere Hotel, Porthloo

Chapter One

The Windermere Hotel, St Mary's,
The Scilly Isles
Late April

'Mrs Locke, it's your mother on the phone,' proclaimed Carrie, holding the handset to her chest.

Geraldine rolled her eyes. Her mother was persistent today. She'd avoided her mother's last two messages left on her mobile, which had obviously forced her mother to call the hotel's main switchboard. Geraldine paused to consider her options.

'Thanks, Carrie, I'll take it in my office,' she said with a sigh.

'Yes, Mrs Locke.' Geraldine walked behind the concierge desk and opened a door marked 'staff only'. She entered a corridor that led to her office. Once she was seated at her desk, she pressed the extension number blinking on the phone.

'Hi, Mum. What can I do for you?'

'Geraldine, I need to see you.'

'What's up?' she said, rolling her eyes again.

'Not on the phone.'

'I'm busy, Mum.'

'This is important, love. Something has happened, but I don't want to discuss it over the phone. I'll come to you if necessary.'

Geraldine didn't want that, but it wasn't like her mother to be so insistent. Theresa Cook had been a woman of restraint throughout her life, and Geraldine doubted her behaviour had changed spontaneously overnight. But she hadn't seen her mother since Christmas, which was four months ago. Their relationship had always been a fragile one, so the further apart they were, the better for both of them. But Geraldine hated going to the mainland, it would be a two-day round trip, and time was something she couldn't afford right now.

Geraldine sighed again, she unconsciously started to twirl her hair between her fingers. There was nothing else for it. 'Alright. I'll fly to Newquay tomorrow. Pick me up at the airport.'

'Thank you, darling.'

Summer was on its way at last. It would be the busiest time of the year for the Windermere Hotel. Geraldine cursed under her breath, then exhaled before booking her flight, relieved there was a seat left on the small aeroplane at short notice. Her flight left at lunchtime, and her return flight was confirmed for the following day. She hated losing two days' work, but flying was faster than going by ferry.

St Mary's was the largest island in the Scilly Isles archipelago. With an area of just 6.58 square kilometres, or 2.54 square miles, it made up 40 percent of the total land area of the Scilly Isles. St Mary's land mass also included four small tidal islands, which connected to St Mary's at low tide. With a population of roughly 1,700 out of a total population of 2,200 throughout the archipelago, it is the most densely populated island.

Geraldine fell in love with St Mary's the first time she came to visit her grandparents as a child. Thanks to her grandmother's bequest ten years ago, Geraldine had turned their stately home into a fashionable boutique hotel.

The Windermere Hotel was situated on the western side of St Mary's, nestled in a small bay called Porthloo. The views were very commanding, stretching out across Porthloo Beach and out to sea. Hugh Town was situated a few miles south across the bay. When the sun shone down on the Scilly Isles, it was paradise. Geraldine liked to believe its rays of sunshine beamed down just for her. She learned to like herself on St Mary's, something she had struggled with until she arrived.

Geraldine cursed again, she had much to do before she left the island tomorrow. She headed into the kitchen in search of the hotel's head chef, Claude Allard. Instead, she found a junior chef, Barbara Eyre, walking out of the freezer, carrying a side of beef.

'Hi, Barb. I need to go over the dinner menu with Claude today as I'm off island tomorrow.'

'No problem, Mrs Locke, he's just out the back having a ciggy.'

'Please call me Geraldine. It's bad enough when Carrie calls me Mrs Locke.'

'Sorry, Geraldine. Old habits. At the Mayflower in London, they were very strict on formality.'

'Well, you're not at the Mayflower now, and you've been here for nearly four months, you're practically part of the family.'

Barbara smiled at the inference. Geraldine was a thoughtful and considerate boss. So far, she had no regrets about moving to the small island. No matter how remote it felt at times.

Geraldine knew better than to disturb Claude during his break. He liked to enjoy his five daily cigarettes in peace. Geraldine was lucky to have him, although she knew he was longing to return to France. This predicament often left him moody most days. Geraldine knew he was lonely and homesick. But there was nothing she could do to fix that, although she empathised with his moodiness and distant longing.

On Claude's return to the kitchen, they sat down together in his office and discussed the specials for the week. Then he complained once again about the thefts that had occurred in his kitchen over the last month. More fish had gone missing. Geraldine suggested locking the back door in the kitchen permanently, which wasn't ideal, considering all the hotel's deliveries came through that service door, not to mention the hotel staff who liked to sit out back during their breaks.

'*Quoi* about *un* security camera?' Claude stated, slipping in and out of his native tongue.

'We can do that. I'll look into it. How much has been stolen?'

'*Un* few hundred pounds at most, but *dat* is not *da* point, Madame. It is an affront.'

Geraldine smiled at Claude's offence. She promised to look into it, she didn't like the thought of someone stealing from her, either.

Claude wouldn't hold his breath. As Geraldine got up to leave, he mumbled something about catching the culprit himself.

After the menu was sorted, Geraldine caught up with Carrie, the hotel's assistant manager and all-rounder. They spent the next hour going through the inventory of all the linen, blankets, towels, tablecloths, and even tea towels that would need to be replaced if they were past their use-by date. Then she remembered the water sports equipment needed to be serviced. Geraldine cringed as she had so much to do. She cursed for a third time. Now wasn't the time to leave on a two-day trip to Newquay to visit her mother.

With the return of summer, tourists would flood into St Mary's and the other Scilly Islands once more. This was the hotel's busiest time of the year, and Geraldine's favourite season. Geraldine would be set on full throttle throughout summer. Just how she liked it.

When Geraldine's youngest daughter Hazel came home from school, Geraldine informed her about her trip to the mainland. Carrie had agreed to keep an eye on Hazel, but Hazel had insisted she wasn't twelve anymore and didn't need a babysitter. Geraldine pecked her youngest child on her head but had no intention of leaving her alone for two days, even at fifteen.

'Dinner's ready,' Geraldine called from the kitchen. Hazel came charging down the stairs, declaring she was starving.

'I'm sorry the dinner's late tonight. I had a lot to do before I leave tomorrow.'

'Is everything alright with Nan?' Hazel asked.

'I'm not sure. She wouldn't say over the phone.'

'Maybe she's sick.'

Geraldine looked at her daughter, alarm appearing for the first time. She hadn't thought of that. *What if it's serious?* Geraldine thought. She had been estranged from her parents for many years. She had tolerated them, for the sake of her children, but their relationship had always been strained. Even after the death of her father a year ago, Geraldine still hadn't repaired her relationship with her mother. But whose fault was that?

'I'm sure she's fine, darling. She would have said.'

Geraldine quickly combed her chestnut, shoulder-length hair and applied the final touches to her make-up. She never applied much make-up, even at forty-five. Her soft, tanned complexion and subtle cheek bones emphasised her beauty. Her slim physique was thanks to her jogging, which kept her sane and fit. She stood no more than five feet six inches without heels, but she was toned, and her legs were slim. Not that she had anyone to show them off to.

Hazel went to the Five Islands Academy, like her older twin siblings Andrew and Vivienne had. But after the summer holiday, Hazel would finish her schooling on the mainland in Cornwall, as the Academy only taught children from four to sixteen. Geraldine was already pining her loss. After summer, all her children would be away at school. Andrew and Vivienne at university, Hazel in Cornwall. They always came home twice a month on the weekends. But lately, they had missed the odd weekend. Geraldine couldn't blame them; they had friends on the mainland. She would never insist that they come home, they were young and had their own lives to live.

Hazel would be coming home each weekend from school, unlike Phillip, her husband. A history professor, he lived in the halls of Southampton University during the week. But these last six months his weekend returns had grown more and more infrequent. Work commitments kept him at the university, so he said. Her family was drifting apart and her nest was emptying. Geraldine knew her children wouldn't want to live on St Mary's after they finished university. They had careers to carve out and adventures to seek. But it didn't make their absence any easier to bear. She couldn't talk to Phillip about it. When he was home, they barely spoke. To Geraldine, they were now simply ships that passed in the night, acquaintances that met fleetingly on the occasional weekend. She often wondered if he only came home to see Hazel. In quiet moments, she often reflected on their loveless marriage. How long had she felt that way? She couldn't say. Which was why she preferred to keep busy. Afforded her a greater companionship than Phillip was able to offer.

Geraldine felt a sadness sweep over her. She quickly turned away from the mirror, picked up her overnight bag, and walked out of her bedroom. She locked the annex and headed into the hotel. The annex was situated beside the hotel, and it was where she lived with her ever-dwindling family. It was two storeys, and contained three bedrooms and two bathrooms upstairs, with a living room, study, dining room and kitchen downstairs. It was comfortable enough, especially considering only Hazel and Geraldine lived there full-time now.

Geraldine found Carrie at the reception desk.

'Have a safe flight,' she said.

'Thanks. Now, call me if anything happens. Anytime. And please check on Hazel, make sure she has dinner in the dining room tonight. I don't want her eating one of her infamous chip sandwiches for dinner.'

Carrie chuckled, 'Don't worry, I'll keep an eye on Hazel and the hotel. Go! We'll all be fine.'

Geraldine smiled at Carrie. She knew she could rely on her.

As Geraldine stepped out onto the road, there wasn't a cloud in sight. She waited for the hotel's minivan to pick her up and take her to the small airport, situated close to Old Town. Nothing was very far from anything else on St Mary's. It was only a few kilometres to the airport. Normally Geraldine liked to walk into Hugh and Old Town, but today she was running late. She was glad she chose to fly to Newquay, rather than take the ferry to Penzance, as the weather report said the water would be choppy. She didn't fancy two hours and forty-five minutes of rolling and pitching all the way across the bay.

As the plane took off, and flew higher and higher, Geraldine looked down on St Mary's. The waters and sky were crystal blue around the archipelago of islands. She took it as a good sign that they would have a long, warm summer. She barely had time to read her book before the captain announced they would be arriving in Newquay shortly. An uneasiness crept over Geraldine. She wasn't sure why. Was her mother really sick? Her father had died suddenly of a heart attack when he was only seventy-one. She wished she could have mourned him better. Geraldine wondered what it would be like to be an orphan, then quickly shook the mawkish thought away.

When Geraldine exited the airport, her mother was waiting for her.

Theresa Cook climbed out of her car when she saw her daughter exit the airport terminal. When Geraldine approached, they pecked each other on the cheek. But they didn't hug.

'Well … are you going to tell me what this is all about?' Geraldine asked, once they were in the car.

'Once we get home. Not here.' The estranged mother and daughter rode in silence, except for the occasional question about Vivienne, Andrew and Hazel. This was fine by Geraldine, who preferred to look out the window as familiar sights came into view. They always brought back the same old memories.

When they walked through the front door, Geraldine was flooded with yet more sentiment. She hated coming home. Theresa walked into the kitchen and put the kettle on. Geraldine followed her. It was about time her mother told her what was so important.

Theresa placed two teacups and saucers on the kitchen table. 'Mum. What is it?'

Theresa turned to face her daughter. She couldn't put it off any longer, so she asked Geraldine to sit down across from her.

'I don't know quite how to tell you this, sweetheart. But I had a phone call last week from a young woman. She said she was your daughter.' Theresa said no more. She allowed Geraldine a moment to register what she had said.

Geraldine felt a flash of heat wash over her. She knew who her mother was referring to. Her heart pounded in her chest. She showed no emotion as she looked across the table at her mother, but on the inside, she screamed with pain. She'd dreaded that this day would come. Geraldine had never stopped thinking about her estranged daughter, not for a single day. It was a painful memory. But after twenty-five years of no contact, she assumed the child didn't want to know her. Her only prayers had been that her daughter was happy and loved.

'Why did she call you?' Geraldine asked calmly.

'After obtaining her original birth certificate, she traced you to St Mary's, but was too afraid to approach you in fear of being rejected. She also didn't want to cause you any embarrassment in case your family didn't know anything about her. So, she traced me and asked if I would speak to you on her behalf. She would like to meet you. She had always known she was adopted, since she was a child. Her parents have recently moved back up north, once they knew Harriet was settled in London. She felt it was the right time in her life to find out who she is, who you are, and who her father is. His name wasn't listed on her original birth certificate.'

Of course it wasn't, Geraldine thought. *You all saw to that.*

'Harriet. Is that her name?' Geraldine said quietly.

'Yes. It suits her.'

'How do you know that?' Geraldine looked defensively at her mother.

'She came here last Sunday. She's a beautiful young woman, and quite like you. We spoke on the phone at first then I invited her to visit. She came with her friend, Ashley. They've known each other for years and share a flat in London. She would dearly like to meet you and get to know you. I said I'd speak to you and if you agree, she'd be happy to come back here, or you can visit her in London. She has an apartment in the Isle of Dogs.'

Geraldine's elbows had been resting on the table; she slowly lowered her head and ran her hands through her hair. She often envisioned this day, but now that it had arrived, she was physically shaking.

'What if she hates me for abandoning her?'

'I didn't get that impression from meeting her. She's had a good life. I've only told her that you were very young and that it was your father and I that persuaded you to give her up for adoption.'

'Persuaded? You insisted.'

'I know you've never forgiven me, Geraldine. But please believe me, I thought it was for the best.'

'I've never forgotten how Granddad made me feel when he found out. I at least thought Nan would be on my side, but you all closed ranks. I never felt so alone in all my life.'

'I'm so sorry, love. I can't change the past, no matter how much I want to. But Harriet wants to know you. This is hard for her, too. I got the impression she would like you to be a part of her life. Do you think you can do that?'

'That's ignoble of you,' Geraldine snapped at her mother. 'Now you're worried about my feelings?'

'I'm sorry, I didn't mean it like that. I wish it could've been different.'

'You all made me feel so ashamed.'

'No. Never that. I ... I was never ashamed of you. I wish you could understand how proud I am of you, for all you've achieved. So was your grandmother, that's why she gave you Windermere Lodge. My father wanted her to sell it and put the money into his law firm. But she refused, she wasn't going to let him have a penny of it. The Lodge was left to her by her parents, and she wanted to give it to you. It was the first and only time she stood up to him. At great cost.'

'I didn't know that.'

'There's a lot you don't know about her. One day I'll tell you.'

The click of a button indicated the kettle had stopped boiling. Theresa stood up and poured the hot water into the teapot, then brought the teapot to the table. Geraldine waited anxiously for her mother to continue. Now was not the time to make tea.

Theresa retrieved the milk from the fridge and sat down again.

'Your grandfather was a difficult man to live with. He demanded obedience and loyalty from everyone around him. Which was ironic because he was a liar and a cheat.'

'Christ! How typical of him.'

'Sorry, I shouldn't have said that. Those things weren't talked about. I admired my mother very much for putting up with him. It would have been difficult for her to up and leave him. But you must believe me when I say, your father and I were only looking after your best interests. You had a chance for a bright future. I dearly wanted you to finish school and go to university. I wanted you to have what your grandmother and I didn't have.'

'You went to university.'

'Yes. But once I was married, I became a wife and mother. Your father didn't want me to work. He wasn't as domineering as your grandfather, but Winston never contradicted anything my father said or did. He admired him and wanted to be a partner in his firm. He never rocked the boat, so to speak.'

Theresa paused for a moment and poured the tea. Then she poured the milk in and added one sugar for her daughter.

'Did I make such a profound error of judgement, Geraldine? I so desperately wanted you to succeed where I didn't.' Theresa stretched out her hand and touched her daughter's, hoping she wouldn't pull it away. Regrettably, she did.

'Oh Mum! It was such a long time ago. I missed not having her in my life. But I also received a good education and now I run a lucrative hotel on an island I love. I don't know how to answer that. Too many years have passed.' Geraldine thought about her first love, Wesley Burrows, she hadn't thought of him in a while – he was another painful memory. She hated dwelling on all the 'what ifs?'

'I loved Wesley, and I knew he loved me. But when I think about how young we were, would we have lasted? He joined the navy, and I ended up owning a hotel. How different would our lives have been if we tried to make a go of it?'

'You'll have to tell him, I'm afraid. Harriet wants to meet him too.'

'I know.'

'I can do it for you. You don't have to see him,' Theresa said, a little too quickly.

'No. I'll do it. It'll be a shock, and I don't want to hurt him or his family. Besides, you never cared for him. He's married with two children, isn't he?'

'Yes.' Although Theresa had recently heard that Wesley was divorced. There was no point in keeping that secret, Geraldine would find out soon enough.

'I met Wesley's mother, Joanna in town last month when she was visiting Wesley's older brother, Samuel. We had a nice chat. All three of her children got married, but Wesley got divorced a few years ago.'

Geraldine was reminiscing as she stirred her tea. Wesley's now divorced. Too many memories were flooding back; it made her head spin as fast as her tea. She needed to meet Harriet first, before she even thought about telling Wesley. Right now, Geraldine's fears of meeting her daughter outweighed any fears of telling Wesley. But she had to address both. Would he despise her for keeping such a profound secret from him all those years?

'What if she's disappointed in me?'

'Why would she be? She just wants to know you. She needs to know. We made mistakes, Winston and I. It's divided our family for too long. I need to make things right, for both you and your brother.'

Theresa wanted to put her hand on her daughter's once again but thought twice about it. She couldn't cope with another rejection. The act was still too intimate.

Geraldine was hit with the stark realisation that she would now have to be honest with both Phillip and Wesley. Everything was converging and being pulled apart at the same time, she felt like she was riding a giant swell and was about to capsize.

When she was ready, Geraldine stepped outside and dialled the number her mother gave her. She paced the garden while she waited for the call to be answered.

Theresa Cook watched on from inside her conservatory. She desperately yearned for her daughter's forgiveness. It had been over a quarter of a century. But she feared this would reignite Geraldine's feelings for Wesley and vice versa. She didn't want either of them to get hurt … again.

The past was best left alone.

Chapter two

St Mary's

Three weeks later – mid-May

'I'm off then. Thanks for staying with Hazel,' Geraldine said to Phillip, picking up her overnight bag as she left their bedroom.

'Say hi to your mother for me,' Phillip said feebly, as she departed. This was Geraldine's fourth visit to the mainland in as many weeks. Phillip doubted his wife was visiting her mother. He had noticed a change in Geraldine over the last few weeks. Giddy with excitement one minute but cagey and aloof the next. He believed something or someone was drawing her away from St Mary's, and it wasn't her mother.

Phillip watched his wife step into the minivan. A light drizzle couldn't even dampen her spirits. He would head back to the mainland himself tomorrow, as he had only come home this weekend to stay with Hazel. The holidays would soon see Phillip back on St Mary's for the duration of summer. He wasn't looking forward to it. He wanted to return to his university life.

Geraldine barely noticed the rain falling on the window beside her. Her hazel eyes were wide with anticipation at meeting Wesley. It would be more than twenty-five years since she last saw him. The short trip into Hugh Town to catch the ferry didn't leave her much time to her thoughts. Carrie had proven herself capable of managing the hotel on her own during Geraldine's absence over the last few weekends. But she hated being deceitful to Phillip and her children. Her family would know soon enough, but for now, privacy was what she craved. She needed time to get to know Harriet and confront Wesley.

As the ferry carried Geraldine to Penzance, she gently moved in time with the swell. It was a calming continuity. She licked her lips as the salty air sprayed on her face, she felt exhilarated but anxious all at the same time. Geraldine prayed their meeting would go well. She'd replayed how their encounter would play out, over and over again, all week. But when do things ever go to plan? If her meeting with Wesley went well, she would invite Harriet to St Mary's to meet her family. She would ask her children to come home in a fortnight's time. She had already set aside a couple of guest rooms at the hotel for Harriet and her mother.

She felt alive. She felt excitement, even delirium, for the first time in years. It had been agreed that if Phillip called her mother on the landline during her visits, Theresa would tell him that Geraldine had gone for a walk without her mobile.

Regrettably, her mind drifted back to Phillip. He had enjoyed St Mary's well enough when they first moved there. Refurbishing the hotel, raising their children in paradise. But she witnessed him slowly grow restless. The hotel was Geraldine's dream and career, not Phillip's. Eventually, he accepted a professorship at Southampton University and their arrangement worked well. Away during the week and home on the weekends, but Geraldine could see over time that their needs and wants were diverging onto different paths. They appeared to have nothing in common anymore. He came home on fewer weekends, finding excuses to remain on the mainland. She often wondered if it was herself and not St Mary's that was too distant and cold for him now.

Geraldine put Phillip out of her mind; today was about Wesley. She tried to stay calm as each rise and fall of the swell brought her closer to him.

On her arrival in Penzance, Geraldine caught the train to Portsmouth. The motion of the train comforted her. She rested her head back in the seat, looked out the window and remembered her first anxious introduction to Harriet two weeks prior.

For their first meeting, Geraldine agreed to meet Harriet in Greenwich Park in London. As she sat on a park bench, waiting for Harriet to arrive, she self-consciously twirled a lock of hair, as she always did when she was anxious. Within ten minutes, a young, attractive woman approached her. She knew instantly who she was. Her heart melted.

At first, they had been shy with each other. Polite and respectful, even. They chatted together on the bench for an hour before they decided to take a walk around the park. They eventually found a café, and during lunch, they peeled away the many layers of their lives as they got to know one another. The day was as sunny as their spirits, but it passed by too quickly for Geraldine, who often caught glimpses of herself in Harriet. These mannerisms only added to Harriet's charm. The movement of her head when she laughed. The slight crook of her smile. Even how she liked to twirl her hair around her fingers self-consciously. Her mother was right; all these unspoken mannerisms made their first meeting surreal. But one inescapable likeness was Harriet's brown eyes. She had Wesley's eyes. It brought back a stirring of emotions that had lain dormant for decades.

For their second date, they agreed to meet at Harriet's favourite restaurant in London. Geraldine wasn't sure what else to call it, other than 'date'. Their clandestine meeting? Sitting across from Harriet, Geraldine was finally confident enough to take the next step.

'Look, I'm going to see your father next weekend. As I told you last weekend, he doesn't know about you, so it will be a shock for him. My parents thought it best to keep it from him, as we were so young.'

'I understand. Truly, I'm alright with the decisions you made.'

'I didn't really have much say in it.'

'It's okay. I've had a good life. My mum and dad are smashing, and I adore them. But my grandmother isn't well, that's why they decided to move back up north to be with her. So once Ashley and I found an apartment, they sold up and left. It's only a train ride to Durham. I called her the other day and told her about our first meeting. She would like to meet you one day. Once the awkwardness dies down.'

'I'd like that,' Geraldine said, insincerely. She wasn't really sure if she wanted to meet the woman who raised her daughter. A pang of jealousy gripped her. Who would Harriet love more? Who would she prefer to call 'Mum'?

'I thought about you often, Harriet. I wanted to contact you many times, but I was afraid you'd resent me. Besides, if you didn't know you were adopted, it would have come as quite a shock. I didn't want to cause you or your family any pain.'

'Same here. That's why Ashley suggested I contact Theresa first. I mean my grandmother. I'm not sure what to call her,' she giggled.

'I think Theresa will be fine. Until you're ready to call her Nan, like my other children do.'

'Alright. But are you okay with Geraldine?'

Geraldine had to think for a moment. She wanted desperately for Harriet to call her 'Mum', but that position was already taken by what appeared to be a kind and lovely woman. She knew this question would be complicated. One woman had loved her, from a distance, from the day she was born, while the other had loved her since she collected her from the hospital. Geraldine had to remind herself – small steps.

'You can call me whatever makes you the most comfortable. Look, I want you to come to St Mary's to meet my husband and children. Why don't you bring Ashley along? It might be a bit overwhelming for you, and it'll be good to have a friendly face around.'

'That would be great. I'd like to meet them. Will you tell them before I arrive?'

'Yes, of course. I'll have to tell my husband Phillip first. But I'll tell the children once they're all together on the Saturday. I think it will be better that way. I'm nervous enough. I'd rather get it over with in the one sitting, if you know what I mean.'

Harriet laughed. She did.

'I hope they'll like me.'

'I know they will.'

'What about my father?' Harriet asked. 'Do you think his children will like me too?'

'If they're anything like their father, yes.'

'I'm looking forward to meeting him. He sounds very nice.'

'Everyone will love you,' Geraldine said. 'I know my children; they'll welcome you with open arms once they meet you. I'll invite my mother too, so you'll have another friendly face. You'll be able to see where I live and why I love St Mary's so much. It's so beautiful this time of year, doubly so in summer.'

'I'd like that.'

'Wonderful. That just leaves me with the task of telling your father.'

Geraldine and Harriet spent the rest of their second date walking through London and trying to catch up on twenty-five years of history. By late afternoon, it was time to say goodbye.

Geraldine caught the train back to Newquay. Her mother wanted to know what they talked about, but Geraldine was reluctant to share her precious time with Harriet with her mother. It was private. She wanted to keep those memories all to herself.

It was now time for Geraldine to tell Wesley about Harriet, in person. A phone call would have been the coward's way. She thought he deserved to hear that he had a daughter face to face. When Geraldine contacted Wesley, he had been surprised, but not unpleasantly. Now, on the train, she kept replaying their conversation over in her head. He hadn't questioned why she wanted to meet him. He had simply agreed to meet.

Wesley was now a commander in the navy and stationed in Plymouth, so they had agreed to meet for lunch at a pub not far from the train station and close to the naval base.

'Please let him forgive me,' she whispered to herself.

When Geraldine arrived in Plymouth, she found the pub without any difficulty. Once inside, she headed straight into the bathroom to fix her hair and reapply her lipstick. She looked at herself in the mirror – she was a quarter of a century older than when she last saw him. She wondered if he would still look at her like he used to. Fear gripped her.

Phillip hung up on his mother-in-law. She was never a very good liar.

He opened his new mobile phone app and watched the little bleep moving through Plymouth. He wondered where Geraldine was going. The last few weeks had her in London – now Plymouth.

Phillip Locke wasn't about to lose everything. He had to know what his options were.

His next call was to his solicitor.

Theresa hung up on her son-in-law. She had done what Geraldine had requested, but she doubted Phillip believed her. She put the kettle on but heard the doorbell chime. She walked out of the kitchen and peered through the sheer curtain to see who it was.

She smiled when she saw it was her granddaughter, Vivienne. She unlocked the door and invited her in.

'Hi, Nan.'

'What a pleasant surprise, Vivienne. What brings you to Newquay?'

'I was visiting a friend nearby and thought I'd drop by and say hello.'

'Your mum is staying with me this weekend. Did you know? But she's out at the moment.'

'Oh! Really. She never said. I can't stay long anyway, but I thought I'd see how you're doing.'

'I'm fine, darling.'

Once the pleasantries were over, they sat in the garden enjoying the glorious spring day. Vivienne waited until she had eaten her sandwich before she broached the topic of why she really came.

Geraldine found a table outside in the garden and ordered a glass of white wine as she waited for Wesley to arrive. She kept repeating her silent prayer, *please don't let him hate me.*

Geraldine looked up as a seagull flew overhead, searching for scraps of food. The gull's cries reminded Geraldine that she wasn't far from the coast. She closed her eyes and breathed in the sea air, which was cool and refreshing. She watched the people sitting at the other tables – laughing, smiling, enjoying each other's company. Then a tall man appeared in the garden. Geraldine didn't need a photograph to recognise Wesley. Not even after a quarter of a century. Her memories of him came flooding back like a tsunami.

He scanned the garden until his eyes fixed upon her. He didn't need to look any further. His smile grew wider when he saw her. If Geraldine had been conscious of anything other than Wesley walking towards her, she would have noticed two female patrons eyeing him as he strode past their table. He cut an impressive figure. Geraldine wondered how he must look in his uniform. Her heart skipped a beat. She wasn't sure if it was only trepidation of telling him her news, or her feelings for him resurfacing.

Geraldine stood up to greet him. They both stared at each other for the longest moment, each waiting for the other to speak. Finally, Wesley took the lead and said, 'Hello.' He placed his hands on her arms as he kissed her gently on each cheek.

'It's been a long time, Geraldine. I was surprised by your call. How are you?'

'I'm good, Wes. And you?'

'I'm well.' Wesley outstretched his arm, indicating that Geraldine should sit, as he sat across from her. He ordered a beer and asked the waitress for two menus. Geraldine could see that his smile hadn't diminished in its tenderness after all those years. The last time she saw him they had been teenagers. Now, in front of her, stood the man he had become. Although he had a few more lines on his face, age had made him more handsome. Rugged with a chiselled face, his charisma oozed confidence. She wondered what he must think of her now she wasn't sixteen anymore, but a middle-aged woman. She realised this was going to be harder than she thought.

'The food is pretty good here,' he said.

'That's good. I'm starving,' she half-laughed.

Wesley had missed her kind smile and remembered how her hazel eyes sparkled in the sunlight. He even recognised the handful of freckles scattered on her face.

There was another awkward moment of silence.

This time, Geraldine took the lead. It was now or never.

'Wes, I've been beating myself up wondering how to tell you why I called you. But I knew I needed to do it in person.'

'The best way is to just say what you need to say, Geri.'

Geraldine smiled. No one ever called her 'Geri' except Wesley. That appellation never felt the same when someone else said it – not even Phillip – which was why she always told everyone she preferred Geraldine. She looked into his soft brown eyes and saw Harriet reflected back at her.

'This isn't easy for me to say,' Geraldine said, and paused. 'Well, when I was sixteen, the reason I left town suddenly … was because … I was pregnant.'

Geraldine took a deep breath. *There*. She said it. She studied Wesley's face, waiting for him to react. Wesley's smile, which had been etched on his face since his arrival, slowly retracted as he took in what Geraldine had just said. Then his face turned ashen. He flinched and looked sternly at her.

'I … I wasn't allowed to tell you,' Geraldine continued. 'I was already five months pregnant when I told my parents. I was scared and confused. It was decided I should go to my Aunt Emily's. Once the child was born, she was given up for adoption.' Geraldine paused and waited again for Wesley to say something.

'What the fuck, Geri!' he leaned away from her.

'I'm sorry, Wes.' *Please don't hate me*, she prayed silently once more. 'The decision to put her up for adoption was taken out of my hands.'

'Why the hell didn't you tell me?'

'You were joining the navy. I wanted to go to university. My parents thought it was for the best.'

'Fuck your parents! Didn't I have a say in the matter?'

'How could we have raised her when we were both so young?'

'Her?'

'Yes. That's why I called you,' Geraldine said. 'Her name is Harriet, and she contacted my mother about a month ago. She wanted to meet me and she wants to meet you, too. I said I would speak with you first. I wasn't sure how you would react. Mum told me you were married but divorced. I didn't want to cause you any trouble.'

Wesley stood up and walked away from the table. He paced around the garden, and as he did, he placed his hands on the top of his head. The waitress arrived with Wesley's beer and two menus, then discreetly left. Wesley needed time to absorb the ramifications of what she had just said. He didn't look at her. This wasn't how she had envisioned their meeting would go. *Please don't hate me, please don't.* After a few minutes, Wesley walked back to the table and sat down across from her. He took a long mouthful of beer. Then he finally spoke.

'You must have been very frightened,' he said. 'But I would have stood by you. You know that, don't you?'

'I do,' Geraldine said with relief. 'But the decision was taken out of my hands. Everything happened so fast. Before I knew it, I was taken to my Aunt Emily's, then after Harriet was born, I was enrolled in a new school. I was made to believe it was better that we didn't meet again. I'm sorry for how they treated you.'

'I should have been told. I cared about you. I know we were young, but I had a right to know. You not only denied me my daughter, but you denied my parents their grandchild.'

'I'm sorry.' Geraldine didn't know what else to say. Tears started to well in her eyes. There was another anguished silence, until Wesley finally broke it.

'When I turned up at your parents' home looking for you, your mother told me you had gone, and that you had an opportunity to study at another school, so you took it. I was made to believe you didn't care about me. I hated you and them for so long.'

'I'm sorry my mother lied. I wish I had been strong enough to stand up to them.'

Wesley looked long and hard at Geraldine, he could still see in her the young girl he loved and lost. He could only imagine what she had gone through alone.

'I have two sons, I've always wanted a daughter,' he said, as his warm smile returned.

Geraldine smiled a sigh of relief. 'She has your beautiful brown eyes. That was the first thing I noticed about her. She would like to meet you.'

'I'd like that.'

'Her name is Harriet Smith. She's lovely. She's had a good life, a happy one, and now lives in London.'

As midday turned to afternoon, Geraldine and Wesley had gotten to know each other all over again. It was like catching up with an old friend. They spent hours talking about their lives. They didn't notice the time until the temperature dropped, and Geraldine shivered. The hour was growing late when they finally said goodbye. Wesley dropped Geraldine off at the train station, where she caught the train back to Newquay. By the time she arrived at her mother's home, she was emotionally exhausted.

Theresa and Geraldine shared a late supper. She probed her daughter about her meeting with Wesley, but Geraldine refused to discuss it with her. Their reunion was private and belonged to them alone. Geraldine climbed the stairs and went straight to bed; she was too tired to socialise with her mother.

Theresa watched her daughter climb the stairs to her old bedroom. She was glad of her daughter's company. Even if it was fleeting. When Winston died, she felt a great loss and emptiness in her life. She did love him. But after the shock subsided, she felt free and independent for the first time in her life. But after a year of solitude, she felt mostly alone. She had a beautiful home, but no one to share it with. She hadn't had any great adventures and wasn't sure what to do with the rest of her life. She never had a career and, at sixty-five, it was too late to start one. Even her grandchildren rarely visited unless they wanted something. She was grateful that Geraldine visited at all. Their relationship had been artificial and strained for so long, she wondered if it could ever be repaired. But since Harriet had come into their lives, they'd slowly developed a greater understanding and respect for each other. Theresa hoped that forgiveness wasn't too far away.

This renewed hope led Theresa to believe she could also repair her relationship with her son, Callum. She often wondered how it went so wrong with her children. She wished she had been stronger and stood by them. She still felt ashamed at the lack of courage she had shown when they needed her the most.

Theresa went to bed with only her regret for companionship. She had decided not to mention Vivienne's visit to Geraldine, despite her concern for her granddaughter and what she had got herself involved in.

As Geraldine lay in bed, the only image she could conjure up before falling asleep was Wesley's sympathetic brown eyes boring into hers from across the garden table. That image made her sleep more soundly than she had done for years.

When morning arrived, Theresa made her daughter a hearty breakfast before dropping her off at the train station.

'Thanks, Mum,' Geraldine said, putting her knife and fork together on the plate. 'I appreciate everything you've done.'

'It's me that should thank you. You've given me the courage to take my next steps.'

'What do you mean?'

'I'll tell you when we're altogether on St Mary's. I've asked your brother Callum to join us, I hope that's alright.'

Geraldine eyed her mother inquisitively but decided not to broach the matter further. Trust was still in its infancy.

'I'll make sure we have a room for him at the hotel,' she said.

Theresa asked delicately, 'Are you still going to introduce Harriet to everyone on St Mary's?'

'Yes, I want it to be in familiar surroundings when everyone is together. There's going to be changes, but we'll get through them as a family. You need to understand that.'

'I, of all people, would never judge you, Geraldine. New beginnings are coming for both of us.' Theresa gently put her hand over her daughter's and squeezed it. The intimacy was warm and comforting. This time, her daughter's hand didn't pull away.

Theresa drove her husband's Mercedes to the train station, where Geraldine would travel down to Penzance for the afternoon ferry back to St Mary's. Theresa hated the big monstrosity. Winston had never let her drive it while he was alive, but she couldn't bring herself to sell it now. At first, she thought of driving it into the sea to spite him, but prudence had restrained her, as always. Maybe she should sell it and buy a small sports car. She'd always wanted one. *New beginnings*, she reminded herself.

A new dawn was about to break over her sleepy family; it was long overdue.

On her return home, Theresa stopped in at the travel agent and booked a flight to St Mary's for a fortnight's time, leaving Friday and returning on the Monday flight.

She was excited by the idea of having all her family around her again. Even Callum, her son, although he thought he was coming to assist his sister.

Theresa prepared her lunch. But before she could eat it, the phone rang. She often let it go to voicemail when she didn't recognise the number. She received too many annoying calls from people trying to scam her out of her money. 'Go fuck yourselves,' she would always say to herself, as she heard her voice off in the distant advising the caller she wasn't at home.

'Theresa. It's Joanna Burrows. I need to talk to you. My son has just told me I have a granddaughter. I'm pissed off and I want answers. You know what I'm talking about. Call me.'

Theresa put her sandwich down. She'd lost her appetite.

Chapter Three

St Mary's

When Geraldine stepped off the bus and walked the short distance to the Windermere Hotel, her mood was upbeat. She passed two of her guests, Mr and Mrs Herbert, who were heading out of the hotel for their afternoon walk. She smiled fondly at them. The couple had been coming to St Mary's for nearly ten years, and the last six at the Windermere. They were predictable, but adorable, in their matching hiking boots and backpacks. James Herbert always walked with a wooden walking stick that was as tall as he was. They liked to visit St Mary's every year in late spring. They were booked in for three weeks and always stayed in room 206. They had arrived yesterday, and Geraldine was disappointed she hadn't been on the island to greet them.

None of her children had shown any interest in hotel management. She often wondered who would run the hotel after she retired. She couldn't bear the idea of selling it.

It wasn't a contentious topic of discussion as she was proud of all her children. But she often wondered who would take over the hotel once she stepped down. Being a boutique hotel, Geraldine wanted her guests to feel at home. It was important that the atmosphere at the Windermere emanated a personal experience for her guests. Geraldine called a number of her guests 'friends', as they returned year after year to St Mary's.

'Afternoon, Geraldine,' the Herberts said in unison.

'How's your day been?' she asked.

'Smashing,' James replied. 'We'll be back for tea.'

Geraldine smiled after them and told them to take care. Geraldine loved the informal familiarity that she had with many of her guests.

When Geraldine arrived at the concierge desk, she asked Carrie to reserve another room for Callum. The hotel was three-quarters full, but during summer, it would be fully booked.

Geraldine's first stop after talking to Carrie was to check in on Hazel. She found her in her bedroom doing her homework. Well, texting and intermittently doing her homework. Phillip had left that morning for Southampton as he had a lecture in the morning. Geraldine kissed her daughter on the head before rubbing her hand through her hair. Something Hazel hated. She quickly pulled away and combed her hand through her hair. Hazel was looking forward to the summer holidays. This year, Geraldine had promised Hazel she could go to France with her best friend, Esme and her family for two weeks. Hazel had been waitressing in the hotel's restaurant for extra spending money.

Geraldine sometimes worried about Hazel, being the only child left at home, she could be solitary. She had a couple of close friends on the island, but she spent most of her spare time exploring the coastline. Hazel was smaller than Vivienne was at fifteen, and worried how she'd settle in at her new school after summer. She wanted to give Hazel the biggest hug she could muster and never let go. She would miss Hazel terribly and wished she could finish school on St Mary's but there were no senior classes on the island, so she had to go to the mainland, like Andrew and Vivienne did.

'Oh ... in a fortnight's time we're having guests come to stay,' Geraldine said. 'I can't say more at the moment, but your Uncle Callum and grandmother will also be here. Please don't make any arrangements that weekend. It's important.'

'Okay. Am I still on restaurant duty while they're here?'

'No. You get a reprieve on the Saturday night. You can work the lunchtime shift if you want, but I suggest you leave Sunday free.'

'Fine. Are you sure Nan is alright?' Hazel asked as her mum stood up to leave. 'You've been going to see her a lot lately.'

'Yes, she's fine, sweetie.'

A spasm of guilt gripped Geraldine, but Hazel would know the truth soon enough.

Geraldine's next port of call was to her office. She spent the next half hour rifling through the unopened post. But she was interrupted when her mobile rang, it was Phillip. She felt another stabbing of guilt, but she answered his call.

'How's your mother?' was Phillip's first question.

'Oh ... she's okay. Spending time together has helped bridge the gap a little.'

'I'm happy for you both. Do you still need me to come next weekend? I have commitments at college.'

'No, that's fine. But the whole family is coming in a fortnight's time. I need you to be here as I have an announcement to make.'

'Sounds ominous,' Phillip said. 'What's going on?'

'I'd rather tell you in person when you return.'

Phillip decided not to push her on the matter.

'I'll see you then. Say hi to Hazel for me.'

'Will do. Bye.'

'Bye.'

Neither said 'I love you' before hanging up. That realisation wasn't lost on Geraldine. She couldn't say when she last felt any physical attraction towards Phillip. He hadn't shown any affection towards her in a long time either. This led Geraldine to believe that he didn't care for her anymore. She wondered if his affection was now centred on someone else.

Geraldine left her office to check that the dinner service was ready for her guests. She popped into the kitchen just in time to see Barbara head out through the service entrance in a hurry.

'Don't ask, *mon amie*,' Claude said to her, without looking up from his work.

As always, Claude was the model of efficiency, although his lack of empathy was trying at times. He ran his kitchen like a captain would his ship. Geraldine had to remind herself she was lucky to have him at the Windermere. She would miss him, if he ever went back home to France. He could have worked anywhere – except France.

Geraldine headed back to the concierge desk, where she found Carrie assisting another guest. When the guest had thanked Carrie and headed to their room, Geraldine asked,

'Is everything alright with Barb? She seemed out of sorts a minute ago.'

'Don't ask me. You know what she's like, hot one minute, cold the next.'

Geraldine gave Carrie a knowing look.

Carrie leaned forward on the desk and said, 'Look, she doesn't confide in me. I don't think she likes me very much.'

'Oh … she just needs time to settle in. I'll speak to her later.'

'Is everything alright with you? You've been going to the mainland a lot lately.'

'I'm fine. It's just family business.'

Carrie knew she'd been visiting her mother lately. Which was unusual as she knew they didn't get on. The same could be said for her husband, Phillip. Carrie honestly believed Geraldine deserved to be treated better. She was concerned for her.

'Mr and Mrs Wright are leaving tomorrow morning. It's their fortieth anniversary today, so I've organised a cake for them after dinner.'

'Thanks, Carrie. They'll love that.' Geraldine didn't know what she'd do without her. 'Look. I'll be busy with my family when they come in a fortnight's time. I would like you to be acting manager for the entire weekend.'

This made Carrie stand a little taller. 'Thank you, Geraldine. I won't let you down.'

'I know you won't. You'll make a great manager one day. Any mainland hotel would jump at the opportunity to employ you. Look, I know I've been off island a lot recently, but things are going to change around here soon – hopefully for the better. I appreciate you stepping in.' Geraldine tapped the concierge desk with her knuckles and headed in the direction of the kitchen.

Carrie watched on after her. She admired Geraldine very much. She had always afforded her respect, something she wasn't used to until she started working at the Windermere. Carrie wondered what all the secrecy was truly about, but she didn't have long to ponder as the phone rang again.

Geraldine checked the kitchen to see if Barbara had returned, but she hadn't. She had an idea where she might be and walked through the kitchen and out the service entrance and down towards the beach. She found Barbara sitting in the sand, in a small bay she liked to frequent, smoking a cigarette. Something she only did when she was agitated.

'Penny for your thoughts,' Geraldine said, as she sat down next to her.

'What? Sorry, Mrs Locke … I mean, Geraldine.'

'Is it something you want to talk about?' They were both looking out to sea. Barbara noticed that the wind was blowing her cigarette smoke towards Geraldine, so she quickly took the cigarette in her left hand and held it away from Geraldine.

'Just family stuff.'

'I'm a good listener, if you need to talk.'

Geraldine noticed clouds were starting to roll in. When that sneaky wind picked up, it could develop a chill fast. Geraldine hoped the colder weather was behind them now.

Barbara discovered soon after arriving at the hotel that Geraldine was a kind woman. St Mary's was the last place she thought she'd ever end up. But when the opportunity arose, she found herself jumping at the chance for a sea-change. She'd worked all hours at the Mayfair Hotel in London, and even though there was a large staff, it was so busy she found it hard to make friends. She often felt alone.

'You know what they say, you can choose your friends, but not your family,' Barbara said, before taking a drag on her cigarette.

'That's true. But we can appreciate them,' Geraldine said, nudging Barbara gently.

'I'm glad I'm well out of it here ... some people shouldn't be parents.'

Geraldine wasn't sure how to respond to that question. Barbara had obviously left London to get away from her life, which is what most people do when they come to an island as small as St Mary's. It could be quite isolating, but some people preferred it that way. Everyone who moved to St Mary's had secrets, even herself.

'Parenting doesn't come with a handbook,' Geraldine said. 'We tend to make it up as we go along. I've made mistakes, but my children know I love them.'

'You're a good mother. They're lucky to have you.'

'Thank you for saying that.'

'I'll be fine, I'm just feeling a little melancholy.'

'I'm here if you ever want to talk.'

'Thanks.' Barbara looked over at Geraldine, then back down at the sand. She wanted to confide in her, but she thought it best to keep her distance for now. It was safer that way.

'I hope you're happy here?'

'I am. It's quiet for one thing, which forces me to think more.' Barbara looked out to sea.

'That's what I love about it. But you're still young, so don't take life so seriously. You never know what's just around the corner.' Geraldine nudged Barbara again, who smiled back in return, despite herself.

'Thanks,' Barbara said.

'Well, I've got guests to attend to, and I think Claude will need you so on your feet, soldier, and put that cigarette out.'

'Yes, ma'am,' Barbara said mockingly. She flicked the last of her cigarette off into the sand and headed towards the hotel.

Geraldine rose and took one more pensive look at the ocean. It was becoming choppy. She wrapped her cardigan around her as the wind had picked up, then she turned her back on it and walked back toward the hotel.

On her return, Geraldine heard a loud bang, which caused her to stop in her tracks. It came from inside the boathouse. She changed course and headed towards it to see what the noise was.

The old boathouse was made of wood and painted dark brown. It had a tiled roof, with a large roller door on the ocean side and two large barn doors on the land side. It was as old as the hotel but had recently been refurbished. The doors of the boathouse were painted red, while all the frames and skirting boards were painted white. It couldn't go unnoticed by her guests. When she opened the door and looked inside, she could see that one of the canoes had fallen from its rack.

Both sides of the boathouse had shelving, which supported six canoes and four rowboats, and two windsurfing boards. The oars, life jackets and other water sports equipment was stacked on smaller shelves on either side of the entrance. The wind was funnelling through the boathouse because the roller door was open, making her shiver. She pressed the button to lower the door, then she walked over to the fallen canoe. A deck ran around the inside of the boathouse and in the middle of the boathouse was a ramp that ran down into the water and out past the roller door. At high tide, the water came right into the boathouse and partially up the ramp. But at low tide, the boathouse was completely dry.

Geraldine tutted as she heaved the canoe back onto its rack. One of the guests mustn't have tightened it correctly. She closed and locked the front door behind her, as she knew no one would be using the equipment anymore today. Then she quickly walked back to the hotel as the wind kept smacking against her back.

Every evening, Geraldine liked to inspect the hotel's ground floor rooms. Her walk would begin in the bar and lounge. She made sure everything was ready for the evening's entertainment. The bar was fully stocked, with plenty of ice in the buckets. The lemons and limes were sliced, and the bar snacks were all placed on the tables. *Thank you, Carrie*, she said to herself as she headed into the dining room.

In the quieter seasons, Geraldine had found Carrie indispensable. She would act as the restaurant's manager, bartender, and concierge. Born on St Mary's, Carrie had been a waitress in a café in Hugh Town before Geraldine offered her a job at the Windermere. Most of Carrie's friends had left the island for university to pursue careers, but Carrie had remained. Under Geraldine's tutelage, Carrie had nearly finished her hotel management course at the Open University.

Some of the Windermere's guests had started to arrive for dinner. Four extra temp staff would start at the beginning of summer, but until they did, it was all hands on deck. She spotted Hazel coming out of the kitchen carrying two plates of Claude's finest cuisine. She winked at her daughter before heading off.

It was going to be a wonderful evening, she thought.

Southampton

Phillip entered the residences hall a little after 9 pm, he was tired but still had work to prepare before his first class in the morning. It had been a long day, catching the morning ferry from St Mary's, and he'd read essays all day. He threw his bag onto his bed and walked over to the drinks trolley and poured himself a scotch whiskey. He took a slow, long swig and sighed after the liquid made its way down his chest.

His reverie was interrupted by a knock at the door. He put his glass down, then opened the door.

'Thought you'd like a night-cap,' the woman said, as she entered his room without being invited in.

'After the day I've had, I hope you brought a full bottle.'

She laughed. 'Poor Phillip.' Clarissa felt sorry for him, always having to trudge back to boring St Mary's and his frigid wife instead of spending his weekends with her.

'I think I can find a way to help you get over your tedious weekend,' she said, as she unbuttoned her blouse. She pulled her hair clip out, which supported a neat bun and let her hair fall down below her shoulders and breasts.

Phillip took her in his arms and kissed her hard on the lips. He'd been starved of affection all weekend. She smelled good. She always did. He removed her blouse, then unclipped and removed her bra. They fell onto the bed where they struggled to pull the remainder of each other's clothes off before finally having hungry, impatient sex.

After, they lay on the bed, sweaty and exhausted.

'I think my wife's having an affair,' Phillip announced, looking up at the ceiling.

Clarissa turned onto her side to look at him. She placed her hand on his chest and played with his nipple.

'How do you know that?'

'She's been coming to the mainland for the last month, supposedly to see her mother. But she's been going somewhere else.'

'That doesn't mean anything.'

'I called her mother to speak with her as she wasn't answering her mobile. Theresa lied for her. She wouldn't do that if she had nothing to hide.'

Clarissa grinned. *About bloody time*, she thought. They could finally be together, officially.

'Then divorce her. Then we can stop sneaking around these blasted halls pretending to be polite co-workers. You love me, don't you?'

Phillip turned his head and looked into her eyes. He loved the sex. He enjoyed what they had together, but he wasn't sure if he actually loved her. Maybe he did but had forgotten what it felt like to love and be loved.

'Of course I do…' he said reassuringly. 'But I have to know what my options are. I'm not walking away with nothing.'

'Of course you won't. You're entitled to half of everything.'

'I'm not actually. The hotel was gifted to Geraldine by her grandmother, along with two hundred thousand pounds for the refurbishment. We sold our house and moved to St Mary's. I'm entitled to half of what our house sold for, which wasn't much after the bank got their loan back. We put the proceeds towards the refurbishment, so I should be entitled to some of the hotel's profits. We live in the annex next to the hotel, but it's owned by the hotel, so I can't claim half of that either.'

'Does it really matter? As long as we're together?'

'Yes, it does. I'm nearly middle-aged. I'm not starting over with nothing to show for it. I'm sure I'm entitled to more.'

'Then confront her and tell her what you want. Then you can both go your separate ways.' Clarissa started to rub her fingers around Phillip's chest hair, gently pulling at them. She had never seen him this agitated before, or this greedy. But she wanted a home with Phillip, and they didn't come cheap.

'If she's pushed into a corner, I'm not sure what she'll do.'

'You don't love her anymore, Phillip, you said so on many occasions. Just tell her you want a divorce and come to an agreement. Then we can get our own place in town.' She kissed his chest, then climbed on top of him. 'She can't make you come like I do … will do.' Clarissa started moving in rhythm on top of him. As always, his mind started to drift in an ecstasy of pleasure. He loved the way Clarissa made him feel.

Yes, he thought. *Yes. Yes.*

Clarissa smiled down at Phillip who was in a dream-like state. She always knew how to place him under her spell. But she couldn't tell if his yeses meant he would move in with her, or that he was simply enthralled by the pleasure she invoked. It didn't matter, she knew what she wanted.

Clarissa would just have to help Phillip make the right decision – for the both of them.

Phillip spoke no more of divorces, or payouts or ungraded student essays. He was lost in Clarissa's spell. He felt young and invigorated whenever he was inside her. *Yes. Yes. Yes.* Now was the time for change.

Chapter Four

Newquay

The following Saturday – Late May

Geraldine kept pacing while she waited anxiously for her guests to arrive. Theresa had prepared a splendid lunch for everyone, but Geraldine had no appetite given that she so wanted Wesley and Harriet to get along.

Geraldine didn't want them to meet in a restaurant or park in London, but for it to be more private and intimate. She suggested Harriet's apartment, but Wesley suggested they meet at Theresa's home. He wanted a confrontation with Theresa, on his terms, at the last place he saw her twenty-five years ago. He had told Geraldine he needed to forgive, but only once he'd confronted Theresa about the past.

'Geraldine, you'll wear a hole in my carpet – do sit down. Wesley will love her as much as you do. It's like any new relationship; it takes time to get to know one another.'

'I know, Mum. But …'

'But what?'

'Forget it.'

'I wish you'd confide in me. That's all I've ever wanted. I hate that you find it so difficult to trust me.'

Geraldine saw the angst-ridden look on her mother's face; she wanted to trust her.

'It's just … seeing Wesley again has stirred up all the old feelings in me. Phillip and I haven't been close in a long while. He only visits St Mary's to see Hazel.'

That wasn't what Theresa wanted to hear. Her fears had been proven right. She wasn't sure how to answer her daughter. She'd only just got Geraldine back, and she didn't want to lose her again. Theresa would have to tread carefully.

'Do you know if he still has feelings for you?' she asked tactfully.

'Who?'

'Phillip, of course.'

'I hope not.'

Theresa's eyebrows were raised.

'Don't look at me like that, Mum. We've been drifting apart for years. We're both too lazy to admit it.'

'Maybe staying at the university all week wasn't such a good idea.'

Geraldine had to agree with her mother on that point. She'd had her suspicions for some time about Phillip. He wasn't getting any affection from her, so he must be getting it from someone else.

'Of course I care about him, Mum, but we've grown apart. We never had that electrifying connection like I did with Wesley … don't laugh.' Geraldine pointed her finger at her mother. She knew what her mother would say, 'How can you know about love at fifteen?' But she and Wesley had a bond from the moment they first met.

'I did love him, don't get me wrong. But Wes made me feel special. He only had to look at me and I'd go weak at the knees.'

'Maybe it's best you leave the past alone, Geraldine. Focus on what's important. Your family. Think about how Andrew, Vivienne and Hazel will feel if you separate.'

Geraldine looked down at her mother. 'I have, Mum.' But their conversation was interrupted by the doorbell.

Theresa got up, walked to the front door and opened it. She found a strikingly tall man standing in front of her. She wasn't that old that she didn't acknowledge an attractive man when she saw one.

She felt a moment's dread wash over her. But she stood aside and let him in.

'It's been a long time, Wesley.'

'Yes. But that wasn't by choice, Theresa,' he said in an even-mannered tone. He made a point of arriving early, to speak with Theresa before Harriet arrived.

Theresa was a bit surprised he addressed her by her first name, but then again, why wouldn't he? The last time she spoke to him, he was seventeen and standing at this same doorstep wanting to know where Geraldine was.

'How are you?' he asked.

'I'm good, thank you. Harriet hasn't arrived yet, but Geraldine is in the living room.' Theresa put her hand on his arm to stop him advancing. 'I want to apologise for how I treated you all those years ago. I was only thinking of my daughter, and I didn't consider your feelings. I'm truly sorry.'

Wesley thought it was too little, too late. But he appreciated her apology. His feelings towards her hadn't changed, but he could see the regret across her face, so for Geraldine and Harriet's sakes, he would try to forgive her. 'You didn't consider Geraldine's feelings either. Did you? But today is about Harriet.'

When Wesley entered the room, his gaze instantly fell upon Geraldine. They remained silent until Theresa asked if anyone would like a hot drink. They both replied no, but she had already left the room to put the kettle on.

Wesley sat down beside Geraldine.

'My mother wasn't happy when I told her about Harriet,' he whispered. 'All she said was, "I knew that family would come back to haunt us one day." I asked her what she meant, but she refused to elaborate.'

'Did she already know about the baby?'

'No. She was surprised, shocked even when I told her.' At that moment, as Theresa walked back into the living room, all eyes were upon her. She stopped in her tracks.

Wesley repeated what his mother had said and asked Theresa for an explanation.

Theresa sat down in her armchair. Everything was happening too quickly, and she didn't want to lose control of the narrative. She mulled over what to tell them.

'If there's something I don't know, I would appreciate the truth, Theresa. You owe me that much,' Wesley said.

'We … we didn't want to hurt you. Either of you.'

'Well, you did. That can't be undone now,' he replied calmly. 'But the truth will be a good place to start.'

Theresa hoped the truth would never need to be revealed. But she knew that was unlikely now. If she didn't, she knew Joanne

Burrows would. But today wasn't the day. This was Harriet's day, and she didn't want anything to spoil it. Theresa decided to withhold the truth for just a little longer. But it would need to be said, and soon. Theresa decided to tell them a half-truth.

'Our families have feuded ever since my father and your grandfather were young men, Wesley. They despised each other. It caused a major rift between our families. Needless to say, my father could hold a grudge. But please let me explain another day. Today is for Harriet. I don't want anything to spoil it.'

'What happened between them?' Geraldine asked, not accepting her mother's reply.

Theresa had to think quickly. 'I … I believe it was to do with your grandmother, Stella Hindmarsh. Both men fancied the same woman, but ultimately, she chose Christopher over my father. His nose was put out of joint and jealousy grew between the two men. No doubt Stella chose the right man.'

'Is that all?' Wesley sighed.

'My father didn't like to lose. He once tried to have your grandfather arrested on some trumped-up charge. But Christopher Burrows had an alibi and the charges were dropped.'

'I wouldn't have put it past him to have planted the evidence himself,' chided Geraldine.

Wesley couldn't believe that a long-standing feud had made Geraldine give up their baby.

Before Wesley or Geraldine could ask any more questions, the doorbell rang.

With relief, Theresa quickly got up and left the room, signalling the conversation was over. She paused for composure before she opened the door. Her mood brightened when she saw her newest granddaughter standing there with an anxious smile on her face.

Harriet was shown into the living room, her heart fluttering with butterflies. Geraldine stood up and squeezed her hands in hers, as she could see how nervous Harriet was. They had a silent moment before Geraldine said proudly to Wesley, 'this is your daughter, Harriet.'

Wesley was standing across the room. He was beaming from ear to ear.

'It's a pleasure to meet you, Harriet. I only wish I could have met you sooner.' He walked up to her and, as he did with Geraldine, placed his large hands on her arms and leaned over and pecked her on the cheek.

'I'm so glad to finally meet you, too. I wasn't sure if this day would ever come.'

Theresa offered Harriet a chair and all four sat down to begin their afternoon.

Harriet and Wesley got on like a house on fire. He marvelled that Harriet did indeed have his eyes and Geraldine's mannerisms. He spoke about his family and gave Harriet a picture of his two boys, Christopher and Charlie, both named after their grandfathers. He promised her that he'd introduce her to them during the summer holidays.

Theresa watched on as the trio laughed all afternoon. They gradually settled down and grew comfortable in each other's company. There was no difficulty or awkwardness. Theresa could only see one unfortunate side-effect to their introduction, that Geraldine and Wesley were re-establishing their friendship and feelings for one another.

When it was finally time to say goodnight, there was no uneasiness or politeness. They were a happy family of three. Harriet had agreed to stay overnight as it was too late to return to London. Theresa was feeling tired and said goodnight to her guests. She slowly climbed the stairs to her bedroom, not realising how weary she was.

Geraldine walked Wesley out to his car. He didn't have far to drive as he was staying with his mother for the weekend.

'She's lovely, isn't she?' Geraldine announced, once they were alone.

Wesley turned from his car and faced Geraldine. 'Yes, she is. She takes after you.' This time Wesley reached over and put his hand around Geraldine's back and drew her near to him. He leant down and kissed her gently on the lips. He didn't care that she was married. He had to kiss her. He had to know if the spark was still there.

It was.

Geraldine didn't pull away, instead she wrapped her arms around him and fell more deeply into his kiss.

It was electrifying.

Chapter Five

Wednesday – Early June
Three days before Harriet's arrival

'Welcome to the Windermere Hotel. I hope you enjoyed your flight,' Carrie said to the newly arrived couple from London, who were still arm in arm.

'Yes, we did, thank you,' the woman said, still smiling at her companion.

Carrie handed them the key card for room 104. 'I hope you enjoy your stay with us. There's always something to do on our small but beautiful island.'

'Thank you, I've been wanting to come here for years,' her companion replied.

'If you're planning on visiting the other isles, please let me know and I'll arrange your transport.'

They both thanked Carrie and headed up to their room.

Carrie watched the couple enter the lift. It was rarely used except when guests had their luggage in tow. Usually, they preferred to walk up and down the grand staircase. Carrie could see on her screen that their surnames were different. She wondered if they were unmarried partners, or secretly having an affair. Some such couples simply used 'Smith' or 'Jones'. Not very original, Carrie often thought, but some guests weren't ashamed of their love trysts and boldly used their own names. Carrie liked to call these types of affairs 'dangerous liaisons'. She'd watched the film far too many times. She wondered who they were betraying. She felt angry all of a sudden – but quickly brushed it off and left the reception desk to begin her walk around.

Carrie took it upon herself to carry out the morning's inspection. At the Windermere Hotel, the ground floor housed the lobby and reception, with Geraldine's office tucked in behind it down a corridor. The dining room, kitchen, bar and lounge area could also be found on the ground level. At the back of the house was a spacious conservatory, which had been added on during the renovation. Geraldine liked to call it her sunroom. The sunroom had large glass window panes which offered panoramic views of the Atlantic Ocean and the Celtic Sea. An indoor swimming pool was built next to the sunroom, nestled in the corner of the hotel. A billiards room and library were also found on the ground floor. There was a small gym and sauna below ground level, along with a laundry, wine cellar and storage rooms. A small number of staff bedrooms were below ground level for the contract staff that came from the mainland during the summer months and for a few permanent staff members.

Level one and two housed twenty-six guest bedrooms. All rooms had uninterrupted views around the island and out to sea. The suites had a sitting room, along with a spacious bathroom. The rooms on level two were known as the loft rooms, as they were built into the attic of the grand old house. They were smaller, but just as comfortable and afforded higher and spectacular views around the island.

Carrie loved the Windermere and saw it as her home away from home. But she would never be the manager here, not while Geraldine continued to run it. She didn't believe Geraldine had any intention of retiring soon. Carrie's options for promotion were limited. If she ever wanted to manage her own hotel, she would have to head to the mainland. She had already made up her mind.

Carrie walked into the kitchen and poured herself a coffee. She smiled as she remembered the time Geraldine took her to London to visit The Ritz and Claridge's in December to admire the Christmas displays. Geraldine admitted that she came every year, as it gave her decorative inspirations for the Windermere.

Carrie had wished her own parents had taken more of an interest in her life and career. She often felt envious towards Geraldine's children, and wished she'd had that same connection with her own parents.

As she drank her coffee, Carrie watched Barbara prepare some haddock for lunch. The restaurant was always fully booked. Even in the dead of winter, when hotel bookings were at their lowest, the restaurant bookings never dwindled thanks to Claude, even if he was a prickly sod.

'Looks good!' she said to Barbara.

'Of course it'll be good,' she replied, without looking up at Carrie.

Carrie decided to give Barbara a wide birth. She could be moody at times and today was no exception. Like herself, Geraldine had seen something in Barbara, although Carrie couldn't fathom why. She surmised that Geraldine must have felt sorry for her.

Carrie shrugged it off and headed back to the front desk.

'That's great. See you on Saturday. Bye.' Geraldine put her mobile down on her desk and leaned back in her chair, smiling up at the ceiling. Harriet and Ashley were booked on the Saturday ferry. This was it. There was no turning back now. Geraldine received an email from her brother, Callum, confirming his flight details and arrival on Saturday mid-morning. Andrew and Vivienne were both flying in at lunchtime on Saturday – the extravagance was warranted as she didn't want them bumping into Harriet and Ashley on the ferry.

Geraldine had endured a few restless nights during the week, thinking about it all. Her emotional clock was wound up so tight that she decided to have a run before dinner. Geraldine left her office and met up with Carrie at reception.

'Have Mr and Mrs Grisham arrived yet?'

'Yes, about ten minutes ago.'

'Great. Are the champagne and flowers in their room?'

'Yes, did it myself.'

'I've placed the orders for the new bedroom linen and beach towels, and Jeff is arriving tomorrow to service the water sport equipment. The pool's filter system is also being serviced. I've also informed the kitchen staff about the Byrd child's dietary needs. He's diabetic, so can you please check that the first-aid kit is stocked with insulin and that it is not out of date. He has his own supply, of course. But it's best to make sure we have a backup supply.'

'Will do. Don't worry, everything is under control.'

'I know it is. Thank you.'

Geraldine headed to the annex and changed into her jogging gear. As she headed off on her run, she decided she would tell everyone about Harriet before dinner on Saturday. That way, they could absorb her news all together, then she would invite Harriet to join them.

Geraldine jogged down Porthloo Lane and onto Telegraph Road, where she ran up to the coastguard lookout tower. It wasn't a long run, but it was refreshing as the cold wind whipped across her face. Built in the early 1800s, the tower had been used as a signal station for the admiralty, but now it was used by Radio Scilly for broadcasting. Once at the top, Geraldine stopped. She was panting, so she put her hands on her hips and bent over. Once she had her breath back, she did a 360 degree turn and took in the view. Why would anyone want to live anywhere else?

As she jogged back down Telegraph Road, her thoughts kept drifting back to what her mother had said or didn't say. She was still holding something back. If her mother wanted a better relationship with her, she'd have to start being honest with her. She decided to press her mother about it on the weekend.

Since returning home on Monday, Geraldine had thought of nothing else except – that kiss. Her whole body was aching to kiss him again. Why didn't she feel guilty? She hadn't felt so much passion in years. Her entire body pulsated for him. She'd forgotten what it felt like. Her feelings for Phillip had changed so slowly over the years, she hadn't realised at what point she had last felt anything for him. Geraldine stopped jogging. She was panting heavily again and tried to control her breathing.

'I still love Wesley.' The finality of what she just said out loud shocked her. She ran upstairs and into her bathroom, where she threw cold water on her face. Then she picked up the hand towel and patted her face dry. She looked at herself long and hard in the mirror.

I'm falling in love with Wes all over again.

Geraldine threw herself onto her bed and lay there with her arms outstretched. A large smile crept across her face. She hadn't felt this giddy and excited about someone in a long time, 'I love Wes,' she said out loud, but quickly put her hands over her mouth, and giggled. She picked up her mobile and dialled Wesley's number. She waited for him to answer, but it went to voicemail.

She was going to hang up, but she loved hearing his voice again. Before she could disconnect the call, she found herself talking into her mobile. Maybe she had more gumption because he wasn't on the other end of the line to interrupt her.

'Hi. It's me. Um ... I wanted to talk to you about that kiss the other night. Please don't play games with me. If you have feelings for me, please tell me. My marriage to Phillip has been over for a long time. We barely speak, even when he's back home. I'm tired of the social proprieties. I deserve honesty. If you feel the same way I do, please tell me ... bye.'

Geraldine disconnected the one-way conversation. She lay flat on the bed and instantly wondered if she had just made the biggest mistake of her life. She'd just ended her marriage. Panic coincided with the rapid beating of her heart as adrenaline coursed through her body. But the thought of Wesley's arms around hers, his lips on hers, warmed and tantalised her whole body.

Geraldine jumped off the bed and walked back into the bathroom to take a quick shower before changing for dinner. She still had a hotel to run and they had a full restaurant tonight.

Southampton

'What did your lawyer say?' Clarissa said, as she hand-fed Phillip a strawberry.

'What I expected him to say. Apart from an equal share in the house we sold, I might have a claim to a share in the profits of the hotel, as I financially helped to build and run it.'

Clarissa had prepared a lovely dinner for Phillip in her apartment, which was only a short walk from the university, but he had only played with his food. He didn't have much of an appetite.

'We both earn enough. Let her have the hotel.'

'That's not the point. It's worth millions now.'

Clarissa was seeing a different side to Phillip that she wasn't sure she liked. 'You'll be free of her. No more trips to St Mary's. All your kids will be studying on the mainland next term, you'll see them more than you do now, it's a win, win for both of us.' Clarissa fed him another strawberry, but he flinched. He'd lost his appetite.

'What's the matter with you?' Clarissa threw the strawberry back into the bowl. Her patience was wearing thin.

'I can't believe she's seeing someone behind my back.'

'Don't be a hypocrite.' Clarissa stood up and paced the room.

'It's not that. She hasn't seemed interested in sex for a long time. Well, not with me anyway.'

Clarissa laughed as she turned around to face him. 'I never had you down as shallow. What bothers you more, that she doesn't satisfy you anymore, or that you don't satisfy her?'

Phillip looked sternly at Clarissa. What did she know about marriage and commitment? She was free to do what she liked.

'I've put ten years of my life into that hotel and twenty-two into my marriage.'

'But that didn't stop you from cheating on her,' Clarissa said. 'Look, I love you. I want us to be together, properly as a couple. No more skulking about.'

Clarissa walked over to Phillip and lowered herself onto him. She wrapped her long legs around the chair and put her arms around the back of his neck. She gently kissed the sides of his neck. Left side, then the right side. She repeated the foreplay until Phillip was receptive to her. Then she started to nibble the sides of his neck, and as she did, she slowly started to caress him with her hand. It aroused him as it always did. He moved her blouse and bra aside to expose her breast, which he gently caressed with his tongue and mouth. Clarissa unzipped his trousers. She knew it wouldn't take long for Philip to forget about his wife.

Phillip, as always, was lost in her seductive supremacy. Why didn't Geraldine make him feel this way? Then he forgot what he had been complaining about.

Phillip carried Clarissa to bed, where they made love. They stayed intertwined in each other's limbs, naked, for the rest of the night.

In the morning, Phillip announced he was returning to St Mary's on Friday afternoon. He would confront Geraldine about her absences. If she's having an affair, then he'd ask for a divorce. But on his terms.

Clarissa hoped rather than believed he would keep his word. Whether or not his wife was having an affair was irrelevant to Clarissa. It was time to move things along.

After Phillip left her apartment, Clarissa opened her computer and Googled flights into St Mary's, Scilly Isles. At thirty-six, she knew what she wanted from life. She was a successful university professor, but she had no intention of being a single mother.

Clarissa first fell in love with Phillip's love of history, then his sense of humour. He was charismatic and charming. Their relationship had been fun, but now she wanted more. She wanted a wedding ring on her finger and a home of her own. She hadn't told Phillip that she was pregnant. She had needed time to get used to the idea herself. Now that she had, she needed Phillip by her side. But she needed to tell him soon. This weekend would be the perfect opportunity. New beginnings for everyone.

Clarissa managed to book a flight on Saturday morning. There were plenty of hotels and bed and breakfasts with vacancies in Hugh Town and Old Town, but her searching brought her to the Windermere Hotel in Porthloo. She had to admire his wife; her hotel was exquisite. She figured that Phillip would need cheering up after his confrontation with his wife. She was never one for underplaying a situation. Smiling to herself, she made a reservation.

But one thing Clarissa knew for certain, their affair was going to be made official by the end of this weekend, one way or another.

Clarissa leaned back in the chair and contemplated her next move.

Newquay

Theresa heard her granddaughter's voice on the answerphone machine and quickly raced to pick it up before she hung up.

'Vivienne, how nice to hear from you.'

'You too, Nan. Are you coming to St Mary's on the weekend?'

'Yes, I'll be there.'

'That's good. I was hoping we could talk further about what we discussed the other weekend.'

Theresa cringed at the thought of upsetting her granddaughter. This weekend was supposed to be for Geraldine and Harriet, not Vivienne's request. Besides, she hadn't heard back from Andrew and had no intention of giving Vivienne her answer until she had spoken to him.

'We'll talk when I arrive, sweetheart. But I haven't made up my mind yet. I need more time to consider.'

Vivienne's sigh reverberated in Theresa's ear. Her granddaughter wasn't pleased. There was a long silence before Vivienne replied.

'Sure. We'll talk on the weekend.'

Theresa had to wonder what her granddaughter had gotten herself caught up in that she would need all that money.

Chapter Six

The Windermere Hotel, St Mary's
Friday – early June
The day before Harriet's arrival

The sunroom was full of the hotel's guests enjoying their breakfast. It was a beautiful, clear day and the guests got to enjoy uninterrupted views of St Mary's, unhindered by fog, mist or rain. Geraldine purposefully had the sunroom added on to the hotel as a separate dining area for her guests to enjoy their breakfast. It broke up the monotony of always eating in the dining room. The light was extraordinary this Friday morning.

The floor of the sunroom was covered with mosaic tiles of various greens and lemons. The tables were intermingled amongst plants of various species, which created a feeling of being surrounded by nature. In summer, the great glass doors would open up and some of the tables would be put outside on the patio.

Geraldine made her way around the room, as she always did, greeting her guests and making sure they had everything they needed. Knowing her guests' names, she greeted them personally.

'Hello, Mr and Mrs Herbert. How did your trek go yesterday?'

'It was lovely, Geraldine, until the rain set in. How's your family?' Joan asked.

'They're great, thank you. They're all coming over this weekend for a family get-together.'

'Oh! How lovely for you,' she replied.

'We're off to St Agnes today. Let's hope the rain keeps off,' ventured James Herbert.

'Well! The weather forecast said it should be fine all day. But they're expecting a late storm tomorrow. So do enjoy yourselves while the weather's good.'

'Thank you,' they replied in unison.

Geraldine continued with her rounds. 'I hope you have everything you need, Mrs Byrd?'

'Yes, we do,' Carol replied.

'The boathouse will be open after 9 am, so you can make your way down there any time after breakfast. You just need to sign out what water sports equipment you're using and record where you're heading in case we need to send out the coast guard if you get lost,' Geraldine chuckled.

'Brilliant,' replied her husband, John. 'I thought we'd do a bit of canoeing around the island, today.'

'That sounds exciting. If you want to take a picnic lunch with you, please let Carrie know at reception.'

'Will do, cheers,' he replied.

Geraldine turned to Lorna and Hugh Grisham, newlyweds from Derby. But as they were leaning across the table whispering to each other, she decided to give them some privacy. The Grishams had finally come down for breakfast after arriving two days ago. Geraldine kept a smile on her face as she continued to walk slowly through the sunroom.

Her smile wasn't only for her guests this morning. Geraldine's spritely gait was thanks to Wesley. She still couldn't get over his reply to the spontaneous voicemail she'd left him.

The night before, as Geraldine slowly drifted off to sleep, her mobile rang. With her eyes still closed, she reached for it.

'Hello,' she said. 'Who is this?'

'It's me, Wes.'

Geraldine's eyes opened wide. She turned over and lifted herself up on the bed and rested on her elbow.

'Hi,' she said. Then she remembered her voicemail.

'I just listened to your message,' he said.

Geraldine remained silent but cringed at the humiliation that might follow.

'I was on a two-day training exercise out at sea. I just got back.'

Geraldine sighed with relief. That's why he didn't reply sooner. She'd thought she'd spooked him off.

'I've missed you too. I wasted so many years being angry with you. If I'd only known why. But when I saw you at the pub, sitting at that table, the anger just drifted away with the tide. I know you're married, but if it's true that your marriage is over, please tell me now. Otherwise, I'll leave you in peace.'

Geraldine allowed her tears to drop down onto her pillow. How could Wes make her so happy in an instant?

'Phillip and I haven't been intimate in a long time. Besides, I think he's seeing someone else.'

'How do you know that?'

'Little things I've picked up on. Sometimes his clothes smell of perfume. I found a receipt once for a dozen red roses in his jacket pocket. Only, I never got any. Strangely, I didn't even care.'

'When can I see you again?'

'Let me talk to Phillip first. He's arriving tomorrow afternoon. The whole family is coming this weekend; I'm introducing them to Harriet. I think it best I get everything out in the open this weekend.'

'Are you sure about inviting Harriet? What if Phillip takes it badly and the children don't warm to her?'

'I thought about that. But I know my children, Wes. They'll understand. They have to meet her eventually. I can't keep sneaking off to the mainland every week. As for Phillip, I think he'll be relieved more than anything.'

'Alright ... I've missed you. Geri.'

'Me too, Wes.'

Wesley couldn't sleep that night. All he could think about was Geraldine. She was going to end her marriage this weekend – for him. He knew what that felt like. It wouldn't be easy. Although his was a relief at the end. But there was Harriet to think about. He wanted to be there for her, too. He hadn't been there for Geraldine when she gave up her baby. He didn't know Phillip or Geraldine's children and couldn't predict how they'd react. He'd only just been reintroduced to Theresa and he still didn't trust her. She was holding something back. Wesley tried to convince himself that Geraldine was right about her children. Only, he wasn't so sure about Phillip.

It was no good. He couldn't get Geraldine out of his mind. He knew what he had to do.

Geraldine had a lot to think about as she strolled through the sunroom. She decided to tell Phillip privately before dinner tonight.

This weekend was going to be truly momentous for everyone involved. But there was no going back now, her mind was truly made up.

Geraldine wasn't afraid – she felt alive with new hope, and she didn't want anything to spoil it. She checked her watch again, which was a habit she attributed to her hectic work days. She had a few chores to attend to before she picked her mother up from the airport at lunchtime.

'I'm telling Phillip tonight,' Geraldine said as she picked up her mother's overnight bag and walked out of the small airport. There was a light breeze but at least the rain had kept away.

'Maybe that's for the best. He should know about Harriet before the children.'

'No, Mum. I'm going to speak to him about our marriage. But you're right. I will tell him about Harriet before I tell the kids.'

Her daughters' news wasn't what Theresa wanted to hear. 'Oh, Geraldine, are you sure about this? You've only just been reunited with Wesley. Are you sure it isn't just your hormones overreacting because of Harriet? Maybe you should leave the past alone for a while. Concentrate on Harriet and the children.'

Geraldine stopped walking and turned to face her mother. 'It sounds like you're still trying to tear Wesley and me apart. Granddad is dead, Dad is dead. Why do you still dislike him so much? You don't know him.'

Theresa was flushed by the accusation. 'I do like him, Geraldine. I'm just concerned about you and Phillip. He's still your husband.'

'Mum, my marriage is over. We've just treading water.'

'And do you think Wesley would move here to be with you? He also has a career.'

'Don't you think I haven't thought of that? All my children will be on the mainland soon, and I'll be here alone.'

'You know Geraldine, maybe you should sell this place, buy another hotel on the mainland? You'll be closer to your children.'

'I can't do that, Mum. The Windermere is my life. Granny gifted it to me; she knew about my dream of owning a hotel. She at least trusted me. I don't want to start over again somewhere else. This hotel is my life.'

Theresa said no more, she had to stop interfering in her daughter's life. This was Harriet's weekend, and she needed to support them both. But she had also come to seek her son's forgiveness.

When they arrived back at the Windermere, Geraldine collected her mother's room key card from Carrie at reception.

'Carrie, you remember my mother, Theresa Cook. Mum this is Carrie, someone I can't do without.'

'Of course I remember you, Mrs Cook. I've put you in room 108.'

'Thank you, Carrie,' Theresa said, accepting her key card, then as an afterthought, she turned to Geraldine and said as they walked off, 'you know Geraldine, if you divorce Phillip, he might have a claim to half the hotel. Can you afford to buy him out? You may have to sell after all if you can't raise the money.'

'I haven't thought that far ahead yet, Mum. I'll discuss it with Callum; he'll advise me on my options.'

Geraldine continued their conversation all the way to the lift, then she pressed the button for the first floor.

'I'll find the cash to buy him out.'

'I'd like to help you if I can. But you never know, maybe one of your children will help you run it, maybe even Harriet, she's studying business management at university.'

Geraldine thanked her mother but declined the offer. The Windermere Hotel was her passion, not her children's. She had no illusions of any of them running it when she finally stepped aside.

Arriving at room 108, Geraldine carried her mother's bag inside and put it on the bed.

'Hazel is at school, but if you pop by the annex, I can fix you some lunch.'

'No. I'll pass if that's okay. I'll order a sandwich if I'm hungry. I just want to put my feet up for an hour or so.'

'Alright, but come to the annex for dinner tonight, at 7 pm. It will be just me, Hazel and Phillip.'

'I'd like that. I might take myself off for a walk later if the weather holds and join you later for dinner.'

Geraldine kissed her mother on the cheek before taking her leave.

Theresa touched Geraldine's face. It wasn't a gesture the mother and daughter were used to. But the action meant more to Theresa than her daughter. *Maybe things need to change after all*, she thought. *I can't interfere with my daughter's happiness. Not anymore.* Once the dust settled, Theresa hoped their relationship would grow into what she always hoped it would be. However, Theresa knew she couldn't put off telling her daughter the truth. Either way, it was going to hurt.

Theresa looked out her window as she thought about her life and her mistakes. She married Winston not long after being introduced to him at a party at their family home. As expected, he became a partner in her father's law firm, and his name was eventually added to the title – Windermere, Hartnell and Cook. Emily, her older sister, married a teacher – without their father's blessing. He told her, 'you can do better, my girl,' to which Emily had replied, 'better than you'll ever comprehend.' Emily was estranged from her parents after that. Theresa envied Emily, who had been happily married for over forty years. But her pity was saved for her mother, who rarely saw Emily after their estrangement. She didn't want to end up like her mother. Her father, Simon Hartnell, had a lot to answer for.

It was a sad day when mothers and daughters became estranged from each other. They shared a sacred bond that should never be broken. Theresa had been proud of her mother when she finally stood up to her father. By the time Theresa's mother inherited her family estate on St Mary's, she was too old to leave her father. Theresa still remembers the day when her mother defied her husband and gave the old house to Geraldine and split the remaining money between her two daughters, Emily and Theresa. Simon Hartnell had ruined his granddaughter's happiness, but Lucinda Hartnell wanted her granddaughter to fulfil her dreams and gifting her Windermere Lodge was her way of helping her achieve that. She would be beholden to no one. Theresa needed to find that same courage in herself now or risk losing her children forever.

Jealousy and prejudice could be dangerous in the hands of a spiteful, bitter man. But this weekend Theresa was going to put things right. Especially with Callum. She was worried about Vivienne, as she appeared to be falling into the same trap that her mother had done. Theresa removed her mobile from her handbag and called her grandson Andrew and asked him for an update. She needed to know more about Vivienne's new boyfriend, Tommy Burke.

'Good news, we had a couple of late bookings after the Johnson's cancelled. We only have one vacant room this weekend, room 116,' Carrie announced as Geraldine walked past reception.

'That's great, Carrie. I'll be in my office if my husband comes looking for me.'

Geraldine knew Phillip would more likely head to the hotel's bar for a drink before he came looking for her. Hazel had texted her to say she was going to her friend's house after school and would be home around five. Geraldine closed her office door for some privacy and rested back in her chair.

Geraldine's thoughts were interrupted by a knock on her door. Her heart skipped a beat; she wasn't ready to confront Phillip yet.

'Enter.'

'Hi, Geraldine,' Barb said. 'You got a minute?'

Geraldine sighed with relief, 'Sure Barb, what's up?'

'John Mumford called, he had a good trip out. He caught some lobster, crab and some John Dory. Wants to know how much we'll take. Chef wants to put lobster on the menu this weekend. He's thinking of a lobster mornay and a spicy lobster and truffle tortellini dish.'

'Sounds good.'

'Great. I'll let him know.'

'Listen, I'm going to be a bit preoccupied this weekend,' Geraldine said. 'All my family will be here. Please let Claude know that Carrie will hold down the fort if the kitchen staff need anything.'

'Oh. Right you are,' she said. 'That must be nice having your whole family home.'

'I hope so. I have a surprise for them. I'm just not sure how they'll take it.'

Barbara nodded and quietly closed the door. She doubted Geraldine would want to confide in her about her private affairs.

Barbara headed back to the kitchen as she had the dinner menu to prepare. Chef was already on the warpath as staff were taking too many smoke breaks. Plus, more food was unaccounted for in the kitchen.

Geraldine looked at her watch. Nearly 4 pm. She reluctantly rose from her chair and left her office. She inspected the dining room, out of habit more than anything else. It was well-presented. Then she walked through the kitchen and exited the hotel via the service entrance, which stepped out into a small courtyard. It was only twenty feet from her own kitchen door at the back of the annex. Guests were not allowed in this part of the hotel. The small rectangular bay area was where staff could sit on old chairs and milk crates and have their cigarette breaks. It also doubled as the loading bay for deliveries.

Geraldine entered her private residence, dropped her keys on the kitchen table and removed her jacket. She helped herself to a glass of wine from the fridge and downed the entire glass in one sitting. She needed it.

The annex was rarely locked, except when Hazel was home alone.

'Phillip? Phillip?' Geraldine yelled, hoping she wouldn't hear a reply.

'I'm up here,' he replied.

Geraldine sighed and climbed the stairs to their bedroom. She found Phillip at his desk by the window. He didn't turn around.

How had they become so distant? Geraldine took a deep breath.

'Can we talk?' she asked.

'Sure.'

'No. I mean talk. Please stop what you're doing and look at me.'

Phillip put his pen down. He knew it. *She's having an affair*, he thought. He hoped so, it would make his announcement less guilt-ridden. He turned around to face his wife.

'I'm not sure how to tell you this. But I wanted you to know before I told the children.'

'You're having an affair, aren't you?'

'What?'

'Your mother's an awful liar.'

'What are you talking about?'

'Well! Aren't you?'

'No. But while we're on the subject of affairs, maybe you can admit to yours.'

Phillip was taken by surprise. How the hell did she know? He had to think quickly, should he deny it? he wondered. No. But his delay in answering told Geraldine he was.

Geraldine studied Phillip. Was it true love for him or just a fling with a besotted skinny young student who couldn't differentiate between love and lust?

'Look! I don't care, Phillip. If you're happy, then I'm happy for you. Let's face it, we've grown apart. I think we have to admit it.'

'That's magnanimous of you.'

Geraldine was flabbergasted by his remark. He's the one having the affair, and he's pissed off.

Geraldine raised her hands in front of her in a gesture of surrender. 'Look, I don't want to fight, not this weekend. There's something else I need to discuss with you, which is far more important to me.'

Phillip eyed Geraldine. What was more important than the disintegration of their marriage? 'Alright. What is it?'

Geraldine was now hesitant to continue. She felt loath to tell him now, but she just wanted it over with. She sat on the end of their bed and took a moment before she began.

'When I was sixteen, I had a child. A daughter. But I gave her up for adoption.'

She watched Phillip's reaction. There wasn't one, so she continued.

'I got on with my life. But a month ago, my daughter contacted my mother, asking to see me. I agreed, and that's why I've been going to the mainland this last month, to see her.' Geraldine took another deep breath and exhaled slowly. She waited for Phillip to say something.

He only laughed.

'Why are you laughing? That's not the response I expected, even from you, Phillip.'

'I'm sorry. I thought you were having an affair. Sneaking off to London and Plymouth.'

'How did you know where I was?'

Phillip stopped laughing. 'I had a hunch. You weren't at your mother's.'

Geraldine eyed him suspiciously.

'Look, I'm not angry, just surprised,' he said, as he rested his arm over his writing chair. 'But this happened long before we met. If this girl wants to get to know you, then I'm happy for you.'

'Good. I've invited her this weekend, so I can introduce her to our children.'

'What?'

'She's going to be a part of my life from now on. If she wants to be. But I'd rather I tell the children all together, then they can meet her on Saturday night. It won't be easy for me to tell the kids. But if they have any questions for me or Harriet, they can be addressed this weekend. She arrives with her friend Ashley tomorrow on the ferry. I've put them in room 204.'

'Well, that's decided then. Thanks for telling me first so I won't be completely embarrassed in front of my kids.'

'Stop it,' Geraldine said. 'This is hard for me. It was painful when I gave her up. I always feared this day would come and now that it has, I want it to go smoothly for everyone, especially the kids. She's lovely, and I think *our* children will embrace her as a sister, in time. We brought them up to be open-minded and respectful, I'm confident they'll understand.'

'Alright. But there's something I need to discuss with you too. But it can wait until the weekend is over.'

'Why not just tell me now. You're having an affair, aren't you?'

Phillip took a moment to answer, but eventually said, 'Yes.' Then, after another long pause, 'but it will keep until Sunday.'

'Please keep what I've said from the children until I've told them on Saturday afternoon.'

'Of course. As you'll keep my affair private until I've told the kids.'

Geraldine nodded her head in agreement. She wasn't surprised or angry. She was actually relieved. She got off the bed and walked out the room. She thought she might sleep in one of the kid's rooms tonight. Now that they were being honest with each other, there was no need for pretence.

Phillip picked up his phone and sent Clarissa a text message:

I've done it. I've told her.

He put down his phone. Within a minute he received a reply:

I knew you could do it.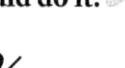

Clarissa put her phone back in her handbag. She was standing in front of a jewellery shop, admiring the diamond rings. She had doubted that Phillip would actually go through with it, but he did. *Good for him,* she thought. He had more mantle than she gave him credit for.

Clarissa had already chosen the church she would be married in and which maternity hospital she'd have their child in. Now, she'd just chosen her wedding ring. All she had to do now was find a house she liked, and Phillip liked, of course – as long as he chose the same one she wanted.

Clarissa thought of cancelling her flight tomorrow but looking down at the diamond rings in the window, she decided not to. The weekend was a long time for something to go wrong. She decided to stick to her plan and make sure everyone else was on the same page she was.

Chapter Seven

Hazel sat silently at the table. The mood at dinner was sombre. She looked around the table, but even her Nan didn't have much to say.

'Well, I hope it's going to be more festive when Andrew and Vivienne arrive tomorrow,' she said, trying to stir up some conversation. She looked from her mother to her father, who sat across from each other, grave and silent.

'Yeah. I'm sure it will be a hoot,' her father finally replied. Geraldine gave him a stern look. Phillip's only reply was to wink at his daughter.

Theresa decided to change the subject. 'Are you looking forward to going to your new school next term, Hazel?'

'Yeah, I suppose. At least my friends will be there too.'

'I'll miss you, poppet,' Geraldine said, looking solemnly at her daughter. *Why do they have to grow up and leave?*

'I'll miss you too, Mum.'

'Don't worry, love,' Phillip said. 'You'll be a three-hour drive from me during the week, if you ever need anything, you only have to call me. Then you'll be here with your mum on the weekends.'

'I know. But we're all separated. I wish we could be together again. Forever.'

'Life evolves, darling,' her grandmother said. 'We can't all stay fixed in one place forever. Life pulls us away sometimes. But think of it this way. You'll have many places to visit.'

'Absolutely,' replied Geraldine, although she felt as solemn as her daughter about her children's separation.

'You never know, you might end up studying at Southampton University. Then I'll see you more often,' Phillip said.

'I'm not sure what I want to do yet,' Hazel replied, although that was a lie. She knew exactly what she wanted to study at university but didn't want to share it with anyone yet. She was afraid they'd disapprove or laugh it off as a five-minute wonder.

'Don't worry about that yet,' Geraldine replied. 'You've plenty of time to decide and there's always a job here for you.'

Geraldine spooned more mashed potato onto her daughter's plate, out of habit than anything else. But the thought of Hazel going away to the mainland to finish her schooling depressed her. She wasn't ready for that, yet. Hazel was still too young. Although she was now the same age that Andrew and Vivienne had been when they left to finish school on the mainland, Hazel seemed younger, smaller, and more fragile. Besides, Vivienne and Andrew had each other.

Geraldine watched Hazel put salt on her mashed potato and play with it. She hoped Hazel would cope with her news tomorrow. She had always been a bright, open-minded young girl. Geraldine turned her attention to Phillip, but he was busy cutting into his meat in a state of agitation.

Geraldine knew at that moment, without a doubt, that she no longer loved him.

After dinner, Geraldine took her mother for a walk. The night sea air was invigorating. Geraldine fed her arm through her mother's as they took a stroll towards Hugh Town. Tomorrow was going to be a busy day for both of them. Even though she was anxious about Harriet's introduction, she also felt a sense of freedom and rejuvenation at what was to come.

As they strolled along, they passed some of the hotel's guests out for their evening walk.

'Good evening, Mr and Mrs Grisham,' Geraldine said.

'Evening,' they both replied, as they walked past. Lorna giggled and snuggled up to her new husband. Geraldine heard her say under her breath, 'I still haven't gotten used to being called Mrs Grisham yet.'

Geraldine watched them arm in arm, shoulder to shoulder, she envied their intimacy. She imagined her and Wesley embracing in the same way. Free to express their love once more.

Locals couldn't walk anywhere on St Mary's without bumping into someone they knew. Tonight was no exception by the amount of 'good evening's' Geraldine said and received on her walk. Everyone knew, and more importantly, cared about each other on St Mary's. Geraldine couldn't imagine living anywhere else. She thought of her grandmother, and wondered how she could have left, especially to marry a man like her grandfather? But that thought made her think about Wesley again. How can they have a relationship when he was stationed in Plymouth and she on St Mary's? Long distance relationships don't work. Her own marriage was testimony to that.

'I never asked Phillip how long he was having his affair,' Geraldine said, matter-of-factly, not looking at her mother.

Her mother sighed, 'Do you really want to know?'

'Yes. I do actually. I want to know how long he felt the need to sleep with someone else. I didn't even ask how old she was.'

'Well, I'm sure, she's younger, and thinner. Isn't that how it always goes?' Theresa meant the jibe kindly. 'If he wasn't having an affair, would you begin one with Wesley? And be honest, Geraldine.'

Geraldine had to think for a moment before answering. She promised herself honesty. 'Yes, I wouldn't be able to help myself. But I would have asked Phillip for a divorce. I wouldn't skulk around behind his back.'

'I admire you, Geraldine. But women have choices nowadays, don't they? Just make sure you make the right one.'

'Evening, Geraldine,' said James Herbert as he and Joan trekked by, heading back to the hotel.

'Evening, James. I hope you both had a good day?'

'Smashing,' he said. Joan Herbert was huffing and puffing and unable to reply. She could only nod.

On their return, they bumped into the Byrd family. John Byrd was carrying his son Bailey, who was half asleep in his arms. His red hair was wild under his hood.

Carol told them that they'd just been to the cinema in Hugh Town. Geraldine reminded them about the open-air cinema. But Carol said it was still a bit too cold for them to stay out in the evenings too long. Geraldine remembered they were from

Queensland, Australia. She made a mental note to check with Carrie that they had extra blankets in their room.

Geraldine entered the Windermere Hotel, walked over to the reception desk and asked the night concierge for a notepad and pen. She left a note for Carrie, who had finished her shift at six. In winter, the phone system was diverted to her own residence after eight o'clock, but for the rest of the year, the reception was manned 24/7.

Geraldine's children all chipped in and worked at the hotel during their summer holidays. Geraldine wondered how many more summers she had left before her children preferred to summer elsewhere. This year may well be the last family summer they shared. That thought depressed her.

Geraldine said goodnight to the night manager and escorted her mother into the bar, where they found a table. She ordered a gin and tonic for herself, and a cappuccino for her mother.

The bar was full that evening. Everyone seemed blissfully happy. Light music was playing in the background as the fire crackled with life. The soft lights scattered around the room on the side-table lamps gave a romantic ambience to the room. The portraits hanging on the walls were originals that had lived at the hotel for well over two centuries. The Herberts were sitting across from the fire, enjoying their coffees. Evan and Judith McCloud were finishing their drinks quietly as they listened to the music. Lorna and Hugh Grisham, the newlyweds, were still intertwined in each other's arms on the couch by the window. The last couple in the room was the London couple. Geraldine had forgotten their names momentarily, but they appeared to be a professional couple. Maybe lawyers or doctors? But they used separate surnames when checking-in. She wondered if they were simply unmarried partners, or what Carrie liked to call 'dangerous liaisons'. Geraldine chuckled to herself at the thought. She remembered how she and Phillip had been in the early days of their marriage. Passionate and in love, but now both were in love with other people. Was she about to become one of Carrie's dangerous liaisons? Geraldine felt a spark of excitement.

Theresa stifled a yawn, so Geraldine finished her drink and walked her mother upstairs to her room and said goodnight. Tomorrow was going to be a very hectic and challenging day for everyone.

Chapter Eight

Saturday morning

'**P**lease just sign this form Mr Budd, then you're all set.'

'Thank you, Carrie,' he said, before handing back the signed form. 'Did you arrange the picnic basket I ordered?'

'I certainly did, I'll go fetch it for you now.'

When Carrie returned to reception, Mr Budd's partner had joined him. Carrie handed him the picnic basket and wished them both a great day sailing.

'We will,' he replied. Only his partner didn't look so confident.

Carrie scanned the signed permission form through the printer and attached the file to their room 104. She wondered how much sailing experience the London couple had. She was in charge all weekend and was determined that nothing should go wrong. Carrie allocated herself a staff bedroom below stairs as she would be pulling double shifts all weekend. She had no intention of leaving the hotel while in charge. This weekend she would prove to Geraldine how capable she was at running the hotel.

A moment later, Mr and Mrs Herbert walked past reception. They had their backpacks secured to their backs, and as customary, Mr Herbert had his lofty walking stick in tow. They nodded at Carrie as they headed off for the day.

'We'll be back for dinner, dear,' Joan Herbert said. They were headed to Tresco today, a smaller island north of St Mary's. The Herberts always stocked up at breakfast with extra pastries and sandwiches for their lunch. They would fill their own flasks with tea and coffee from their room. Carrie was astounded by their endless energy, considering they were in their late seventies.

Geraldine had another restless night. She had been too excited to sleep, but now she just felt drained. She had slept in this morning, something she rarely allowed herself, but when she looked at herself in the mirror, she saw big bags under her eyes. She quickly jumped in the shower to wake herself up.

What if Phillip decides to tell the kids before I do? What if he spoils everything? Geraldine shook the thoughts away. He wouldn't do that. He wasn't a spiteful man. Her head was full of too many scenarios as she stepped out of the shower. She looked long and hard in the mirror once more and said to herself, 'You can do this. Just breathe.'

After breakfast, Geraldine walked over to the hotel to check that Carrie had the rooms ready for her guests. She had requested fresh flowers in Harriet and Ashley's room, along with a box of chocolates. She had texted Ashley during the week to find out Harriet's favourite.

Carrie reassured Geraldine that everything was under control and she should go be with her family. She didn't know why Geraldine was making such a fuss about these two guests. Whoever they were, they were making Geraldine giddy with excitement. Carrie wondered if one of them was Andrew's fiancée.

'Hi there, good looking!'

Geraldine spun around to find her brother, Callum, standing in the foyer.

She rushed up to him and gave him a tight hug.

'I'm so glad you're here, Callum.'

'Hey, come on now. Is everything alright?'

'Sorry,' she said, releasing him. 'I'm a bit emotional this morning. I'm just so glad you came. So is Mum.'

'Is *she* already here?'

'Yes.' Geraldine frowned at him. 'Our mother *is* here. She arrived yesterday. Come on,' she said putting her arm through his. 'I'll take you up to your room, you're in 202. There's a lot going on this weekend. I'm glad you're here to share it with me. I'm going to need your professional advice on a delicate matter. But it can wait until later.'

'Sounds intriguing.'

Geraldine walked her brother upstairs, unlocked his door and gave him his key card. She left him to unpack and walked back downstairs to her mother's room and knocked on her door. The only time her mother ever had breakfast in bed was when she stayed in a hotel. The Windermere was no exception.

'Come in, the door's unlocked.'

Geraldine opened her mother's door and walked into the room.

'I hope you enjoyed your breakfast.'

'I always do when I don't have to cook it myself.' Theresa took another sip of her tea.

'Callum has just arrived on the early flight.'

Her mother put her teacup back on the saucer.

'I'm expecting another guest today,' Theresa said. 'I wasn't sure if he would come, but he confirmed last night that he's arriving this afternoon.'

'Sounds intriguing. Who?'

'Khenan.'

Geraldine raised her eyebrows. She wasn't expecting that. 'How did you manage that?'

'I lied to him. It's about time I put things right with Callum.'

Geraldine wanted to cry. She put her hand on her mother's.

'Oh, Mum. You know they've been separated for a long time.'

'I know. But only because Callum was angry and confused, which had nothing to do with Khenan. I'll speak to him before dinner. It's a private matter and Callum doesn't need everyone to hear what I have to say. I'll say hello before Khenan arrives.'

'Alright.'

'Please don't tell Callum, if you see him. I want it to be a surprise.'

'My lips are sealed. Don't forget dinner is at six tonight.' Geraldine left her mother to finish her breakfast.

Geraldine's adrenaline was growing with every skip she took down the stairs. She started singing under her breath. She always preferred to use the staircase instead of the lift, as it saved her from going to the gym.

After giving final instructions to Carrie, Geraldine went back to the annex and found Hazel and Phillip still eating breakfast. She kissed her daughter's head and gave a slight nod at Phillip. The ferry didn't arrive until after lunch, so Geraldine wasn't quite sure what to do with herself.

Once the breakfast dishes were washed and put away, Geraldine kept pacing the living room. She walked back into the kitchen and wiped down the already clean kitchen surfaces again. She finally received a text from Andrew confirming their flight was on time. He and Vivienne would be arriving just before lunch. Geraldine sighed with relief.

After her children had arrived, Geraldine would walk down to Hugh Town and wait for the afternoon ferry. She decided to prepare lunch now – she knew her children would be hungry when they arrived. As she gathered some salad ingredients from the fridge, she heard Phillip's phone chime. Moments later, she heard him swear, before he rushed past her and out the back door.

Geraldine wondered what had agitated him so much. She doubted it was work. Before she could put any more thought into it, Hazel entered the kitchen, 'What's up with Dad? He jumped out of the chair and stormed out of the room.'

'It could be work, sweetheart. Don't worry about it,' she said, trying to sound reassuring.

She kissed Hazel on the cheek.

'Today's going to be a complicated day for everyone,' Geraldine said. 'But I hope in time it will prove to be a good one. All you need to know Hazel, is that I love you very much.'

'You're scaring me, Mum. Is something wrong?'

'No. No, sweetheart. Everything's fine,' she said, stroking Hazel's hair. 'It's just, life can sometimes throw us curveballs. But that doesn't mean they're bad curveballs.' Hazel only nodded at her mother, who was talking in riddles again. She grabbed an apple on her way out of the kitchen. She had somewhere she needed to be before Vivienne and Andrew arrived. Shaking her head, Hazel wondered if her parents were going to separate or get a divorce. She wasn't blind. When her dad did come home, her parents barely spoke to one another anymore.

Carrie left the reception and headed to the kitchen to make herself a coffee. Neither Claude nor Barbara was in the kitchen. When she asked one of the kitchen hands, they said Barbara was outside having a smoke. Carrie walked through the kitchen and found Barbara sitting on a milk crate, smoking. She appeared to be in a daze. She didn't reply when Carrie called her name.

'Barbara,' she had to repeat, even louder.

Barbara finally looked up.

'I wanted to make sure you and Claude have everything you need this weekend.'

'I'll let you know if we don't.'

Carrie could see Barbara was in one of her moods. She deserved more respect from her.

'By then, it will be too late. I'm running the hotel this weekend. It's important to me that everything's just right.'

Barbara answered slowly so Carrie wouldn't misunderstand her. 'We have everything we need. I'll let you know if we need anything more.'

Carrie's dislike for Barbara grew daily. If she had her way, she would have sacked her months ago. Carrie didn't know why Geraldine put up with her moodiness but decided to change the subject. 'I think it's great that all of Geraldine's family are coming over this weekend. I think she has something important to tell them. She's been taking a lot of time off lately.'

'That's her business, not ours.'

'There are two young women arriving today. They're Geraldine's personal guests.'

Barbara didn't want to hear any more about Geraldine's family reunion. She took one more long drag of her cigarette before putting it out in the sandbox. 'I'm sure we'll find out soon enough, if Geraldine wants to tell her staff her personal business.'

Barbara never took to Carrie, she found her clingy and too nice for her liking, it felt like a pretence at times. Besides, she had her own problems to deal with. She stood up and stretched before heading back inside the kitchen.

'Are you fucking kidding me?' Phillip yelled into his mobile, once he was outside the annex and out of earshot of Geraldine and Hazel. He was pacing around in circles about twenty feet from the kitchen.

'Relax. I wanted to surprise you. You've told your wife about us, and I thought you could use some morale support this weekend. Besides, there's something I need to talk to you about.'

'Couldn't it wait until I get back on Monday?'

'No. It can't!' Clarissa replied sharply.

'Fine, let me know where you're staying and I'll try and get away.'

'No need. I've booked myself in at the Windermere.'

Phillip stopped pacing. *Shit, shit, shit,* he mumbled under his breath. 'What the hell are you playing at?'

'If your wife is also having an affair, then it's a fresh start for both of you. Now, we all know where we stand – don't we?'

'She isn't having an affair.'

'What? You confronted her about it?'

'Yes. If you can believe this, she had a child when she was sixteen and she wants to introduce her to the family tonight, she's arriving today on the bloody ferry.'

'Holy shit!' Clarissa said, chuckling.

Phillip was getting annoyed. His life was about to be turned upside down and Clarissa found it amusing.

Phillip's silence implied caution. Clarissa stopped laughing. 'Oh, come on, Phillip. We've been sleeping together for over a year now. Your marriage was dead long before that, otherwise you wouldn't have cheated on her.'

'But now it's about to become a reality. Divorces can be messy. I have to handle this just right, and I have the kids to think about.'

'They're not kids anymore, Phillip. They'll handle it. I'm at the airport now, and I'm flying into St Mary's this afternoon. We'll talk then.' Clarissa hung up, before she said something she would regret.

Phillip cursed himself, but instead of walking back into the annex, he took himself off for a walk along the beach to calm himself. When he returned, he entered the hotel and found Carrie on reception talking to a guest.

'You're welcome, Mr Burrows, and I hope you enjoy your short stay with us.'

'I hope so too.' The guest picked up his overnight bag and placed it on his shoulder before walking up the staircase.

'Ah, Carrie,' Phillip said. 'Could you please tell me if a Clarissa Montgomery is a guest this weekend?'

'Certainly, Mr Locke.' Carrie brought up the reservations list and checked the name. The colour drained from his face when she confirmed Clarissa Montgomery would be in room 201.

'Thank you,' he said. He left the hotel and walked the short distance to the annex. Before returning home, he let out a loud yawp of pent-up frustration.

What is Clarissa playing at? he wondered. Clarissa could be confrontational when her back was up. She was used to getting her own way. Although, that was Phillip's inability to say no to her. *No. She would never cause a scene where his children were concerned.* But he did worry about what his children would say once they found out about Clarissa. But it wasn't his fault that he fell in love with another woman.

Then his mind drifted to Clarissa's long legs and how they could wrap tightly around him. Her soft skin against his. Her touch. Her breasts. Her kiss.

He deserved happiness too.

Room 202

Theresa knocked on her son's door. When he opened it, there was a moment's silence between them. Callum knew he was expected to talk to his mother at some point during the weekend, but he didn't expect it would be this soon. He stood aside to let her in. But there was no motherly hug or kiss, she simply entered the room, then turned to face him.

'How have you been?' he asked.

'Well. And you, dear?'

'Fine,' he replied, flatly.

'Look, Callum. We can go around in circles all weekend with polite chit-chat, or we can have a serious talk.' Theresa took a deep breath. 'I'm sorry. So deeply sorry for what happened with your grandfather, and how he hurt you and Khenan. And I'm sorry your dad and I didn't step up when we should have.'

'Mum. Stop. It was a long time ago. Sorry has long since passed, don't you think?'

'It's never too late to say sorry. Please let me explain.'

Callum shrugged his shoulders but indicated that his mother should sit down. This was Geraldine's weekend, whatever his mother had to say, needed to be said before tonight.

'I thought we could discuss this over lunch, so I took the liberty.' As if on cue, there was a knock on the door. Callum walked over to answer it. A waiter was standing there with a trolley of food and cutlery. He sighed at her temerity.

'Thank you,' Theresa said to the waiter, as he pushed the trolley into the room. 'I'll serve it up.'

'Very good, madam,' he said, and walked quietly out of the room.

Theresa took the food off the trolley and put it on the table. Once this was done, she sat down at the table and gestured to her son to join her.

'I was shocked by your grandfather's cruelty, but I had no say in how the law firm was run. And my opinion never counted for anything where he was concerned. But I was so proud of you the day you announced that you were gay and in a relationship with Khenan. I'd always known, of course, but the fact that you felt you could tell everyone – I have never been so proud of you.'

'My illustrious grandfather wasn't, and neither was my own father, come to that. Both were clearly ashamed of me. So ashamed that Granddad sacked Khenan at work, in front of everyone. I couldn't stay after that. Neither of them could look me in the eye.'

'Your grandfather hurt many people in his life. Mainly his family. Your father was a good lawyer, but not a strong man. He always held my father in high esteem. It's a shame he died before he could put things right, he so wanted to. He loved both you and Geraldine very much.'

'Are you saying I should forgive him?'

'No. I'm hoping you'll understand him. All I've ever wanted was for you and Geraldine to succeed and be happy. You're a lawyer now. You're twice the lawyer your grandfather and father ever were. Windermere, Hartnell and Cook changed when my father took over the reins and not for the better.'

Callum was quiet for a moment.

'I know you and Khenan have separated, but you belong together,' Theresa continued. 'You both had a dream of starting a law firm together. There will be a lot of secrets coming out this weekend and your sister will need your support. I hope by the end of the weekend we can find common ground and start again. All I have is my children, and I would die to protect either of you.'

Callum wanted to be angry with his mother, but he couldn't.

'What's going on with Geraldine? She was anxious when I saw her this morning.'

'The past has caught up with us again, but I'm going to put it right. I only hope it's not too late.'

'People pay me for legal advice every day, but to love someone, unconditionally, is free. So, you would think there would be more love in the world.'

Theresa couldn't agree more.

They ate lunch quietly together. It was a start. By 1:30 pm, Theresa said goodbye to her son and walked back to her room.

When Andrew and Vivienne arrived at the airport, Geraldine greeted them with her biggest hugs and kisses. She'd missed them so. Her twins were growing up fast. Both looked well, though. She couldn't ask for anything more than that. They were both doing well at university, but Geraldine knew her children had their own careers to carve out.

Andrew was sporting a three-day growth. Geraldine wondered if he was trying to grow a beard or if he was just being lazy. She rubbed her hand on his cheek and said, 'What's this, then?'

'Don't worry, I'll shave before dinner tonight. I've been studying late into the night all week and couldn't be bothered shaving.'

'I thought it'd taken you a month to grow that thing,' Vivienne said, teasing.

'Leave him be. He's still my handsome boy.' Geraldine linked her arms through both her twins' arms as she directed them to the minivan. She was so happy they were home again.

Sitting in the minivan, Vivienne turned on her phone again to see if there were any new messages. Disappointedly, she put her phone in her back pocket of her jeans and stared out the window.

Back at the annex, Vivienne and Andrew dropped their bags in the living room and saw Hazel watching television. She quickly turned it off when they entered.

'Hi ya, squirt,' Andrew said, as he sat down on the settee.

'I'm glad you're here,' she said. 'Mum and Dad have been acting stranger than usual. Mum has an announcement to make but wouldn't say what it is until you were both here.'

'I think I know what it is,' Vivienne announced solemnly.

'What?' Hazel asked. Vivienne looked at her twin, who nodded she should continue.

'I think Mum and Dad are getting a divorce,' she whispered.

'What?' Hazel snapped, sitting upright. But she was half expecting it. She was just surprised Vivienne and Andrew knew before she did.

Andrew looked at Vivienne again, 'Tell her.'

Vivienne leaned forward and whispered softly to Hazel. 'A few months ago, I was in Southampton, and I thought I'd stop by and surprise Dad at work. He wasn't in his rooms, but the bursar said he saw him walk down to the lake, so I went down there. I found him alright. He was lying on the grass with another woman. A younger woman. They were kissing.'

'Argh … you mean a student?' Hazel asked distastefully.

'No. She was older than that. In her thirties, I'd say.'

'Did you tell Mum?'

'No,' answered Andrew and Vivienne simultaneously.

'We decided not to. We didn't want to hurt her.'

'What if they get a divorce?' Hazel asked, growing anxious at the thought.

'Maybe it's for the best. Dad's rarely here anyway. Mum can get on with her life. Maybe find someone else, too.'

'What about me?'

'You're going to be fine, squirt. You're going off to school after summer. Then to university. Mum will be here by herself.'

'Everyone's leaving,' she said fretfully. 'I hardly see you two anymore.'

'I'm sorry, Hazel,' Andrew replied. 'We have a lot of studying to do and it's time-consuming having to travel half the day to come home on the weekends.'

Vivienne could see Hazel was upset, but there wasn't much she could do about that.

'I know it seems worrying now,' she said, reassuringly, 'but when you're at your new school, you'll feel differently. We were anxious at first when we left.'

'Yes, but you had each other.'

'You'll have fun and meet new friends,' Andrew said. 'Life has to go on. We both love the Scilly Isles, but we want careers too, which we can only achieve if we work on the mainland.'

'I know.' Hazel lowered her head. She understood what her brother and sister were saying, but she wasn't ready to accept it. She wanted to study Marine Biology. She'd been fascinated with marine life ever since they moved to St Mary's. She had often dreamed of visiting the Great Barrier Reef, in Queensland, Australia. But when she first mentioned it to her father in passing, he brushed it off, telling her that it was a nice hobby, but not a worthwhile career, so she never brought it up again.

The whole family ate lunch together, but on seeing how quiet Hazel was, Andrew jumped up and said, 'Come on. Let's go down to the beach and see if we can spot any seals. We can also search for more seashells to add to your collection.'

'Okay...' Hazel said, a little more upbeat. 'There's something I want to show you.'

Vivienne checked her watch. She needed to be somewhere later in the afternoon. But she had time now, so she grabbed her sister's hand and pulled her out of the chair. Together, they all headed to Pelistry in search of seals.

Geraldine watched her three children head off down the beach together. She remembered how it was when they were young, Vivienne and Andrew would both hold Hazel's hands as they strolled along the beaches looking for seashells. Would this be the last time? She loved how they were all together again. She dearly wanted this weekend to go as planned. She decided to prepare dinner, which was simple enough. She cleaned the vegetables and peeled the potatoes and put them in a saucepan of cold water. She took some lard from the fridge and dropped small amounts into a cupcake tray to make Yorkshire puddings. They were Hazel's favourite. Geraldine couldn't go wrong with a roast beef dinner. Her only exception was to buy an apple pie for dessert, as she didn't have time to make one herself.

Geraldine kept an eye on the time. She needed to leave soon to meet the ferry when it arrived. She would use the hotel's minivan for the second time that day.

Geraldine stood anxiously near the ferry wharf as she waited for Harriet and Ashley to disembark. When she saw them, she waved excitedly to them. Harriet's face lit up when she saw Geraldine, her anxiety melting away on seeing her smile. She reassured herself that they had to like her. *What's not to like?*

'I hope your crossing wasn't too rough?' she asked.

'I'm alright, but Ashley's looking a little peaky.'

Geraldine chuckled. 'Well, let's get you back to the hotel and you can rest up. But it's best to sit upright in bed and not have your head down. Slow deep breaths will see you right, Ashley.'

Geraldine took Ashley's carry bag and walked them to the minivan, which was waiting in the bus bay.

As they walked off, a young man brushed past them. He had only a small rucksack slung over his shoulder. He was in a hurry and headed into town. He didn't seem too pleased to be on St Mary's. He sniffed the sea air but turned his nose up at the saltiness. He pulled up the collar of his jacket as he headed off. As he walked, he was sending a text message. He didn't act like a tourist.

Geraldine escorted Harriet and Ashley into the hotel. Both women were impressed by the grandeur and architecture of the old house. Harriet scanned the foyer and all the old paintings on the walls and the antique furniture, but what impressed her the most was the grand staircase leading up to the first floor.

Carrie was checking in another set of guests who had arrived on the same ferry. Once she'd finished, Geraldine introduced Harriet and Ashley to her before asking for their room key cards. Carrie welcomed them and gave them their key cards for room 204.

When they headed off to their room, Carrie didn't need a second look at Harriet to realise she was related to Geraldine. Carrie wondered if she was Geraldine's big surprise. Her likeness to Geraldine was uncanny.

Geraldine opened the door to their room and showed Harriet and Ashley inside. It was beautifully decorated, in a colour palette of soft lavender. There was even a scent of it in the room. The small attic windows faced the ocean. They had an uninterrupted view for miles out to sea.

'I was thinking,' Ashley said, 'I'm here for morale support, but I don't think I should be there when you introduce Harriet to your family. I mean, it will be confusing enough for everyone.'

'If you're sure,' Geraldine replied. Both Harriet and Ashley nodded their agreement. 'I thought I'd tell everyone about you before dinner, Harriet. Hopefully, everyone would have absorbed my news by the time we sit down to eat. If everyone is receptive to the idea, I'll call you and you can come and join us.'

'What if they aren't receptive? Angry at you, even?' Harriet asked.

'Phillip already knows, I told him last night. He took it well. I'm sure my children will too. But, if it all goes pear shaped, and my children need a little more time, well, they'll be here all weekend. But don't worry, Harriet. I know my children.'

'I hope you're right,' she said.

'Hazel is inquisitive and will ask a thousand questions but will ultimately like the idea of another older sister. Andrew is very reserved, but he has a kind heart and will understand. Vivienne may take it the hardest. She wears her heart on her sleeve and may think it is a betrayal of her father somehow. But she's matured a lot since being at university and I think she'll understand.'

'I just don't want to hurt anyone,' Harriet said.

'You won't. You've restored a kind of balance in my life. I feel like I'm cruising on an even keel. My children will love you, just as Wesley's sons will.'

'Alright,' Harriet said, feeling more reassured.

'Are you sure you don't want to join us, Ashley?' Geraldine asked.

'No, thanks. But I'm here if Harriet needs me. I'll take myself off for a walk once I've found my sea-legs.'

On returning to the annex, Geraldine took off her windbreaker and put her mobile down on the kitchen workbench. As she put the potatoes on the stove to parboil them, she wondered how her mother and Callum had gotten on.

Geraldine laid the table for dinner. She decided to use her best china for the occasion. While she walked around the table, laying the delicate pieces neatly in front of each seat, she thought of Wesley and wondered what he was doing at that very moment. She smiled at the thought of him back in her life again. She wanted to touch him, smell him, kiss him. She had missed the sensualness of love.

Wesley scanned the horizon from his window. The loft room was a corner room that offered two amazing aspects from the front of the hotel, out across St Mary's and down to Hugh Town, and out across the crystal blue waters of the archipelago. Wesley had watched Geraldine step out of the minivan with Harriet and Ashley. He wanted to open the window and call down to them but stopped himself from doing so. He didn't want to complicate Geraldine's weekend. His only reason for coming was to protect Harriet. That's what he kept telling himself. If he had known Ashley had accompanied her, he wouldn't have come. Then he realised, if Geraldine checked the guest list, she'd know he was here. He cursed himself under his breath and realised he should have stayed at another hotel. But what was the point in that? He had acted impulsively, booking his flight and accommodation. Something he rarely did. But he was concerned for Harriet and wanted to be near her. That being said, he was secretly pleased to be close to Geraldine, too.

As the sun burst through the windows and reflected off the aqua marine waters, he understood Geraldine's love for St Mary's. He'd always felt the pull of the ocean, ever since he was a child, when his grandfather had first taken him fishing. It was entrancing to be a part of the rise and fall of the ocean, at its calmest and even at its most malevolent. It wasn't difficult to get caught up in it. The navy had been his calling, but now, he felt another type of pull.

He decided to be discreet and have dinner in his room tonight. He would only make himself known if Harriet needed him. Then he would quietly leave on the Sunday morning flight.

He couldn't imagine anything bad happening in such a paradise.

Theresa opened her door to her grandson. He was turning into a handsome young man, although, he could have done with a shave and a haircut.

They hugged each other, before she invited him in.

'Did you manage to find out anything about that young man?' she asked Andrew, straight off the bat.

'Yes, I asked around the university about him. I don't trust him, Nan.'

'I thought so.'

'If Vivienne is asking you for access to her trust fund, it would be for him. He's a schemer. Of what I could find out, he invests in get-rich-quick schemes that go nowhere. But he only ever goes after the girls who can fund them. Vivienne appears to be his prey now. But she's truly in love with him, I hate to see her get hurt again.'

Theresa frowned. 'What do you suggest I do?'

'Be direct and tell her no. If he can't get the money from her, he'll get it from someone else and leave her alone.'

'Alright,' Theresa said. 'I created your trust funds for your future. I just don't want Vivienne giving it all away to a fraudster. She can access it when she's twenty-five, but only earlier at my discretion or death.'

'Then you made the right decision. He won't hang around that long if there's no cash. I did try to warn her about him last weekend, but she won't hear anything bad about him. She just thinks I'm being over-protective.'

Theresa was mindful of when to tell Vivienne, she thought it best to speak with her before dinner tonight. This weekend belonged to Geraldine and Harriet. It was better that Vivienne knew her answer sooner rather than later, to rip the band-aid off in one go, as her mother had always said.

'Thank you, I'll call her and ask her to come and see me,' Theresa said. 'How are you? I haven't seen you since Christmas.'

'Sorry, I've been studying hard. I think Mum has something important to tell us, tonight. If they're getting a divorce, I'm okay with it.'

'Oh Andrew, how much do you know?'

'Only that we think Dad is seeing someone at his uni. But I'm more worried for Hazel, she's afraid of losing everyone.'

Theresa now knew her daughter's assumption was correct about Phillip's affair, but it didn't sit well with her. She felt an uneasiness stir.

'Are you alright?' he asked, seeing her drift away from their conversation.

'Yes, fine, darling. I'm sure Hazel will adjust to the news in time, she's still young, but your Mum will explain tonight. Just remain open-minded like you always are.'

Andrew hugged his grandmother then left. Vivienne would be upset by her decision, but she hoped she wouldn't take it out on their mum. She knew Vivienne was an intelligent, but young woman who was love-struck, and Tommy Burke was obviously rotten to the bone.

Theresa exited the lift and walked up to the reception desk.

'Carrie, isn't it?'

'Yes, Mrs Cook, how can I help you?'

'A guest is arriving this afternoon. His name is Khenan Metcalfe. Could you please let me know when he arrives, I'll be in the bar.'

'Of course, Mrs Cook.'

Carrie made a note and checked his name on the guest register. He wasn't listed. Was this another family surprise, she wondered?

'Thank you.' Theresa didn't feel like staying in her room until dinner. She wanted to be a part of the hotel's atmosphere, so she walked into the bar and ordered a red wine.

There were only a few guests in the lounge. It was such a beautiful day, Theresa assumed everyone must be out enjoying the archipelago of islands. The weather report still confirmed a storm would be rolling in, later that evening, but for now, the sun shone bright.

There was a solitary woman sitting by the window, she appeared to be in a hypnotic stare. Theresa knew the ocean could do that to a person, with its smooth, never-ending resonance. She had spent many summers on St Mary's as a child. The woman appeared to be in her early to mid-thirties. She had slender long legs that were criss-crossed at the ankles. Her sandy blond hair was tied up in a neat bun. On the table next to her was an orange juice, or more likely a screwdriver.

'Afternoon,' Theresa said, as she sat down across from her.

'Afternoon,' the woman replied, but turned her head back towards the ocean.

After a few minutes of uncomfortable silence Theresa asked, 'Are you here alone or with your partner?' Theresa knew the correct term nowadays was partner, it covered any number of categories.

'It's hard to say. We'll see once the weekend is over.' The woman half smiled and picked up her drink and took a sip.

Theresa wasn't sure how to respond to that, but when the waiter arrived with her wine, she took a long, slow mouthful of the claret. She was resolved to deal with Vivienne's new boyfriend. She was hopeful about Callum, too. They had a civil lunch together. At least he didn't ask her to leave. That was an improvement. She was starting to believe this weekend was going to work out well for everyone. Earlier, she'd watched Callum, from her bedroom window, head off down to the beach. Her heart ached for him. She hated seeing him so alone.

Theresa looked over at the woman and smiled. The woman was rubbing her stomach the same way she herself did when she was pregnant. Theresa concluded it must be an orange juice.

'When will you be summoned downstairs?' Ashley asked Harriet, feeling a little better.

'Geraldine will tell them before dinner, around 6 pm. If they're receptive, she'll call me and I'll go down and join them for dinner. If not, then I'll meet them later, once the storm has abated.'

'Okay, but don't let them intimidate you or make you feel uncomfortable. Come back upstairs.'

'I'll be fine,' Harriet chuckled. 'Geraldine will tell me if it doesn't go as she thought. I'm a little nervous, actually. Meeting my first lot of half-brothers and sisters. I've been an only child all my life. Now I have five of them.'

'With my three sisters, until I got my own apartment, my clothes and make-up were never my own, unless they needed washing or replacing.'

Harriet laughed. 'I would have liked that.'

'No, you wouldn't.'

Harriet smiled at her friend. She was grateful to Ashley for coming. She would have been too nervous to come alone. Ashley could always be relied upon to boost her morale.

'I'm going to order room service tonight. I might go for a walk now that I'm feeling better.' Ashley picked up the room's booklet and started to breeze through its pages. It displayed pictures of the Windermere before and after it had been renovated. It listed all the islands in the archipelago, and things to do while on St Mary's and on the other islands. The hotel boasted a swimming pool, and gym. There were water sports down by the boathouse and walking treks all around the island. Ashley was impressed and thought it would be a lovely place to come for a holiday.

Ashley turned to the room service menu page and scanned down the list. She knew what she wanted and hoped her stomach did too. The hotel's menu boasted the finest seafood in England and the head chef, Claude Allard was apparently one of England's finest. Ashley grinned to herself as he sounded French.

Harriet said she was going to have a long hot bath to relax herself. She grabbed her toiletry bag, walked into the bathroom and closed the door.

Ashley jumped off the bed, put her sneakers back on and picked up her red windbreaker.

'I'm just going for a walk,' she said. She grabbed her phone and room key and left the room.

Chapter Nine

Saturday – 3.50 pm

'There she is, Mr Metcalfe.' Carrie showed Khenan into the bar, which had become very populated.

On hearing his name, Theresa stood up too quickly and had to steady herself. 'Khenan, thank you for coming.' She had forgotten how handsome he was. His mother was Jamaican and his father English, along with a sprinkling of French somewhere in the mix. His skin was a smooth, unblemished, soft tan colour, but he was broad shouldered and stood over six foot. He cut an impressive figure. Theresa remembered he had a soft and gentle voice that could put any client at ease. She had never seen him angry or even with a raised voice. Although, she hadn't seen him in a few years.

'I came as soon as I could, Theresa.'

'Would you like a drink?'

'I'll have a beer, thank you. You said on the phone it was an urgent legal matter regarding the hotel. You said you didn't want Callum involved.'

'That was a lie to get you here.'

Khenan's face turned ashen. Anger lines grew across his face. He didn't like being lied too. Especially by Theresa Cook.

'Please …' Theresa pleaded, raising her hands in front of her. 'Let me explain, I needed you here this weekend because I have something important to say to both you and Callum.'

'You never said Callum was here.'

'I lied again – I'm sorry for the deceit.'

Khenan sighed deeply, he was about to turn around and leave, but Theresa caught his arm. 'Please don't leave, Khenan.'

'It's been over between us for some time now, Theresa.'

Theresa asked him to sit down, then she walked over to the bar and ordered him a beer. When she returned, the solitary woman was gone. She sat down across from him.

A moment later, Ashley walked into the bar and scanned the room. She saw Theresa and waved, but when she saw her talking to a man, she decided to give her some privacy, and headed outside to begin her walk. It would keep.

'I was hoping we could talk before we meet Callum.'

'He won't be pleased to see me.'

'My father's bigotry cost you your job and my son's affection. He and my husband are dead now, and I've come to realise how dependent I was on both of them. I can't remember when I lost belief in myself, it was so long ago. I should never have allowed Winston or my father to be so domineering, now my children are suffering for it.'

Khenan let Theresa have her say, she had obviously gone to a lot of trouble to organise his visit.

'I need to repair my relationship with my children. Especially Callum. I love him dearly and I hate that he's unhappy. When my father fired you and gave Callum that ultimatum, I was so proud of him when he walked away from Windermere, Hartnell and Cook. I have never seen my son happier than when he was with you.'

Khenan interrupted Theresa, 'But he never got over what his grandfather did. And what you and Winston didn't do. He was made to feel so ashamed of who he was. Can you comprehend how your son felt afterwards? He had finally found the courage to tell everyone who he truly was, only to have that happiness ripped out from under him by those he loved. That resentment drove us apart. He stopped liking who he was, so why should anyone else like him?'

Theresa wanted to cry, if only she had been stronger like her sister, Emily and stood up to her father. 'My father would have made it difficult for me to see my mother if I defied him. My mother had already lost Emily to his narrow-mindedness.'

'I appreciate that, but Callum has to learn to love himself before he'll let anyone else love him again.'

'That's why I invited you here this weekend,' Theresa said.

'It's not as easy at that.'

'But it can be. I have a lot to make up for. We all need to forgive each other and ourselves.'

Khenan could see the desperation in her eyes.

'I do miss him. I wanted a future with him. A partnership, like anyone else.'

'I'm glad you said that, because I have something I want to give you both,' Theresa said. 'Shall we go up and see if Callum is back from his walk?'

Khenan eyed Theresa. She was up to something, but he didn't believe there was anything she could say that would change Callum's mind. His hurt ran deep. Khenan was not immune to bigotry, but he hated Simon Hartnell for what he did to him and Callum. However, Theresa wasn't any better for not defending her son. Khenan agreed to go upstairs with Theresa, if not for any other reason, than there should be a finality to their relationship. There was much unsaid when Callum left, and Khenan knew if Callum ever wanted happiness again with anyone, he would need to be honest with himself and those he loved.

A few minutes later, they were standing in front of room 202. Theresa knocked on her son's door. Thankfully, he had returned from his walk. He opened the door to see his mother standing there once again, ready for round two.

He stepped aside and walked back into his room without saying a word. Once Theresa entered, she held the door open, and Khenan appeared at the door.

Callum was momentarily taken aback, 'Khenan! What the hell are you doing here?'

'I was summoned by your mother under false pretences.'

Callum leered at his mother, who had a cheeky but pleading look on her face. Callum didn't know whether to be angry or pleased by her actions. He gave Khenan a stern look as if to say, 'what the fuck is going on?' Then Callum conceded the battle and watched his mother take a seat on the couch.

Theresa patted the chair beside her, indicating they should both sit.

'Callum, I need to make right what happened to you. You and Geraldine are the two most important people in my life. I'm standing by Geraldine this weekend, no matter what happens and I want to make things right with you, too. You found happiness with Khenan and your family poisoned it.'

'Mum. It wasn't just because of you that Khenan and I separated.'

'Yes, it was. You're a far better lawyer than your father and grandfather ever were. You should have been running Windermere, Hartnell and Cook by now.'

'That's all in the past. I've moved on.'

'Winston was my father's golden boy, whether he was up to it or not. I was so proud of you. But I was foolish to believe my father would see it that way.'

'Yeah, but I was the only one to tell him to go fuck himself.' Theresa chuckled.

'There's a story I need to tell you. I hope by the end you'll understand what I'm trying to do this weekend.' Callum conceded the conversation and allowed his mother to continue.

'My grandfather started the law firm as Windermere and Son. But alas, his son died, which only left my mother to continue his legacy. She married your grandfather, Simon Hartnell. The firm then became Windermere and Hartnell.'

'I know all this, Mum!' interrupted Callum.

'Please let me explain in more detail. My father was disappointed not to have sons of his own, and when Emily walked away, it fell to me. I married your father, Winston Cook and the firm became, Windermere, Hartnell and Cook. You were expected to eventually take the reins, followed by Andrew. But that will not happen now. Your father's share in the firm came to me. But my father's share was left to Andrew in the hope he too would study law at university one day, but Andrew wants no part in the firm, so I bought Andrew's share in the firm from him late last year. George Windermere, your great-grandfather, left his share to his daughter, my mother, not Simon Hartnell. On her death, it went to Emily and me. But he had written a codicil in his will, that the firm could not be sold unless the majority of the partners were in agreement, which is now Emily and me. We have just sold our partnerships in the firm to John Harrow and Sons.'

Both men sat stunned by Theresa's story.

'I brought you both here this weekend because I'm giving you both the proceeds of the sale of the firm so you can start your own law firm.'

'What?' Callum said, flabbergasted.

Khenan raised his eyebrows and whistled. He knew Simon Hartnell would be rolling in his grave right now if he knew. Khenan couldn't help but smile.

'Your grandmother gave Geraldine this house and some money to start this hotel, she deserved it after everything we put her through. I'm now helping you. I want you and Khenan to become partners, in every sense of the word.'

Callum frowned. 'Mum. I couldn't take a penny from that man, even if I was penniless.'

'It isn't from your grandfather; it's from your grandmother and me. Besides, call it poetic justice. You are two of the most talented lawyers in the country, you deserve to have it.'

All three remained quiet for a long minute, until Khenan finally broke the silence.

'Callum, it's what we always wanted. Our own law firm.'

Callum looked at Khenan, shaking his head.

'My father sacked you, remember,' Callum said. 'Just because I loved you.'

'Yes, and this country used to imprison men for being homosexual until 1967,' Khenan replied. 'Men like us were prosecuted, even executed centuries ago. It's time we all moved on from the past. Our relationship fell apart because you have always struggled to accept who you are. You've always feared being judged. You were so demoralised by how you were treated you crept back into your secluded existence and stopped everyone from entering. We fight for justice. You gave up on fighting for yourself long ago.'

'All I've ever wanted was to be allowed to be myself.'

'And you can, my love,' pleaded Theresa. 'Please take what I offer. I'm trying to right a wrong the only way I know how. I wasn't brave enough back then. I now have the power to make things right. Please take it.'

Callum looked at Khenan. He'd missed him these last few years, his calmness, his intellect, and most of all his tenderness. He didn't want to be alone, not anymore. But he hurt Khenan when he walked out on their relationship. He punished himself, too.

Theresa felt her son's remorse. 'Am I really too late?' Theresa said, growing worried by her son's silence.

'No. You're not,' Khenan replied, on behalf of Callum. 'I've missed you, Cal. But I couldn't reach you anymore. One of us was bound to leave eventually. I hoped for a long time you'd find your true self and come back but you didn't.'

'I've been miserable without you,' admitted Callum.

'And I'm miserable for both of you, so please take what I'm offering. You're good together. Use the money to start again. Then hopefully you'll remember why you both fell in love in the first place. Small steps can lead to a marathon. Besides, you're in paradise, anything can happen.'

Theresa's mobile rang. She reached into her pocket to see who was calling her. She let it go to voicemail.

'I'll leave you two alone then,' Theresa said, standing up. 'There's a family dinner tonight around 6 pm. Geraldine has something important to tell everyone. But I'm sure she'll understand if you can't make it. I'll fill you in later.'

'Is she alright?' Callum asked.

'Yes. But that might be short-lived.'

'What do you mean?'

'Your grandfather had a propensity to hurt people. Even now from the grave. But I'm trying to make it right.'

Callum stood up and faced his mother.

'Thanks, Mum.' He walked her to the door and leaned in to embrace her. Theresa's eyes swelled with tears as she squeezed her son tight. She'd longed for this moment for so long.

Theresa said goodbye, she needed to rest before dinner. She was suddenly tired and overwhelmed. This weekend was proving extremely emotional for her. Once she was back in her room, she put the kettle on and sat on her bed. Then she remembered the call that went to voicemail and removed her mobile from her jacket pocket. She'd never truly mastered the contraption, but her grandchildren had insisted she get one, in case she was out alone and had an accident.

She retrieved her phone and played the message. It was from Ashley. She was concerned about Harriet, who was getting more anxious by the minute. Theresa placed a call to Harriet, but it went straight to voicemail. She decided to pop by before she went down to dinner. After making herself comfortable on the bed, Theresa picked up her tea and took a long, slow drink. *That's the trick*, she thought. She heard a knock on her door. She grumbled as she got off the bed, then remembered Vivienne was supposed to come by before dinner.

When Theresa opened the door, her granddaughter was standing there, arm in arm with a slightly older man, who could only have been Tommy Burke. She instantly grew angry at his intrusion; she hadn't expected him to be on the island. Theresa invited them in, but she took an instant dislike to him.

As he strutted in, his eyes scanned the room. His expression of the guest room was one of disdain. He obviously didn't appreciate other people's talent or taste, unless it aligned with his own. Theresa figured him out in twenty seconds.

Vivienne introduced Tommy to her. Theresa cordially responded, although she was tired and just wanted the conversation over with. She had to assume Vivienne invited Tommy to the meeting. Unless he invited himself in the hope of persuading her to hand over the money. This vexed Theresa, as she had promised herself that she would never be man-handled again. She offered them a seat across from her. Tommy slung his rucksack on the floor, slouched down beside Vivienne and crossed one leg over the other.

'So, Tommy. What do you study at university?'

'Oh. This and that.'

'Is that a degree now?'

Vivienne eyed her grandmother. 'He's studying philosophy and history, Nan.'

'I see,' Theresa decided to get right to the point.

'Can you tell me why you want your trust fund early, Vivienne?'

Vivienne looked embarrassed by the question.

'Um, Tommy and I have plans, you see. We're going into business together. He has a great idea and we don't want to miss the boat, so to speak. You should hear him talk about it; it sounds so exciting.'

'I see,' Theresa replied. 'But I asked you why you wanted all your trust fund. You still have two years left at university and neither of you is qualified to run a business.'

'Because I'll be setting it up for her,' Tommy interrupted, 'and once she's finished school, we'll work together as partners.'

'I see. But you're not studying business management, so how will you manage it?'

Tommy didn't like the insinuation; he began fidgeting uncomfortably beside Vivienne, who was growing redder by the minute.

'I'm an ideas man, and when you have an idea, you run with it, or someone else will beat you to it.'

'How much are *you* putting into this venture?'

Tommy was getting irritable at Theresa's questions. He never answered her.

'At least I've done my due diligence,' Theresa continued, 'and have been led to believe that your previous schemes have failed. So why should I believe this one won't? Especially considering it wasn't your money you gambled away and lost previously. I guess you walked away lightly.'

'Nan, that's unfair,' snapped Vivienne. Tommy was growing angrier by the minute. He knew where the conversation was heading.

'Who have you been talking to? You can't believe everything you hear,' he said.

'Someone I trust, actually. I was told you recently schemed money out of another young woman and once the money was gone, so were you. There's no way in hell I'm handing over my granddaughter's trust fund to her any time soon, just so she can give it to a piece of driftwood like you.'

'Nan!' yelled Vivienne, utterly embarrassed.

But Theresa's statement had rung true as Tommy sat very quiet. His stare was cold and deliberate at Theresa. She saw through him like a wafer.

'If you wish to discuss your trust fund with me again in the future, Vivienne, we will do so in private. But my answer today is no.'

'That's unfair, Nan, it's my money. I should be able to do what I want with it.'

'And rightly so. When you're twenty-five.'

'Come on,' said Tommy, who stood up and walked to the door.

Vivienne couldn't believe what her grandmother had just done. She turned to look at Tommy, then back at her grandmother. But when she turned back around, Tommy had already left the room.

'How could you embarrass me like that?'

'He isn't for you, sweetheart, he's only after your money. He's done this before. I need you to understand that.'

'What the hell do you know?' Vivienne ran from the room and down the corridor after Tommy. She caught up with him as he walked through the foyer.

'Tommy ... Tommy ... slow down,' she pleaded.

'That bitch had no intention of giving you your money. She only wanted to embarrass me. She thinks I'm not good enough for you.'

Tommy stormed out of the hotel and started walking toward Hugh Town.

Vivienne hurried on behind him. 'But you are. It's a delay, that's all. It's only a few years.'

'Oh, grow up. I can't believe I wasted an entire weekend coming here. You said she would give you the money.'

'So did I. What did she mean about the other woman?'

Tommy looked down at Vivienne, then up at the hotel. His contempt and disdain for the beautiful hotel was etched across his face. He threw her hand away when she tried to touch his face and told her to grow the fuck up. Then he stormed off.

Vivienne was left alone in the middle of the road, tears running down her face. People were looking at her, she felt embarrassed and used. She wiped her eyes, then ran back to the annex and straight up to her room. She didn't know who she was angrier with: Tommy, or her grandmother.

Phillip left the annex and headed down to the boathouse. He zipped up his jacket and pulled the hood over his head. The wind was picking up and the sky had grown dark. It was threatening to rain. The storm was on its way. He made sure the water-sports equipment was all secure but noticed one sailboat was still missing. He could see storm clouds off in the distance, the guests would need to get back soon. When he exited the boathouse, he looked up at the hotel and scanned the windows until he found the window for Clarissa's room. He checked his watch. He decided to stretch his legs before dinner. He stretched them all the way up to room 201. As he tapped on her door, he quickly scanned the corridor nervously until the door was finally opened.

He stepped inside quickly.

'What do you think you're playing at?'

'Nice to see you to, Phillip,' Clarissa said calmly, as she walked back to the bed.

'My whole family is here. What if they see you?' he said, eyeing Clarissa's polo neck sweater and admiring the shape it presented over her breasts.

'Relax, they don't know who I am. You're the only one who's drawn attention to us by knocking on my door.'

Point taken, he thought. No one had yet met Clarissa.

'There's a lot happening tonight, I'm going to sit down with Geraldine tomorrow and work out the finer details of the separation.'

Clarissa laughed at his banal response to the ending of his marriage. She knew she needed to tell him her news now.

'Sit down Phillip, I have something more important to tell you.'

Phillip obliged, but he didn't know what could be more important than his separation. He sat down on the end of the bed beside Clarissa. She smelt nice. Her scent always lured him to her.

'I'm pregnant,' she announced, then waited for Phillip's reaction.

It took him a moment to register, but at least he didn't fall off the bed. His mouth was open but nothing came out. He stood up and paced the room.

'But we've been careful. Haven't we?'

Still calm, Clarissa replied, 'Yes. But life has a habit of finding a way, Phillip. Are you okay?' She found his reaction amusing, if not a little childish.

'I know what I want. I want marriage. I want this baby, and I want you. So, if we're going to be together, then you better leave your wife officially before I leave this island tomorrow.'

'I've already got three grown kids. I just didn't expect to go through the nappy fiasco again. I'm forty-seven years old.'

'And I'm nearly thirty-six. You have until tonight to let me know your decision. You know mine.' Clarissa stood and walked over to the door and opened it, indicating that their conversation was over. Phillip knew there was nothing left to say. He needed time to get his head around Clarissa's bombshell. He was drawn to her room in the hope of sex. But left more confused and frustrated than when he arrived.

He left without saying goodbye. He walked back along the corridor and down the staircase. He walked into the bar and ordered a scotch, which he downed in one gulp. He left the hotel via the front entrance but walked past the annex and up the road. The cold evening air woke him from his stupor. For some reason, he felt like he'd just jumped out of the frypan and into the fire.

Phillip checked his watch. He needed to get back to the annex for dinner. As he walked back home, he looked up at the impressive hotel and realised in that very moment that St Mary's was no longer his home.

The knock at the door roused Theresa from her nap. She climbed off the bed and walked to the door. She opened it, thinking it might be Vivienne again, in the hope of changing her mind. But it wasn't.

'Yes. Can I help you?'

'I need to talk to you.'

When Theresa closed her door she was confused and physically shaking. *It can't be*, she thought. She didn't want to alarm Geraldine. But when Theresa retrieved her mobile, she called the only person she thought would know what to do, Ashley.

'There's proof,' Theresa said, almost at a whisper.

'Did you see it?' replied Ashley.

'No.'

'Then you need to. Do you want me to come with you?'

'No. I must be discreet. I don't want Geraldine or Harriet learning of this. There has to be an explanation.'

'Call me when you've seen it and we can investigate it together.'

Theresa agreed, then quickly changed for dinner before heading downstairs. She found who she was looking for outside the hotel.

'You said you had proof, well, I want to see it.'

'I don't have it on me, but I can get it for you.'

Theresa looked around her and noticed a light on in the boathouse. 'I'll be waiting in the boathouse. You can show me then.'

This can't be happening, she thought. No one was going to ruin her daughter's weekend. Theresa needed to resolve this mess and quickly. There had to be a mistake. She decided to see the evidence first, before speaking to Ashley again.

What if it was true?

Chapter Ten

Saturday, 5:55 pm

Theresa opened the boathouse door and stepped inside. She was dressed for dinner, but the wind blew fiercely through the boathouse, creating a cold wind-tunnel, which caused her to shiver. She quickly wrapped her shawl around her shoulders and neck and waited anxiously for her guest to arrive. There had to be a rational explanation.

She looked around the boathouse, the racks were full except one. She wondered who was still out sailing. The sky was growing dark with cumulonimbus clouds that were growing by the minute. She knew it was going to be a stormy night. She patted her hair, worried at the state it would be in by the time she arrived for dinner.

Then she heard the door creak open behind her. She turned around to see who had entered.

Theresa spoke first. 'I'm not sure what you're playing at, but you've made a terrible mistake. You see that, don't you?'

'I have proof. I know it's true. You don't think I'm good enough for your family, is that it?'

'I'm not saying that. I'm only thinking of my daughter, she's been through enough. Please show me your proof.'

An envelope was produced and handed over to Theresa. Theresa read it, then sighed with disbelief.

'How in the world did you get this?'

'It's mine.'

'It's not.'

'You wish it wasn't.'

'I didn't mean it like that. I'll sort this out. Please don't speak of this to Geraldine, not until I've discussed it with her.'

'Why not?'

'This weekend is important to her. I'm only thinking of her happiness.'

'What about my happiness?'

'Please, just stay away from Geraldine this weekend,' commanded Theresa. She grabbed her visitor's arm in a plea for understanding. 'Please don't ruin it.'

'Why would it be ruined, if it's the truth?'

'What do you want? Money?'

'Fuck you!'

Theresa's guest turned to leave, but her grip tightened, more so out of desperation. The blow came quickly and without warning. Theresa was propelled back against the door of the boathouse. Profound dizziness and pain spun all around her. She called out, but no one answered. She staggered. Then darkness.

'I'll keep her steady while you climb out.'

Sofia stepped unsteadily out of the sailboat but kept a firm hold.

Sailing around the island all day had been more thrilling and enjoyable than she thought possible. When she and Harry set out in the morning, her only thoughts were of seasickness and capsizing. But she had to admit, Harry was a great sailor. It wasn't until the wind picked up in the afternoon that she grew concerned. But they were back now, and Sofia was looking forward to a hot bath before dinner.

Sofia looked at her watch: 6:10 pm. She wanted to call Francesca, her daughter, before dinner. She was staying with her parents for the week, but each night she called Francesca before dinner.

Once Harry lowered the mast, Sofia helped him pull the boat up the ramp. But Sofia gasped when she saw a woman lying on the ramp, partially submerged in water.

'Oh, God, Harry. Come quick!' Sofia let go of the sailboat and ran up the ramp. The tide was coming in fast and it was about to consume the woman.

Harry ran up to Sofia and knelt down beside the woman. He checked her pulse and quickly moved her further up the ramp and out of the cold water before he started CPR.

'Call an ambulance, I don't know how long she's been lying here.'

Sofia called 999 and ordered an ambulance immediately to the Windermere Hotel boathouse. She took off her wet weather jacket and placed it over the woman's body to keep her warm.

Harry continued CPR. There was blood across the woman's face and head, it flowed as freely as the tide did around her. Sofia ran back to the sailboat and removed a tea towel from the picnic basket. She folded it and placed it over the wound and kept pressure on it.

Finally, the woman stirred and coughed. Harry quickly turned her on her side as she continued to cough up seawater.

'I don't know how much water is in her lungs. Or how long she's been unconscious. We have to hope there's no brain damage.'

'She must be a guest at the hotel.' Sofia tucked her jacket more securely around the woman and stroked her hair. A few minutes later, they heard the ambulance. Sofia got up and ran out of the boathouse to greet it.

Harry explained to the paramedics how he found her and what he'd done for her. The paramedics placed an oxygen mask over her face and took the woman's vitals. Then they gently placed her on the gurney. Harry agreed to stay with them while Sofia ran back to the hotel to inform them of what happened.

Everyone had finally gathered in the Locke's living room. Callum and Khenan had arrived ten minutes ago. Andrew, Vivienne and Hazel were pleased to see their uncle and Khenan reunited again, although their uncle had stated it was early days and they had both agreed to take small steps. No one had noticed their father's arrival shortly after they arrived. He had gone straight to the drinks trolley and fixed himself a drink. The only family member missing was Theresa Cook.

'Shall I go and find her?' Hazel asked her mother when she entered the kitchen.

'No. I'll just call her on her mobile,' Geraldine said, a little surprised her mother wasn't already here. Geraldine went back into the kitchen and dialled her mother's number but it went to voice mail. She put her mobile back on the kitchen table and walked back into the living room.

Phillip half-expected his mother-in-law to make a grand entrance, now that she had her whole family together in one place. *Probably for the last time*, he thought, before saying, 'We're all here, just tell everyone your news, Geraldine. Your mother already knows.'

'No,' Geraldine said, 'we need to wait.'

Andrew asked if anyone needed a top-up as he walked over to the drinks trolley. Vivienne asked for a wine, she had been sulking since returning home that afternoon. She wanted to go to a pub in Old Town and get blotted, but her mother had asked her to stay. Only Andrew knew why but decided to give his twin a wide berth. He handed Hazel a Pepsi.

Geraldine wasn't sure what was keeping her mother. Harriet would be waiting in her room for a call. Geraldine checked her watch again, it was 6:15 pm. She couldn't wait any longer. Harriet might be thinking the worst.

'Look! Can I have everyone's attention, please?'

Everyone turned their attention to Geraldine. 'There's something I need to tell you all. I was going to wait until your grandmother arrived, but I can't wait any longer.'

'Are you getting a divorce?' interrupted Hazel.

'What?' Geraldine replied. Everyone looked to and from Geraldine and Phillip for an explanation.

'Shush,' Vivienne said to Hazel. 'Go on, Mum.'

'Oh, God!' this was proving harder than Geraldine thought. Hazel wasn't entirely wrong. She looked to Phillip, had he said something? But he nodded to indicate he hadn't.

'This is hard for me to say. But I need you all to be open-minded,' Geraldine said, taking a deep breath. 'When I was sixteen, long before I met your father, I had a boyfriend which resulted in a baby. But I had to give her up for adoption.'

The only person in the room not surprised was Phillip. Everyone was talking at once, until Geraldine shushed everyone down and continued.

'About a month ago she contacted your grandmother and said she wanted to meet me. That's why I've been going to the mainland so often lately. I've been meeting her. But this weekend I want to introduce her to you all. Her name is Harriet Smith and she's here now at the hotel. She's very nervous about meeting you all. But if you're okay with it, what I'd like to do is invite her to dinner tonight so she can meet you all.'

Off in the distance, an ambulance could be heard.

Geraldine looked at her children, one by one. Andrew, then Vivienne and lastly Hazel.

'This has been hard for me, as I didn't have a choice back then. But she never held it against me. She's had a good life and has always known she was adopted. Andrew, Vivienne, Hazel, what do you say?'

'Um … it'll take some getting used to, I guess, but I'm okay with it,' Andrew said. 'That must have been hard for you. Why didn't you tell us about her before?'

'Because it was painful for me. I was afraid that if I contacted her, she wouldn't want to know me. So, I thought it best you didn't know.'

The sound of the ambulance grew louder and louder.

'Vivienne, Hazel? What about you? How do you feel about it?'

'I'm okay with it, I guess. It'll be strange having an older sister,' Vivienne replied, although she appeared a little distracted and sullen. She sat back down on the sofa and finished off her wine. Only Hazel seemed a little unsure. Geraldine went up to her and put her arm around her youngest.

'Maybe you and I can have a long talk about this later if you like. I wanted to invite Harriet to dinner, but if that's awkward for you, I'll call her and cancel.'

'No, don't do that. I think I'm okay with it. Where does she live?'

'London.'

Callum walked up to his sister. 'That's why you went to live with Aunt Emily halfway through the school year. You never said…'

'I didn't want to go. I had no choice.'

'Let me guess. Our fucking grandfather.'

Sofia ran into the hotel. She found Carrie behind the reception desk with someone she recognised as the night manager. She told them what had happened and asked if they had a guest staying at the hotel matching the woman's description. Carrie said it sounded like Theresa Cook, Geraldine's mother.

'Where can I find Geraldine now?' Sofia asked.

'She's in the annex next door, having a family gathering. Do you want me to call her?'

'No. I'll do it myself. Thank you.'

Sofia ran out of the hotel and headed to the annex. She was used to giving bad news to strangers of loved ones that had died, but this felt strangely personal.

'Hazel, could you please go to the hotel and check on your grandmother, and hurry her along. I don't want the vegetables to get cold.'

'Yes, Mum.' Hazel jumped up and headed for the front door. Geraldine was reluctant to call Harriet until her mother had arrived.

When Hazel opened the door, she found a guest standing there, out of breath, about to knock on the door.

'I need to speak with Geraldine Locke. It's an emergency.'

Hazel showed the woman into the living room. Everyone stopped talking and looked at Sofia as she entered the room, dishevelled and out of breath.

'Can I help you, Ms Faraday?' Geraldine said, finally remembering the woman's name.

'A woman, in her mid-to-late sixties was found injured in the boathouse. She's wearing a black jacket and a black shawl with poppies over it. Could it be one of your guests?'

A flicker of recognition crossed Geraldine's mind. She'd given her mother a black shawl with poppies on it last Christmas. Then she remembered the sound of the ambulance.

'Oh, God! Yes, it could be my mother. But I don't know what she'd be doing in there at this time of night. What happened?'

'I'm sorry to tell you, we found your mother unconscious about ten minutes ago. She sustained a head injury, and we found her partially submerged in the water. My partner has given her CPR and she's now breathing on her own.'

'No!'

'The paramedics are with her now.'

Geraldine raced out of the room, followed quickly behind by Callum and the rest of her family. Geraldine met the paramedics as they were about to put her mother into the ambulance.

'I'm coming with you,' she yelled, as she climbed straight into the ambulance. The paramedics said only one family member could ride with them, so Callum said he would follow on behind her. The paramedics thanked Harry for all his help and closed the ambulance door. Theresa's family were huddled together, shivering in disbelief as the ambulance sped off. Their family reunion was over before it began.

'Come on, we'll meet them at the hospital,' Phillip said to his children, as he put his arm around Hazel. Khenan put his hand on Callum's back and reassured him that Theresa was as tough as nails. Callum wanted to believe that, but she looked so frail in the ambulance.

Phillip ran into the hotel, retrieved the minivan's keys and drove everyone to the hospital.

Sofia reappeared by Harry's side and once everyone had departed said, 'Do you think it was an accident?'

'It's hard to tell,' he replied. 'She could have simply tripped and hit her head. It's dark in there and the light wasn't on.'

'Or someone could have hit her and placed her in the water.'

'I'm sure with your detective mind and my forensic one, we'll figure it out. Let's just hope she wakes up and tells everyone what happened. It could be a simple, senseless accident.'

'Do you think she'll pull through?'

'It depends on how long she went without oxygen. In cold water, it has been recorded that a person can be brought back after two hours, if the right steps are taken in recovery. But that head injury looks bad. I can't say for sure.'

'I want that boathouse locked, just in case,' Sofia said. 'No one else is to go inside without my approval.' He nodded in agreement and walked back to the boathouse and secured the sailboat before closing the roller door on the ocean side, retrieving the key from the hook on the wall and locking the two large doors on the island side. He put the key in his pocket and walked with Sofia back to the hotel. The tide would have already washed away any evidence around where the woman was found. But he would check the boathouse thoroughly in the morning for any evidence of foul play.

'Where have you been?' Harriet asked Ashley when she re-entered their room.

'I went for a long walk. I told you I would when you went into the bathroom to take a bath. What's wrong?'

'I'm nervous, Geraldine hasn't called. She would have told them by now.'

'Don't get worked up,' Ashley replied, as Harriet kept pacing the floor. 'Maybe there's a delay.'

'Should I call Geraldine or Theresa?'

'Maybe you should give it a little longer.'

'Geraldine was going to tell them before dinner. It's a quarter past six. What if they're angry and don't want to meet me? I think this was a mistake coming here.' Harriet was almost spinning in circles around the room.

'Calm down. Geraldine knows what she's doing. Look, maybe it's taken her a while to explain, and her children are still getting used to the idea. Give it till six-thirty then call.'

Harriet wasn't convinced but agreed. It was nearly six-thirty when they heard the sound of an ambulance off in the distance.

Harriet looked out the window but couldn't see where it was heading. Harriet had a bad feeling and couldn't wait any longer, she picked up her mobile, but she cursed aloud when it wouldn't turn on – it was dead. She had forgotten to charge it again. She walked over to the bedside table and plugged it into her charger.

'Can I borrow your phone?'

Ashley handed over her mobile, and Harriet sent Theresa a text message.

I'm concerned. How did it go?
Harriet

'Who was that to?'

'Theresa. She'll let me know what's happened.'

'Now relax. Everything will be fine.'

Ashley didn't like seeing Harriet distressed. She had agreed to help Harriet find her birth mother, but now she was concerned it might not turn out the way Harriet envisioned it.

'Something's happened, Ash.' Harriet turned to her friend. 'I feel it. What about that ambulance we heard? What if someone in Geraldine's family is hurt?'

Ashley got up and put her arm on Harriet's back and said, 'I'm sure everything's fine. It might have been for a guest at the hotel.'

'What if it's not? That could be why she hasn't called.'

'You stay here. I'll go down and ask.'

Ashley left their room and trotted down the stairs. A tall man rushed quickly past her, up the stairs. She was startled momentarily as she had been looking down, but when she looked up at him, she had a flicker of recognition. Where had she seen his face before? She brushed off the thought and ran down the final flight of stairs and walked up to the reception desk.

Wesley dashed up the stairs two at a time. He saw Geraldine running towards the boathouse, followed by her family. Something was wrong. He raced upstairs to avoid being seen. He cursed himself for being a fool. He shouldn't have come.

Ashley arrived at reception and tapped on the little bell and waited for someone to arrive. She tapped a second time and waited impatiently.

'I'm sorry. How can I help you?' Carrie said, as she came through a door behind reception. The sign read, *Staff Only*.

'I don't want to pry, but we saw an ambulance drive off. Is everything alright?'

'Unfortunately, Mrs Locke's mother had a fall in the boathouse and sustained a head injury. If it wasn't for one of the guests knowing CPR, she would have drowned.'

'Shit!' Ashley turned white. This couldn't be happening. She had only spoken with her half an hour ago. The blood drained from her face as she considered, what if it wasn't an accident? She wondered if she should call the police and tell them about Theresa's rendezvous.

'Was it an accident?'

'Of course,' Carrie replied. 'Why would you say that?'

'I need to speak with Geraldine now. It's important. Can I have her mobile number?'

'She's just left in the ambulance. I doubt she had her phone with her, and I don't think now is the time. Do you?' Carrie was surprised by the woman's lack of empathy.

'What about her husband. Can I speak to him?'

'Mr Locke has just left for the hospital with his children. What is it you need to ask them about?'

Ashley hesitated. She wasn't sure what to say.

'If Geraldine contacts you, please tell her I need to speak with her. My name is Ashley Lamb; I'm in room 204. You should have my mobile on file. I'm sharing a room with Harriet Smith.'

'Alright, Ms Lamb. I'll let her know.'

Ashley walked off towards the staircase and slowly ascended the stairs.

When she arrived back in their room, she told Harriet what happened to Theresa. Ashley convinced Harriet to stay in their room tonight. They would speak with Geraldine in the morning.

Reluctantly, Harriet had agreed, it was a family matter, and even though she was fond of Theresa, it wasn't the introduction to Geraldine's family that she was hoping for.

Ashley lay on her bed, fearful for Theresa. Regret swept over her. If she had gone with Theresa to the boathouse, would she be safe right now? Was it just an accident? Who had she spoken to? Who would be angry enough to hurt Theresa?

St Mary's Hospital

The small waiting room was overcrowded when the nurse informed Theresa's family that she was still critical. Phillip didn't want the children to stay all night at the hospital, so he said he would take them home. Callum said he wanted to stay a little longer with Geraldine, so Phillip left with Khenan and the children.

Theresa was eventually moved to the only ward in the tiny hospital. The doctor informed Geraldine and Callum that she had a skull fracture and would remain unconscious for some time. She lay in a hospital bed in an induced coma. The brain scan showed no bleeding on the brain, but they were still concerned about her head injury. They had treated her for hypothermia and had successfully removed the remaining seawater from her lungs.

On returning home, Phillip said goodnight to his children at the bottom of the stairs. Hazel asked her dad, in an anxious voice, if her Nan would die. He tried to explain to Hazel that while her grandmother was in a coma, she was quietly repairing herself. He hoped rather than wished that was the case. Andrew and Vivienne said goodnight and walked Hazel upstairs. Phillip found the living room cold and empty. He walked into the kitchen and found the back door open. He quickly closed it and looked at all the uneaten food. He put the roast in the fridge and cleaned up the kitchen.

He then poured himself a stiff drink, sat down on the sofa and took a long, slow gulp. He thought about going to Clarissa, but he would have to go through the hotel lobby, given the service entrance at the back of the hotel was locked this time of night. He didn't want the night-manager to see him skulk up the staircase. Phillip closed his eyes and thought about the mess he was in.

Phillip texted Clarissa:

I've had a shitty day

Clarissa texted Phillip:

Well, you better come up. I'm sure I can make it better.

Phillip was tempted by her invitation, but on second thought decided against it. What if Hazel needed him in the night? Maybe tomorrow.

Chapter Eleven

Phillip's phone chimed. It woke him out of his drowsy state. It was a text from Geraldine:

**I need to speak with you urgently
Meet me in the boathouse now**

Phillip had to re-read the message again. He had assumed Geraldine would be at the hospital all night. Why couldn't she talk with him once she got home? He thought it was all a bit too melodramatic, but then thought, that perhaps Theresa had died and Geraldine couldn't face telling the kids. Maybe she wanted him to tell them.

He pulled himself up and walked through to the kitchen, where he grabbed his coat and stepped outside. He texted:

On my way

He was grateful the storm had passed as he walked down to the boathouse. A light drizzle was still falling, but the night was calm.

When Phillip arrived at the boathouse, it was unlocked. He thought Geraldine had already arrived, so he opened the door and stepped inside, but it was in darkness. He reached over to turn on the light, but he didn't get the chance. A terrible pain tore through the side of his head. He was dead before he hit the ground.

Phillip's killer placed Geraldine's mobile phone back on her kitchen table and left quietly without being seen or heard. The incriminating text message had been deleted.

Chapter Twelve

The Windermere Hotel

Sunday, 7:20 am

Harriet woke up and enjoyed a long, slow stretch in bed. When she finally opened her eyes, she remembered where she was. Then she remembered Theresa was hurt and in the hospital. She turned onto her side and faced Ashley's bed. It was empty.

Harriet closed her eyes and enjoyed the peace and solitude of the morning before she had to face Geraldine's family. Although under the circumstances, she wondered if she should leave. But she was now a part of Geraldine's family and decided to text Geraldine and find out how Theresa was doing. She reached over and picked up her mobile phone from the side table and sent a text message.

Dear Geraldine,

Could you tell me how Theresa is doing?

I'm happy to leave and return another weekend.

Thinking of you,

Harriet.

Harriet put her phone down and turned over, she was facing the bathroom. The door was open and the light was off.

'Ashley? Are you in there?'

Silence.

'Ashley!'

Harriet sat up and looked around the room. Ashley's phone was missing, and so were her clothes. She'd known Ashley for many years and knew she wasn't an early riser. She jumped out of bed and went to the window. There was a light fog drifting across the island and out to sea. She couldn't tell where land ended and the sea began. She strained to see anything, or anyone. Harriet grabbed some clothes and entered the bathroom. She was washed and dressed within ten minutes.

When Harriet exited the bathroom, Ashley still hadn't returned. Harriet called Ashley's mobile, but it went to voicemail.

'I'm heading downstairs, where are you, Ash?'

Jogging down the stairs, Harriet decided to head straight for the breakfast room. She didn't believe Ashley would be in there eating breakfast without her, but she checked all the same. Confirming her suspicion, Harriet headed for the reception desk. She tapped the bell anxiously and waited for a response to her plea.

Carrie walked through the door behind the reception, wondering what the urgency was. When Carrie saw who it was, she assumed Harriet was after news on Geraldine's mother.

'I'm sorry, but there's no news on Theresa Cook yet.'

'Oh, thank you. But I seem to have misplaced my friend, Ashley Lamb. I woke up this morning, and she was gone. I've looked everywhere for her, and nothing. Her mobile is switched off, which isn't like her.'

'She may have gone for a walk.'

Harriet chuckled. 'You don't know Ashley. Not this early and not in this weather.'

'I've only just come on duty. I haven't seen her.'

'Do you have CCTV coverage? Could you check to see if she left the hotel?'

'I'm not sure I can do that. I would need approval.'

'Please, could you get it? I'm concerned. She hasn't answered her mobile.'

'Mrs Locke is still at the hospital. I don't think I should disturb her – do you?'

'Sorry, of course. But if she knew I made the request, she would agree. Who's in charge while she's at the hospital?'

Carrie frowned, 'I am.'

'Then can't you make that decision. Please, I wouldn't ask but after Theresa's assault and the fog outside, I'm worried.'

Finally, Carrie agreed. She asked her when she last saw her friend. Harriet said around 11 pm last night, when she turned off the bedside lamp.

'Go have some breakfast, and I'll come find you in the conservatory once I've checked.'

'Thank you.'

Harriet decided to take a look outside the hotel before heading into breakfast. What if she had gone for a walk and got caught in the fog and couldn't find her way back? Harriet had to zip up her jacket as the cold air took a bite out of her. It was threatening to rain at any minute. She quickly jogged down to the beach, but she saw no sign of Ashley.

Harriet began to feel uneasy. Ashley had been unusually quiet last night. On her way back to the hotel, the fog began to drift away, and the boathouse came into view. She saw Ashley standing by the boathouse door. She recognised her bright red jacket. She was just standing there gazing down at something inside the boathouse.

Harriet ran up to her, asking her why she hadn't responded to her calls. Ashley only turned her head towards Harriet, fear etched across her face. Harriet took a few cautious steps towards the door and looked inside. She stiffened when she saw the body of a man lying in a pool of dried blood. Then she let out a scream.

Hazel trotted down the stairs for breakfast. She was already dressed as her father had promised to take her back to the hospital that morning. Andrew entered the kitchen shortly after and made himself some coffee and toast. Neither sibling was concerned about their father's whereabouts until Hazel ran upstairs to ask him to get up. He wasn't there. He wouldn't have gone without her, so she had to wonder if he had gone for a walk. Not that he ever did that on any other given morning. But as Hazel was getting anxious, Andrew called his father, but it went to voicemail. Andrew agreed to take Hazel in the minivan.

Hazel quickly ran back upstairs and put some of her mother's things in a small bag: a change of clothes, a hairbrush, a toothbrush and toothpaste.

'Hurry up, squirt. The hotel will need the minivan for the guests.'

'I'm hurrying,' Hazel yelled as she came stomping down the stairs. On her return to the kitchen, she saw her mother's mobile phone on the kitchen table and picked it up and put it in her bag.

Andrew drove Hazel to the hospital, then returned the minivan to the hotel. He wanted to talk to Vivienne about Tommy Burke before they headed back to university. He needed her to see reason, but with their mother's revelation last night and Theresa's accident, it had completely slipped his mind.

Carrie entered the conservatory and did a walk around as Geraldine often did, making sure her guests had everything they needed. She was all smiles and pleasantries, but word had spread about Theresa's accident, and the guests kept asking her how she was. She thanked them for their well-wishes and said she would pass on their condolences to Geraldine and her family.

As she finished her walk around the room, she could just make out Harriet running through the fog, from the direction of the boathouse. She was waving her hands in the air, yelling something she couldn't quite hear.

But as she came closer, she understood the word, 'HELP!'

A female guest approached the conservatory's giant windows and opened one of the French doors. She stepped outside quickly to calm the woman down.

'The boathouse … the boathouse … there's a dead body in the boathouse!' Harriet tried to catch her breath.

Sofia asked her to calm down and to take her to the body. She turned around and waved at Harry to join them. Carrie quickly followed them, after alleviating her guests of any alarm.

Gratefully, the fog was snaking its way out to sea, but it was still reasonably thick by the boathouse. Ashley was still standing near the door; she hadn't moved an inch. Harry quickly stepped inside and checked the body. He was careful not to disturb anything. But it was obvious from the man's appearance that he had been dead for several hours.

When Harry reappeared, he nodded confirmation to Sofia. He walked over to Carrie and asked if he could show her a picture of the deceased man in the hope she might recognise him as a guest at the hotel. She reluctantly agreed.

Carrie grew alarmed when she recognised the man in the photo. She confirmed the dead man was Phillip Locke.

'I tried to bring her with me, but she wouldn't move. I think she's in shock,' Harriet said to Sofia, not quite knowing what to do.

'It's okay, Harry will help her. My name is Sofia Faraday, I'm a Chief Inspector at Scotland Yard, and Harry is a forensic pathologist in London.'

Harry went up to Ashley and asked her name. He then asked her to take some deep breaths. Ashley managed to comply, but she was shaking. Harry had to remember that most people had never seen a dead body, and they could react in any number of ways. Ashley was frozen with disbelief; the image was still too surreal for her to comprehend what she was looking at. Harry motioned for Harriet to stay with her, while he pulled out his phone again, and called his forensic lab in London.

There was no doubt in Sofia's mind that it was murder. She called the local police and informed them that a murder had been committed and instructed them to cordon off the entire boathouse. Sofia knew the St Mary's local police didn't have the resources to handle a murder case, and it would inevitably be handled by Scotland Yard, but she would need approval from London before instigating the investigation.

'How's she doing?' Hazel asked her mother when she arrived by her side. Geraldine was sitting in the chair by her mother's hospital bed. She stretched her neck on both sides to alleviate the stiffness.

'No change. But no worse either, sweet pea.' Hazel could see how tired her mother was and leant down and gave her a hug.

'She's tough, Mum. She'll pull through.'

'I hope so.'

'Here you are!' she said, removing her mother's mobile from her bag. 'You left it in the kitchen. I also brought you some things from home.'

'Oh, Hazel. Thank you.'

Geraldine turned her phone on and saw a message from Harriet. Geraldine's emotions built up all of a sudden, and she wanted to cry. She'd forgotten all about Harriet. She excused herself for a moment, saying she needed the bathroom. Geraldine walked out of the ward for some privacy and sent a reply. Then she rested her head against the wall and prayed that her mother would recover.

She wished Wesley was here.

Harriet was momentarily distracted by the pinging sound on her mobile, telling her a new text message had arrived. She quickly flicked it on. The text said:

My Dear Harriet,

Your grandmother is in a coma. She's breathing on her own, but doctors are concerned about her head injury. Please don't leave. I'll call later.

Geraldine.

It was strange to hear Theresa being referred to as her 'grandmother'. It was such a very personal inference, but one of inclusion. But then she realised Geraldine didn't know yet that her husband was dead.

She showed Sofia the text.

'Geraldine doesn't know,' Harriet declared.

'Once the local police arrive, I'll coordinate with them, then I'll go to the hospital and inform her. She'll want her family to know as soon as possible, as word will spread fast through the hotel and island.'

Harry gestured to Sofia to come with him. She excused herself from Ashley and Harriet and followed Harry away from the boathouse.

'I had a quick look inside the boathouse,' he said. 'I can see blood spatter on the wall by the door. But I'll need to run DNA tests to discover whose blood it is. It could be either Phillip Locke's or Theresa Cook's, or both. But one thing I know for sure, I locked that door after Theresa was taken to the hospital, and the lock hasn't been broken.'

'Thanks, Harry. When is your team arriving?'

'They'll be here after lunch. If the blood is Theresa's, then she sustained her injury by the entrance to the boathouse and not where we found her. She either staggered down the ramp then passed out, or someone dragged her to the water line and left her there to drown as the tide came in. My team will thoroughly check the entire boathouse. But I'm pretty sure Phillip was killed by the door.'

'Do you think they were assaulted by the same person?' she asked.

'It's too early to tell. I have to ascertain how he was killed and with what. These two incidents might not be related.'

'I don't like coincidences, Harry. So, find me a link.'

'Don't worry. I'll find out what happened.'

Sofia turned back to Harriet and asked her to take Ashley back to their room, order her some breakfast and make sure she ate something. She asked them not to speak with anyone until she spoke to them again. Harriet nodded and escorted Ashley back to their room. She turned her mobile to silent and put it in her jacket pocket.

Sofia turned her attention to the boathouse – her romantic week away with Harry had just come to an end. She could hear police sirens off in the distance. Her next phone call was to her Chief Superintendent.

Chapter Thirteen

The Windermere Hotel

Sunday, 9:15 am

'Yes, sir. I understand,' Sofia said to the Chief Superintendent at Scotland Yard and hung up. She was now in charge of the investigation. Her next call was to her Sergeant, Carl Brooks. It was Sunday and his day off; she knew he wouldn't be pleased at her early call.

'Guv, what a surprise. You're supposed to be on holiday.'

'Not any more. There's been a murder.'

'That could only happen to you,' Carl said.

'As I'm already here, the chief super has asked me to head up the investigation. I need you on St Mary's pronto. Bring the team up to date and have the incident room ready by tomorrow morning.'

'Right, guv.'

'We may be looking at two crimes,' Sofia said. 'But I'm unsure yet if they're linked. A Theresa Cook was found barely alive in a boathouse with a head injury on Saturday early evening, and her son-in-law, Phillip Locke, was found dead this morning at the same location. We're not sure yet if her injury was an accident or an assault. She's in a coma and may not recover. Theresa Cook wasn't local but was here visiting her family, and Phillip Locke is the husband of Geraldine Locke, the owner of the Windermere Hotel. I'll update you more once I've informed Mrs Locke of her husband's death.'

'Right, guv.'

Sofia read out a list of what she needed Carl to bring with him.

'The weather is unpredictable here, it's foggy and it looks like it wants to rain. The ferry may be cancelled so you'll need to fly in.'

'Thank goodness for that,' Carl said, knowing he would likely puke his guts out on the ferry.

Sofia rolled her eyes. Her sergeant was never comfortable outside of London.

'What about forensics?'

'Harry's team is on the way and I'm coordinating with the local police.'

'So Harry's already there?' he said, cheekily.

'Yes, as you very well know.'

In fact, her whole team knew, even though Sofia had been very discreet about her relationship with Harry, nothing got past them.

Carl knew the drill. First, they would profile the victims and their closest relatives and friends. They would also begin a timeline leading up to each victim's assault.

'I'm going to talk to Geraldine now. But you will need to coordinate with the local police to interview all the staff and guests currently staying at the hotel as soon as possible, as some may be leaving today. I want alibis and witness statements taken before anyone leaves.'

'Okay, guv. I'll do it now.'

'One more thing. Check both victims' phones, I want a full list of calls and text messages from their telecom providers ASAP and check if they're still active. Neither victim had their mobiles on them.'

'On it.'

Sofia's team at the Yard was made up of five police officers: DS Carl Brooks, DS Shirley Smith, DC Devish Das, DC Ronnie O'Farrell and their newest team member, DC Hillary Hubbard. Sofia hand-picked her team after she was promoted to DCI. She believed them to be the best investigators at the Yard.

When the local police arrived, they quarantined the boathouse with the standard yellow police tape. Sofia updated them on what she knew, then headed to the hospital to speak with Geraldine. The hotel was already abuzz with rumours of a murder, although they didn't know who was dead.

As Sergeant Oliver Ives escorted Sofia to his car, a man in his mid to late forties ran up to her.

'Are you the detective?'

'Yes. I'm Chief Inspector Sofia Faraday.'

'Please, I need to know who was killed. Was it Geraldine Locke, or Harriet Smith?' The man seemed overly concerned to simply be another guest. Sofia knew the victim's name would be all over the hotel soon enough, but she was obliged to notify the next of kin first.

All Sofia could say was, 'No. It was a man's body. What is your name, and your connection to those two women?'

The man's relief was palpable. 'Thank Christ!' He ran his hands through his hair, then he realised his insensitivity. 'Sorry. My name is Wesley Burrows. Harriet Smith is my daughter. Geraldine Locke is her mother.'

'So you've known Geraldine a long time then?'

'Yes. When we were young. We've only just re-connected. Please? Who was murdered?'

'I can't tell you that right now. What room are you staying in, Mr Burrows?'

'Room 208.'

'Please don't leave the hotel until I've spoken to you again. It might not be until later today.'

'Of course. I'll need to contact my work as they're expecting me back tomorrow, I'm a commander in the Royal Navy, stationed at Plymouth. If I'm not back on Monday, they'll think I'm AWOL,' he managed a wry smile, but was unsure why.

'That's fine, but please don't leave the hotel.'

'I … yes, I understand.'

'Why did you think the victim was Geraldine or Harriet?'

'I heard about Theresa's accident. Now there's a murder, I'm a cautious man by nature, Chief Inspector. I tried to call Harriet, but it went to voicemail. I was concerned.'

Yesterday, Wesley had felt embarrassed about being so overly protective of Harriet, but now he felt justified. Wesley headed back inside the hotel; he hoped to God the dead body had nothing to do with Geraldine.

During their short drive to the hospital, Sofia asked Sergeant Ives to obtain a full list of the staff and guests at the Windermere. She wanted each guest and staff member interviewed and he was to coordinate his interviews with DS Brooks. He was to start with the guests that were scheduled to depart today.

'Yes, ma'am,' he said, excitedly. Then he realised his insensitivity and apologised. He'd lived on St Mary's for almost ten years and was responsible for the entire Scilly Isles. In all that time he had never had a murder. A couple of drunken brawls and assaults but never a murder.

'It's alright Sergeant, and its DCI Faraday or simply guv, I hate ma'am.'

The duty nurse directed Sofia to Theresa Cook's bed. The hospital only boasted ten inpatient beds in a single ward, plus a minor injuries unit which was open 24 hours a day. Theresa's bed was at the end of the ward away from the other three patients in residence. A curtain was drawn around her bed for privacy.

Sofia turned to the nurse and asked her if Geraldine Locke had been here all night.

'Yes, first in the waiting room, then by her mother's side.'

'What about her husband?'

'No. He left last night around 11ish.'

'Did he leave with anyone?'

'Yes, he left with his children and another man. Geraldine and her brother stayed, but he left around midnight. He only returned about half an hour ago.'

Sofia could see Geraldine's daughter sitting beside her mother, while a man she recognised from Saturday evening was on the other side of Theresa's bed. Sofia asked the nurse if there was somewhere quiet that she could talk to Geraldine. The nurse suggested the staff canteen as it was unoccupied.

Sofia approached Theresa's bed quietly, then waited a moment before introducing herself.

'Excuse me, Geraldine Locke, could I speak with you?'

Geraldine looked at the woman with recognition from last night.

Sofia pulled out her warrant card and said, 'I'm Chief Inspector Sofia Faraday. I was on holiday with my partner, Harry Budd. We found your mother yesterday in the boathouse.'

'Of course, I remember you. Thank you for saving her life.'

'That was all Harry,' Sofia said. She looked at Hazel, whom she recognised as a waitress in the dining room. 'Do you think we can speak privately for a moment?'

'If it's about my mother's accident, you can talk in front of Hazel,' she said.

'I will need to speak to you about that, but I need to talk to you about a more serious matter, Mrs Locke. I think we should discuss it in private.'

Geraldine looked up at Sofia, a little confused. Then she looked at Hazel and then at her brother, Callum.

'My name is Callum Cook. I'm Geraldine's brother and a lawyer. Is this a formal interview, Chief Inspector?'

'No. But it must be done in private.' Sofia looked down at Hazel, indicating she shouldn't be present.

'It's okay, Callum,' Geraldine replied, then turning to Hazel, 'I'll be back in a minute, sweet pea.'

Sofia led Geraldine out of the ward and into the staff canteen. She always hated being the bearer of bad news. It was heart-wrenching to see families suddenly torn apart by a tragic event, with only a few delicately chosen words.

'I don't understand, what's going on?' Geraldine asked, once Sofia had closed the door.

'I'm sorry to have to tell you this at such a trying time, but your husband Phillip was found dead this morning in the boathouse.'

'What?' Geraldine seemed confused and shocked. She heard the words but couldn't comprehend their meaning. Then her hands went immediately to her mouth. 'He can't be. Are you sure?'

'Yes, his body has been formally identified. But I now have to treat your mother's fall as suspicious until proven otherwise. She may have been assaulted and left to drown. I don't know if the two crimes are linked, but I don't like coincidences.'

Geraldine was scared. 'Oh, God!' Her hands were shaking. She wanted to cry for Phillip, but she couldn't manage it. Hearing of his death felt dreamlike. Geraldine understood the police \woman's words, but she hadn't registered their full meaning yet.

'I'm sorry to have to ask now, but has your mother or husband mentioned anything to you about being threatened recently?'

'No. They're ordinary people. We're ordinary people. I don't understand … I've got to tell my children.' Geraldine started pacing the room, her fingers kept reaching for her mouth then around her ears; she didn't know where to put them.

'It's okay, Mrs Locke, I'll have the police sergeant escort you and Hazel home. But I'll need to talk to you again today, if you're up to it, and I'll need to speak with your family once they've recovered from the shock, it's important I do that. They may know something or saw something that might help with our inquiries.'

'You don't think they had anything to do with this? That's absurd!'

'It's just routine, Mrs Locke, please don't be alarmed. We need to retrace your husband's last steps and speak with anyone who was in contact with him and your mother.'

Geraldine nodded her understanding, but nothing felt real.

'Sergeant Ives will take you home.'

'What about my mum?'

'The nurses and doctors will look after her. Your brother is here, he'll call you if anything changes. You can return once we've completed our interviews. What did the doctor say about your mother? Will she be transferred to the mainland?'

'No. They don't want to move her, not with a concussion. But she's stable at the moment. If you hadn't found her when you did, it would have been an entirely different outcome. She just needs to wake up. The doctor isn't sure how long it will take.'

'Then let's give her time. She may or may not remember what happened. It's common after a head injury. I'll organise for a police constable to be at the hospital at all times. She'll be quite safe here.'

Geraldine looked even more shocked. 'Are you saying someone might try to kill my mother?'

'It's a possibility. If she wakes, hopefully, she'll be able to tell us what happened in the boathouse.'

'This can't be happening!'

Sofia led Geraldine back into the ward. Callum could see by Geraldine's altered demeanour that she had received more bad news, but he decided to wait until she had taken Hazel from the room before speaking to the police officer.

Sofia didn't envy what Geraldine had to do next.

Geraldine gathered her belongings, but before she left, she leant down over her mother and gently kissed her on the forehead. Tears were running down her cheeks.

'I'll be back later, Mum.' Geraldine squeezed her mother's hand.

'What's wrong, Mum?' Hazel asked.

'I'll tell you once we're home, love. Come on.' Geraldine wrapped her arm around Hazel and they left the ward.

Callum looked up at Sofia. 'Chief Inspector, what's going on?'

'We found the body of Phillip Locke this morning in the boathouse. He has been murdered.'

Callum's face turned ashen.

'Christ! Poor Phillip. I assume you'll want to question my family?'

'Yes, but later this afternoon will be fine, if they're up to it. Tomorrow at the latest.'

'I'll be present during those interviews, Chief Inspector.'

'Understood, Mr Cook. We'll advise you when we need to talk to them. But I'll have to speak with Geraldine today at some time.'

Sofia called the local police station and asked for a patrol car to collect her from the hospital.

The fog had cleared, but a light drizzle made the day feel miserable and cold. By the time Sofia arrived back at the hotel, the atmosphere was sombre, but respectful. Guests were either keeping to their rooms or resting in the lounge, quietly talking amongst themselves. She wanted to believe that it was the rain keeping people indoors. As she approached the reception desk, her mobile rang and she excused herself before answering it.

'Carl. Where are you?'

'I'm boarding my flight now. Should be with you in an hour.'

'That's great.'

'I've applied for a Digital Evidence Access Order, with the warrant to follow for the call and text logs for Theresa Cook, Geraldine and Phillip Locke's mobile records. I've also requested the transcripts for their email accounts. They should come through today or tomorrow, being Sunday an' all.'

'I'll keep an eye out for them. I'll fill you in on developments when you arrive.'

Sofia returned to the reception desk and asked Carrie what room Harriet and Ashley were staying in.

'Room 204, Inspector.'

'Thank you. My sergeant is arriving this afternoon. Can you find a place for us to work where we won't be disturbed? I need to set up an incident room at the hotel. Preferably with a locked door.'

'Of course.'

'Have you given the list of all staff and guests to Sergeant Ives?'

'Yes, done.'

'Before your shift ended yesterday evening, did anything suspicious or unusual happen in regards to the Locke family or Theresa Cook? Did you see Theresa Cook that evening?'

'No, sorry, I was very busy.'

'Did anything stand out at all, no matter how small?'

'Well, Phillip Locke did come to the reception yesterday afternoon and ask if a woman was staying at the hotel this weekend. I checked and said yes.'

'Do you remember her name?'

'No, but hang on,' Carrie brought up the reservations list and scanned the room details. 'Her name was Clarissa Montgomery, room 201.'

'Did anything else stand out?'

'A man arrived, a Khenan someone or another, sorry I don't remember his last name, he was here to see Theresa. He wasn't listed on the hotel guest list, but she knew him and they talked in the lounge. And later that afternoon Vivienne walked through the hotel with a young man I didn't recognise. I only mention it, because they stormed out shortly after. He was pissed at Vivienne about something.'

'Thank you, you've been most helpful. My sergeant will take a full witness statement from you when he arrives this afternoon. Are all Geraldine's family here this weekend?'

'Yes, her mother arrived Friday afternoon, her brother Callum and her children, Andrew and Vivienne, arrived yesterday. Then Geraldine personally escorted two guests to the hotel yesterday, Harriet Smith and Ashley Lamb.'

'Thank you. I'll also need to see all security footage in and around the hotel from yesterday afternoon to around six this morning.'

'That might be tricky. The security videos went down late yesterday evening.'

Sofia grew concerned at another coincidence.

Carrie sensed Sofia's mistrust and informed her that during storms the power can go out and the security cameras don't always reset automatically when it comes back on again. The generators kick in immediately, but they have to manually reset the video surveillance system sometimes.

'How often do the security cameras go down?'

'Not often, mainly during storms. Everything appeared fine this morning. The night manager would have turned them back on. I'll ask him and get you the footage we have.'

'Thank you, Carrie. Who else has access to the security room and video surveillance equipment?'

'Most of the staff I'm afraid, it isn't locked.'

'Great, I'll have the local police interview your staff today. Please advise your guests we will need to speak with them before they depart the hotel and let the police know if any of your staff is not on roster today that was working last night.'

'No problem. I'll arrange it. A couple of our guests have asked to leave the hotel. They're a little anxious. I said I'd try to find them another hotel in town. Is that okay?'

'If any guests are uncomfortable staying here, they can leave once we've interviewed them. Please don't take any more bookings for accommodation for the next few days, as the police will be busy at the hotel.'

'Right, Inspector.'

'Thank you. You've been a great help. Please let me know when my sergeant arrives.'

'It's my pleasure. Anything to help catch who killed Geraldine's husband. And your incident room will be ready by the time your sergeant arrives.'

'His name is Carl Brooks. He'll also need a room for the next few nights.'

'No problem.' Carrie checked the hotel's room availability. A couple of guests were checking out that morning, but with other guests indicating they wanted to leave, she had more availability to choose from.

Sofia headed upstairs to speak with Harriet Smith and Ashley Lamb.

Sofia knocked on the door of room 204.

Harriet opened the door and stepped aside to let her in. Ashley was sitting on her bed, looking a lot better than she did early that morning.

'I'm going to need to ask both of you some questions. I need to know your connection to Theresa Cook and Phillip Locke.'

Harriet told Sofia that she was the link. She looked at Ashley, who only smiled and nodded that her friend should tell their story.

Sunday, 11:15 am
Interview with Harriet Smith and Ashley Lamb

Harriet 'Geraldine Locke is my birth mother.'

Sofia 'How long have you been acquainted with Geraldine?'

Harriet 'Only a month.'

Sofia 'I see.'

Harriet 'I first contacted Theresa, my grandmother, a little over a month ago. I wanted to meet my biological parents and Theresa acted as the go-between for me with Geraldine and Wesley. I met Geraldine a couple of times in London and once in Newquay when I first met Wesley. I've only met Theresa a couple of times.'

Sofia 'When did you find out you were adopted?'

Harriet 'I've always known, since about seven years old. My parents didn't want any secrets between us.'

Sofia 'I see. What brought you both here, this weekend?'

Harriet 'Geraldine was going to introduce me to her family. Ashley came along for moral support. She's good like that.'

Sofia 'What about your father?'

Harriet 'What about him? He's in Durham with my mum?'

Sofia 'Sorry. I meant your biological father, Wesley.'

Harriet 'I've met him once. He said he'd introduce me to his sons during their summer holidays. I was looking forward to it. I was nervous about coming here this weekend, but Geraldine was so excited for me to meet her children. Now, I think it might be best if we left.'

Sofia 'Did you know Wesley is staying at the Windermere this weekend?'

Harriet 'What?'

Harriet couldn't keep the surprise off her face. Ashley finally realised who she passed on the stairs the evening before, but she kept that to herself.

Sofia 'I met Mr Burrows early this morning, he was concerned about you. I take it you were unaware of his presence.'

Harriet 'Yes. Geraldine never told me he was coming, too.'

Sofia wondered why Geraldine would invite Harriet's biological father. Unless she didn't.

Harriet 'Ashley, what made you go to the boathouse this morning?'

Ashley had been in a daze but brought herself around when she heard Sofia say her name.

Ashley 'Um ...'

She looked at Harriet but wasn't sure what to tell her.

Sofia 'Anything at all relating to our two victims is important, no matter how trivial.'

Harriet   'Two victims?'

Sofia   'Yes, I believe Theresa may have been assaulted and left to die in the boathouse. These two attacks could have been committed by the same person.'

Harriet looked at Ashley, who was starting to unravel again.

Ashley   'I know this will sound stupid, but I went to the boathouse to look for evidence of a crime. But when I opened the door, that man was lying there.'

Sofia   'What made you believe a crime had been committed?'

Apologetically, Ashley looked at Harriet.

Ashley   'Theresa called me last night and said someone had come to her room with accusations that Harriet was a fraud. It was nonsense, but this person said they had proof. Theresa was going to confront them. She must have asked to meet in the boathouse. If she had told me where she was going, I would have gone with her.'

Now Sofia thought she was getting somewhere. All crimes have motive, now she may have found one for Theresa's assault.

Sofia   'Was the boathouse door open or closed when you went in this morning?'

Ashley	'It was closed but unlocked. I simply opened the door and stepped inside. Then I saw him…'
Sofia	'When was the last time you spoke to Theresa?'
Ashley	'Around five-thirty, maybe a quarter to six, she called me. I asked her to call back after she confronted this person, but she never did. I knew she was having dinner with Geraldine and her family at six, so I didn't worry about it. Not until Carrie told me that Theresa had been taken to hospital.'
Sofia	'Did Theresa say who approached her?'
Ashley	'No.'

Sofia would check Theresa's phone records, but if she met her attacker earlier in person, then there wouldn't be any digital record of the meeting.

Harriet had been quiet while Ashley spoke with the inspector. But she couldn't hold her tongue any longer. This was the first she'd heard about these so-called accusations.

Harriet	'What are you talking about, Ash? Why would someone accuse me of being a fraud? It took me months to find the courage to call Theresa. I have my original birth certificate, she's seen it – you've seen it. Christ! I even look like Geraldine.'
Ashley	'I don't know.'

Ashley shrugged her shoulders, yet something was niggling at her. She couldn't put her finger on it. Her intuition was directing her towards Harriet's investigation into her adoption. Something must have happened.

Sofia   'How many people, apart from you and Ashley, knew of your relationship with Geraldine?'

Harriet   'Geraldine said she told her husband on Friday night. Apart from Theresa and Wesley, nobody knew, not even her brother. She was going to tell everyone before dinner last night.'

Sofia   'That's all for now, but I'll need to talk to you again. Please remain on the island. I'm going to interview Wesley Burrows now. He asked to see you. Are you happy for me to give him your room number?'

Harriet seemed a little confused but nodded her agreement. Wesley would never call her a fraud, he was too genuine in his affections towards her, and he appeared so proud of her. She had to wonder; how well did she know any of them?

Harriet wanted to go home. But she didn't want to abandon Geraldine either.

Sofia knocked on the door of room 208.

Wesley was a tall and striking man. Sofia had to wonder if Geraldine still felt any affection toward him, and vice versa. She couldn't blame Geraldine if she did. But that could ultimately lead to a motive for murder.

Sofia entered and formally introduced herself to Wesley.

'This conversation will be recorded, but my sergeant will take a formal statement from you once he arrives. You can request a lawyer to be present, if you feel you need one.'

'That won't be necessary, Chief Inspector. Ask your questions.'

Sofia saw a softness in his brown eyes, accentuated by his calm, but confident demeanour. Sofia wondered how much the navy's discipline had contributed to his disposition and what was drawn from his own character.

Sunday, 11:35 am
Interview with Wesley Burrows

Sofia   'Geraldine was going to introduce Harriet to her family this weekend. Did she invite you to join her?'

Wesley   'No. I invited myself. I didn't even know Harriet existed until two weeks ago. I don't know Geraldine's family and I was concerned Harriet's introduction wouldn't go as Geraldine hoped. I felt protective of Harriet and wanted to be here to support her. But I didn't know her friend Ashley had accompanied her. I wouldn't have come if I had known.'

Sofia   'Have you ever met Phillip Locke or Theresa Cook?'

Wesley 'No, I've never met Phillip, but I was re-acquainted with Theresa a few weeks ago at her home in Newquay. I hadn't seen her for over a quarter of a century.'

Sofia 'Did you get on with her?'

Wesley 'I've always hated her. She separated Geraldine and me. But that was over twenty-five years ago. But learning about Harriet, and the adoption, I can't imagine what Geraldine went through back then. That only added to my disdain for Theresa and Winston. Why all the questions about Theresa? You don't think her accident was in fact an accident, do you?'

Sofia 'No. I don't. Two assaults, in less than twelve hours, raises flags in my book, Commander Burrows.'

Wesley 'Wesley, please. Look, I was angry with Theresa, but I would never hurt her, or any woman for that matter, Chief Inspector. The act is contemptible.'

Sofia had always been a good judge of character, and she wanted to believe him.

Sofia 'When did you re-connect with Geraldine?'

Wesley 'A few weeks ago. She came to Plymouth and told me about Harriet. Then we met at her mothers in Newquay. We've also spoken on the phone a few times.'

Sofia   'Are you married, Wesley?'

Wesley   'Divorced.'

Sofia   'And what is your relationship like now with Geraldine?'

Wesley took a moment to respond. He looked down at the floor, wondering how much to say. He didn't want to be insensitive, but he also didn't want to lie, there had already been far too many lies told between their families.

Wesley   'It took a long time to get over Geraldine – I was in love with her. But we both married other people. My marriage is over now, and I believe Geraldine's was coming to an end. She believed Phillip was seeing someone else. So, I think they planned to separate.'

Sofia   'Do you care for her now?'

Wesley didn't need a moment to consider his reply.

Wesley   'Yes. I'm falling in love with her all over again.'

Sofia   'Thank you, that's enough for now. My sergeant will be in touch later today to take your statement.'

Wesley seemed relieved.

'Alright. Is Harriet safe here?'

Sofia thought that a strange question. 'Has she been threatened?'

'No,' Wesley replied. 'But I don't believe in coincidences either.'

Chapter Fourteen

The Windermere Hotel

Sunday, Noon

Carrie was on reception when Sofia returned downstairs. 'How is Geraldine coping?' she asked. 'I wanted to offer my condolences, but I didn't want to intrude.'

'Geraldine left the hospital to tell her children about their father. I think it's best that she be left in peace.'

'Of course. How is Mrs Cook this morning?'

'She's holding her own at present.'

Carrie was visibly relieved. She hated the thought of Geraldine suffering. She thought it would be a kind gesture if she had the kitchen prepare lunch for Geraldine and her family. She picked up the reception phone and called Claude's office extension, but there was no answer.

Sofia was a little lost as to what to do. She had no forensic evidence yet and wouldn't until tomorrow at the earliest, and Carl wouldn't arrive for another hour or so. She couldn't enter Theresa's room until forensics had inspected it. She decided to have an early lunch and call her daughter, Francesca, to find out how her weekend was going. She needed a pleasant distraction. Before walking off, Sofia asked Carrie if she had set up an incident room, as she requested.

'Nearly. I've spent most of the morning reassuring anxious guests. Some were supposed to check out today, they had morning flights. I've had to reschedule them and ferry tickets.'

'I'm sorry for all the extra work, but it can't be helped. They can't leave until they've been cleared.'

'I understand. I should have it ready for you by the time your sergeant arrives.'

Sofia thanked her and headed back to her room, where she would eat lunch in private and start writing up her notes before Carl arrived.

Carrie decided to head into the kitchen and speak to Chef Allard in person. She found him barking orders to his staff as they prepared the lunch orders. Their work never stopped, not even during a murder investigation.

'*Comment Geraldine s'en sort-elle?* Sorry. How is Geraldine?'

'Hanging in there.'

'*Et* her mother?'

'No change, Claude.'

'If she's like her daughter, she'll pull through.'

'Let's hope so.'

'If *dere's* anything we can do for her, *s'il te plaît* let us know,' he said.

'Thanks. Actually, in case any of you don't know, the murdered man is in fact Phillip Locke, her husband.'

'*Mon dieu*,' Claude said, crossing himself.

Barbara dropped her knife on the floor. She quickly picked it up and took it to the sink, then returned to her station. She felt pity for Geraldine.

'I thought you could put together some sandwiches for Geraldine and her family. They're all in shock over Phillip's death, so we could help them out a little.'

Claude agreed and said his staff would organise the sandwiches.

Satisfied, Carrie left the kitchen, but not before she heard Chef Allard bark more orders at his staff.

'I want *dat* chicken on *da* grill within five minutes.'

'Yes, chef,' yelled Barbara.

'Why aren't those herbs crushed and in *da* soup?'

'Sorry, chef,' replied another junior chef. 'I can't find the pestle.' He held up the mortar, but the pestle was missing.

'*Mon dieu*, check *da* dishwasher.'

'It wasn't in there, chef.'

'Then crush *dem* with *da* mallet.'

'Yes, chef.'

Carrie quickly exited the kitchen. She knew Claude was a gifted culinary genius, but she wouldn't want to be on the receiving end of his never-ending orders. Carrie made her way back to reception, relieved that she would never have to work in a café or kitchen again.

Clarissa sent another text to Phillip asking after his mother-in-law. She hadn't heard back and feared she had scared him last night with her pregnancy news. Clarissa supposed Phillip was busy with his children – still, she didn't like being ignored.

She looked out of the window and saw a lot of activity down by the boathouse. Wasn't that where Mrs Cook had her accident? Why so many police? Morning sickness had taken hold when she woke, so she had eaten her breakfast in her room.

Her thoughts were interrupted with a knock on the door. A young sergeant introduced himself and asked if he could come in. Clarissa opened the door wider and allowed him to enter. He asked her to confirm her name and where she was yesterday afternoon until early this morning? Did she have an alibi? When she asked why all the questions, the answer made Clarissa's blood ran cold.

All her poise and dignity drained from her face as she fell down on the sofa. Clarissa's future had just been ripped out from under her.

The sergeant asked her not to leave St Mary's. It was clear to him that she knew the victim very well.

Chapter Fifteen

Sunday, 1.00 pm

Sofia hadn't spoken to Harry all day. She was tempted to go back to the boathouse to check on the forensic team's progress. But considering they had only just arrived she decided to let them get on with it. When Sofia returned to the reception desk, Carl walked through the foyer carrying an overnight bag and a large cardboard box. Seeing Carl made the investigation all the more real. She was no longer a tourist; she was now a Chief Inspector of Scotland Yard.

'Am I glad to see you,' she announced.

'Couldn't help yourself, could you?' he said, shaking his head. 'If you wanted me to join you on holiday, you could've just asked.'

'Very funny. You're going home on the ferry.'

Carl's face turned ashen.

Sofia turned to Carrie. 'Is our incident room ready yet?'

'Yes, I've set you up in the function room, it's used for conferences and weddings. Geraldine's office is a bit small for both of you. I've put a *Do Not Disturb* sign on the door and set up a whiteboard and printer. There are extension cables and extra adaptors if you need them. I have also put a landline in the conference room, so you have a direct line to the reception desk and the mainland.'

The acting manager had thought of everything.

'Thank you, that's perfect. This is Sergeant Carl Brooks. This is Carrie Ford, she's the acting manager this weekend. Anything you need, I'm sure she'll be able to accommodate.'

Carl's attention was immediately drawn to the attractive young woman behind the reception desk. But that wasn't unusual, he was often attracted to beautiful young women. Sofia used to call them 'fleeting fancies' as she could never keep up with his latest girlfriend. But lately Carl had been quieter than usual. When she asked him about his moodiness, he simply shrugged the question away, so Sofia never pressed him on the subject. He would say when he was ready.

'Hello,' Carl said, in his softest manly voice.

He would have run his hand through his hair, but his hands were full.

Carrie blushed a little and walked them to the function room. It was a large square room, with at least twelve round tables and dozens of chairs stacked one on top of the other in the corner of the room. Carrie had set up two tables with chairs in the middle of the room.

'Perfect. Does the room have a lock?' Sofia asked.

Carrie handed Sofia two key cards, then left the room. Carl walked over to one of the tables and set the box down.

He began unpacking as Sofia brought him up to date on what she already knew.

'Are the local bobbies equipped to monitor Theresa Cook round the clock?'

'I think so. They're keen to help. They're not happy that someone was murdered on their unsullied little island.'

'Yeah, especially now that summer's coming. Bad for business.'

'Partially true. But they care about the community here on St Mary's. Theresa Cook and Phillip Locke might not be Scilly Isles natives, but it's still personal for them.'

'Understood.'

Carrie returned with some tea and coffee facilities for them. Sofia thanked her before she left the room again.

'Okay. Who am I interviewing first?'

'I need Geraldine's family interviewed first. Callum, her brother, is a lawyer and wants to be present.'

'Great. There's always one around when you don't want one.'

Sofia chuckled. 'Harriet said no one knew about her visit or who she was before her arrival on the island, except Theresa, Wesley and Phillip. Geraldine told the rest of her family on Saturday night, around six. Even if her children knew, I can't see any cause to warrant the attack on their grandmother. Or kill their father, for that matter. Unless there's something sinister going on that we haven't uncovered yet.'

'Jealousy and abuse are often motives for murder.'

'True. But I think it has to do with Harriet in some way, that's why Theresa went to the boathouse. I just can't see anyone in her own family attacking her. I watched them when I told them about Theresa's accident. They all appeared shocked.'

'Well, if Theresa and Phillip knew about Harriet, then one of them might have told someone else. When do you want me to interview the children? Do you want them brought in here, or would you rather I interview them in their own home?'

'Bring them in here,' Sofia said. 'It's more formal that way, but only if they're up to it. We might need to wait until tomorrow, just see how they're feeling.'

'Got it.'

Sofia also filled Carl in on what Ashley said about Theresa's mysterious visitor and the accusation of fraud. That line of enquiry would need to be investigated.

Carl walked over to the columns of chairs and carried three more over to the centre of the room. Then he dragged one extra table over and placed the chairs around it for the interviews.

'The local police are interviewing the guests and staff as we speak. I've told them to forward everything to you,' Sofia said.

'Alright.' Carl finished emptying the contents of the cardboard box onto his and Sofia's new desks, then headed to the annex to collect Geraldine for his first interview.

Sofia logged on to her computer to see if the mobile phone records had arrived. She was a little disappointed at the delay, so she decided to head over to the boathouse and see what Harry had discovered so far before they interviewed Geraldine Locke.

'Hello, you. Do you have anything significant for me yet?' Sofia asked Harry when she arrived at the boathouse. She had donned a plastic jumpsuit, hairnet and shoe coverings before entering.

'Not much, I'm afraid,' Harry said. 'I don't think the killer came right into the boathouse. It's pretty clean so far. But I'm confident both attacks happened by the entrance. We have two different and distinct blood spatters. Phillip's killer was probably waiting just inside the door when Phillip entered.

We've taken fingerprints all around the entrance, but I hope Phillip's body will tell us more. I've already taken Harriet and Ashley's fingerprints, and Ashley's are a match on the door, but there are also a few others. I'll need fingerprints from the staff and guests, but they could have used the boathouse at any time during their stay. But I can categorically say, I locked that door yesterday evening.'

'Ashley said it was closed but unlocked. So the killer had access to a key,' Sofia said.

'Maybe Phillip brought it with him, or his killer, but it isn't here now?'

'Do you think both our victims were attacked with the same object?'

'No way of knowing yet. But both Theresa and Phillip were struck on the right side of the head, indicating the attacker was left-handed. I'll know more once I've done the autopsy. I'll stop by the hospital to photograph Theresa Cook's injuries and gather her clothes. The hospital has bagged everything she came in with, so I'll take them with me.'

'Let me know if you find her mobile phone. Your team said it wasn't in her room.'

'Will do.'

Harry's team hadn't found Theresa's or Phillip's mobiles in the boathouse. Even after the tide had gone out, there was no sign of them.

'We'll be finished later this afternoon,' Harry said. 'We have a private flight booked to take us back to the mainland as we'll miss the last scheduled flight. I'll have answers for you tomorrow.'

'I'm sorry our holiday has been cut short.'

'It's not your fault. I'm glad I actually got to save someone's life for a change.'

'I do love you, you know.' Sofia wanted to kiss Harry right there in the boathouse, but restrained herself, as his colleagues were still working the room.

'Right back at you,' he winked at her. 'We'll make up for it another time.'

'Thank you.'

'I'll see you before we head off.'

They stared at each other for a few moments. Their mutual smiles inferred, *I love you*.

Sofia spent some time looking around the boathouse. It felt different in the daylight somehow – peaceful. Finally, Sofia headed back to the hotel. It was hard to believe a brutal murder had taken place here.

Sofia decided to conduct Geraldine's interview herself. The mobile phone records had just arrived, and she wanted to see Geraldine's reaction to her questions. She made three copies of the mobile records and handed one copy to Carl.

Before she began, she offered Geraldine a hot drink.

Sofia busied herself at a rectangular table by the wall that Carrie had set up for them with an assortment of different teas, with coffee and sugar sachets, and a jug of cold milk. She provided a kettle and small packets of assorted biscuits. She'd thought of everything.

Sofia watched Geraldine, while the kettle boiled. She appeared aloof and distant. She was dishevelled compared to her usual attire and immaculate appearance. Sofia didn't envy her having to tell her children about their father. She could only imagine the suffering that was festering in the little annex, next door.

Sunday, 2:10 pm
Interview with Geraldine Locke

Sofia   'How is your mother doing? Any news?'

Geraldine 'No change, I'm afraid.'

Sofia   'We won't keep you long. Then you can get back to your family. There is counselling available if your children need it. The nature of their father's death can be traumatic.'

Geraldine 'Thank you. I'll keep an eye on them. They're in shock as you can imagine. But we'll get through this together as a family.'

Sofia understood all too well. But sometimes children can hold back their feelings in order to protect themselves or a parent or sibling. She could predict Francesca's reactions and mannerisms in certain situations, but she was still capable of holding back her emotions, especially where her father was concerned.

Geraldine 'We were all so happy yesterday, now everything has fallen apart. My children still can't believe he's dead. Why would someone kill Phillip?'

That was the million dollar question Sofia needed to solve. She brought three coffees to the interview table for Geraldine, Carl and herself.

Sofia   'I don't know yet, but I promise you, we'll
find out.'

They sat quietly drinking their coffees, until Callum arrived.
Sofia introduced him to Carl before he sat down beside his
sister, and asked Geraldine if they'd already questioned her. She
shook her head in the negative.

Carl asked Callum if he would like a coffee, but Callum
declined the offer.

Sofia began her questioning.

Sofia   'I need to know if you had your mobile
with you the whole time since your
mother was taken to hospital?'

Geraldine 'Um … no. I didn't.'

Sofia   'When did you last use it?'

Geraldine 'Early yesterday afternoon. No, this
morning. I used it around six o'clock
last night when I called my mother to
see where she was, then I put it down
somewhere. I think I left it in the
kitchen. It wasn't until Hazel handed it
to me in the hospital this morning that
I realised I never had it.'

Sofia   'So, to be clear, you didn't use it after six
o'clock yesterday, until your daughter
brought it to you in the hospital this
morning?'

Geraldine 'Correct. You arrived to say my mother had been hurt and I ran out the house and I got straight into the ambulance. Why is it so important?'

Sofia 'Phillip received a text message asking him to go to the boathouse late last night – it was sent from your mobile.'

Geraldine was awash with shock and confusion. She turned to her brother; she wasn't sure what to say. He appeared just as shocked as she was. But he brought his emotions under control, professionally.

Callum 'Only a fool would use their own phone to lure someone to their death, Chief Inspector.'

Sofia had to agree with him. It would be foolish, but also clever.

Sofia 'Did everyone follow you to the hospital last night?'

Geraldine 'Yes.'

Callum 'I can confirm the whole family was at the hospital until late Saturday night, Chief Inspector.'

Geraldine 'I don't usually lock the back door to the kitchen. I suppose anyone could have come in and used it. Maybe when we were at the hospital.'

Sofia	'Possibly. Do you have it with you now?'

Geraldine removed her mobile from her jacket pocket and showed it to Sofia. Carl retrieved an evidence bag from his desk and asked Geraldine to put it in the bag.

Carl	'We'll need to check it for fingerprints, but unfortunately, it may only show yours and your daughter's. But we need to be thorough.'
Callum	'My sister isn't a malicious person. Plus, she was at the hospital all night.'
Carl	'The nurses couldn't have watched her all night. She could easily have slipped out, and then returned without anyone being the wiser, this is a small island. But we'll check the CCTV cameras at the hospital to verify who came and went and at what times.'
Sofia	'We have to investigate all the victim's acquaintances, Geraldine. Had anything been going on between your husband and your mother, a falling out or disagreement? Were they involved in anything, business wise or personal?'
Geraldine	'No nothing. I've only just reconnected with my mother. We haven't been close in a long time.'
Sofia	'Can I ask why?'

Geraldine looked down at the table, then at Callum before answering.

Geraldine   'I never forgave my parents for making me give Harriet up for adoption. It was a long time ago, but some wounds don't heal.'

Sofia   'Harriet said she first contacted Theresa to act as a go-between before meeting you. Can you tell me about that?'

Geraldine   'There's not much to tell, really. Harriet obtained her original birth certificate before adoption from the General Register Office and Ashley helped her trace me. But because I was married with children, she didn't want to just turn up on my doorstep, so she contacted my mother. I met Harriet in Newquay and in London a couple of times. She wanted to know who her birth father was and so I had to contact Wesley Burrows and tell him he had a daughter.'

Sofia   'So he was unaware that you had a child together?'

Geraldine   'Correct. My parents thought it best he didn't know. Our families hadn't been on good terms. Stupid pride and prejudice nonsense. My grandfather wasn't a nice man. I think he was more livid that I was pregnant by a Burrows than anything else. He insisted I terminate it, but as I was already six months pregnant, it was out of the question. In the end, my parents persuaded me to put her up for adoption.'

Carl   'That must have been hard for you.'

Geraldine 'It was. But I was young and scared. I stayed with my aunt and uncle during the final months and then I was shipped off to a boarding school for the remainder of the school term. Then I lived in Oxford when I was at university, that's where I met Phillip. But I couldn't face Wesley again.'

Carl   'Was he angry when you told him?'

Geraldine looked directly at Carl.

Geraldine 'Yes. He was. But he understood how frightened I must have been and felt bad he wasn't there to support me.'

Sofia   'Were you angry that he turned up this weekend?'

Geraldine 'What?'

Sofia   'He's here, staying at this very hotel.'

Geraldine 'I had no idea.'

Geraldine looked around the table, lastly at her brother. Fear gripped her momentarily, a pain appeared in her chest, she wasn't sure why.

Sofia　'I spoke with him earlier, he came on an impulse, as he was worried about Harriet.'

Geraldine lowered her head again and started to cry. She was grieving for Phillip, but so desperately wanted to hold Wesley in her arms. Her heart lifted momentarily on hearing that Wesley was so close. But a prevailing fear hung over her like dark clouds. Someone killed Phillip?

Carl　'What about your husband, Mrs Locke? How did he react to your news about Harriet?'

Geraldine wiped her eyes before continuing.

Geraldine　'My husband didn't appear too concerned when I told him on Friday night. He's been having an affair with a work colleague. I had my suspicions for months, but he confirmed it Friday night. He actually thought I was having the affair. Can you believe that?'

Geraldine finished her coffee, her throat was dry and she was feeling anxious. She couldn't look at Sofia or Carl any longer. So she stared down at her empty coffee cup.

Sofia　'Do you know who your husband is having an affair with?'

Sofia tried to be as delicate as she could.

Geraldine   'No. He only said it was someone at work.'

Sofia   'Thank you, Geraldine. That will be all for now.'

Geraldine and Callum rose to leave, but Geraldine turned back to ask a question of her own.

Geraldine   'What about my mother? Do you think she's in danger?'

Sofia   'If she remembers who assaulted her, then yes. But I've spoken to the local police and they'll be keeping an eye on her at the hospital. She's safe there.'

Geraldine   'Thank you, Chief Inspector Faraday.'

Carl returned to his desk to type up his notes, when Sergeant Oliver Ives entered the room. Sofia introduced Oliver to Carl before he told them his news. He flipped over his notepad.

'Guv,' Oliver said, 'We've spoken to all the guests that are checking out today, most couples were together around the island, some frequented Hugh Town and Old Town at restaurants and pubs, etcetera. They showed me electronic receipts paid for on their mobiles. Others were in the bar and lounge, or up in their rooms. It was a stormy night, so some never ventured out. I have their details and room numbers. Some have already missed their scheduled flights and are not happy. They want to know if they can leave now on the afternoon ferry.'

'Did anything stand out in their interviews that would warrant detaining them any further?'

'No.'

'Did you take down their personal details?'

'Yes, Carrie gave me a printout of all the guest's details, plus the staff.'

'Okay, cross-reference their numbers against the call logs of Theresa and Phillip's mobile numbers. If they appear, we'll need permission from the guests and staff before we can access their mobile records. Also, reception keeps a list of everyone who uses the water sport equipment. Check the log and see who used them on Friday and Saturday. We'll need fingerprints from anyone who entered the boathouse this week to eliminate them from our inquiries.'

Sofia handed the sergeant a printout of Theresa and Phillip's mobile logs. There weren't many numbers in the call registry, so the task wouldn't take long.

'Thank you, guv. Oh, one couple did say they saw Phillip Locke enter room 201 yesterday afternoon, around 5:30 pm. The guest's name is James Herbert, he's staying in room 206. They stay at the Windermere every year, in fact they always request the same room. He recognised Phillip but didn't think anything of it.'

'Good work. Have you spoken to the guest in room 201 yet?'

Sergeant Ives quickly checked his notes, then said, 'Yes, guv. Clarissa Montgomery. She was in her room all night, but when I told her who had been murdered, she appeared very shocked. I think she knew Phillip Locke personally. But, then again, a number of guests were in shock.'

'Thank you, Sergeant,' Sofia said, looking at Carl quizzically.

'I'll check the call logs to see if her mobile number appears on Phillip's mobile,' Carl said, then turning to Sergeant Ives, he said, 'Have your notes typed up and email them to me once your team has finished.'

'What do I tell the guests? They keep approaching my officers for updates, they're a little anxious to leave,' Sergeant Ives enquired.

'As long has your team has questioned them, the guests can leave, all except Clarissa Montgomery. We'll need to speak with her in more detail.'

'Will do,' Sergeant Ives quickly gathered up his notes. He was grateful to be a part of the murder investigation. Not much happened on St Mary's or in the whole of the Scilly Isles for that matter. He ashamedly felt excited to be doing some 'real' police work for a change.

Sergeant Ives hurried out of the conference room.

Sofia watched him leave. She smiled at his eagerness; she had been just as enthusiastic when she was assigned to her first homicide case.

Carl checked Clarissa's number and confirmed it appeared many times on Phillip's mobile log. 'I have a large number of calls and text messages from Clarissa to Phillip and vice-versa. The last one was earlier today, asking how Theresa was and when was he coming up to see her?'

'I think we better go up and speak with her, she's scheduled to leave this afternoon. If Phillip Locke was her lover, she's probably in pieces.'

'Unless she already knew,' replied Carl.

Carl had a point. Until proven otherwise, Clarissa Montgomery was now a suspect. Although Sofia didn't know how it related to Theresa Cook's assault, unless she learned of their affair and confronted one of them.

Carl pointed out that he couldn't imagine a guest simply walking into Geraldine's home in the middle of the night to use her mobile. It would have been a brazen act. How would they even know the mobile would be there?

Sofia wondered the same thing. 'They could have taken it earlier that evening, when everyone left for the hospital. Or simply entered late in the evening and used it to send the text message.'

'True. But if everyone was home by then, it would still have been risky.'

'There's a 'Find my Phone' app on most phones. I have one on Francesca's phone so I know where she is. Please check if Geraldine or Phillip have one on their phones.'

'Will do.'

'If there is one on Phillip's he would have known where Geraldine was going while on the mainland, but not necessarily who she was with. Hence, why he thought she was having an affair. Maybe their separation wasn't as amicable as we were led to believe.'

'Spying on your wife would suggest a possessive husband. But if he was having an affair, then why should he be jealous?'

'Carrie told me that Phillip seemed shocked when she told him Clarissa was staying at the hotel. Obviously he didn't invite her. Maybe there was animosity between them and she came to confront him. Choose or lose.'

'Well, she's got balls, to stay at his wife's hotel. That's brazen,' Carl said, shaking his head.

'I want to speak with her next, before we interview the Locke children. I want confirmation of their affair and who knew about it.'

Carl checked his emails and found one from the telecom companies confirming Phillip and Theresa's mobiles were both still switched off.

They spent a few more minutes reviewing the call logs and text messages.

As Sofia scanned down the list of Theresa's call logs, she noticed a matching mobile number. It was Ashley's, confirming what Ashley had told her earlier.

'I want the mobile records for Harriet and Ashley made a priority as well. Add them to the warrant.'

'Will do,' replied Carl. 'I'll get on to the providers straight away. Hang on, there's also a text message from Ashley to Theresa at 6.35 pm on Saturday, but it was signed by Harriet. It says: *I'm concerned. How did it go? Harriet.*'

'That could be Harriet asking about the dinner,' Sofia said. 'She was supposed to join them once Geraldine told her family about her.'

'You don't think Phillip attacked Theresa Cook, then someone attacked him in revenge?'

'That's a possibility, but what reason would Phillip have to attack his mother-in-law?'

Before Carl could give a sarcastic remark to her last question, Sofia pointed her finger at him and narrowed her eyes.

'What about a jealous lover?' Carl offered up instead.

'Why don't we ask her?'

But Carl was referring to Wesley.

Clarissa climbed off her bed when she heard the tap, tap, tap at her door. She opened it to find a man and woman standing in the hallway.

'Can I help you?'

'My name is Chief Inspector Sofia Faraday, and this is Sergeant Carl Brooks.' They both produced their warrant cards.

'You better come in then.'

Clarissa removed her arm from the door and casually turned around and walked back into the room. She was obviously expecting another visit from the police. Geraldine could see she had been crying. Her eyes were blood-shot. She wore white, slim-lined three quarter length trousers and a light blue turtleneck top with no sleeves. She was an attractive and sensual woman and she obviously knew it. Her movements were graceful and implied sensuality.

'I heard about the attack on the old woman, it's terrible. I met her yesterday in the bar. Now there's been a murder. Not such a sleepy little hamlet, after all.'

Sunday, 3:10 pm
Interview with Clarissa Montgomery

Sofia   'Could I ask if you left the hotel at all from Saturday afternoon until this morning?'

Clarissa half-chuckled.

Clarissa   'You don't suspect me, do you? I only met her twenty-four hours ago.'

Sofia   'Please just answer the question.'

Clarissa   'I was in my room all night and didn't see or hear anything.'

Sofia   'Is there anyone who can corroborate your alibi?'

Clarissa 'No. Phillip came to my room Saturday early evening, but he didn't stay long.'

Carl 'What time was this?'

Clarissa 'A little before six. I ordered room service which arrived about seven.'

Clarissa sat down on the sofa. She lifted her legs up in front of her and rested her arm over the top of the sofa. Her slender, long legs hadn't gone unnoticed to either police officer.

Sofia 'You would have been told by the sergeant who interviewed you earlier today that the victim was Phillip Locke. Were you and Phillip having an affair?'

Clarissa admired directness, but the words were hard to hear, now that Phillip was gone.

Clarissa 'Yes, for about fourteen months.'

Sofia could see Clarissa was trying to stay in control of her emotions.

Carl 'It didn't bother you that he was married?'

Clarissa 'No. Maybe you should have asked Phillip that question. He was married, not me, Sergeant.'

Sofia glared at Carl, he was out-of-line.

Sofia 'I apologise. But we need to ask some delicate questions. Why did you come to the island this weekend, and stay at the Windermere, of all places. Was it Phillip's suggestion?'

Clarissa 'No. I decided to surprise him.'

Sofia 'Was Phillip planning on leaving his wife, for you? His text messages to you suggest he was.'

Clarissa 'Yes. He was in love with me, Inspector. He finally agreed to tell Geraldine this weekend. He was tired of the charade that was their marriage and wanted to make a clean breast of it.'

Sofia 'Did Geraldine know about Phillip's intentions before this weekend?'

Clarissa 'I don't think so. I was surprised that he finally told her on Friday. I didn't think he had the bottle. That's why I came, to make sure he did...'

Sofia 'Was that why Phillip came home this weekend? To tell his wife about you.'

Clarissa 'No.'

Sofia 'Can you elaborate?'

Clarissa 'Phillip thought his wife was having an affair, but he told me on the phone on Saturday that his wife had a love child.'

Carl 'What time on Saturday?'

Clarissa   'After I arrived, I texted him and he called me back shortly after and told me about his wife's long-lost daughter.'

Clarissa chuckled.

Sofia   'What's so amusing, Ms Montgomery?'

Clarissa   'He was the one having the affair, but he naturally accused his wife of having one because she was no longer interested in him. Phillip said he told Geraldine about me on Friday night. Everything was out in the open, they agreed to a separation, so Phillip and I could now be together, officially. There was no need to sneak around anymore behind anyone's back.'

Sofia   'Why did he think his wife was having an affair?'

Clarissa   'She had made numerous trips to the mainland recently. Something Phillip said she hated doing. She said she was visiting her mother in Newquay, but she went to London instead.'

Carl   'How would he know that?'

Clarissa just realised she said too much, she stood up and wrapped her arms around herself for comfort.

Clarissa   'I'd like you to leave now.'

Sofia wasn't quite finished, but she stood up to indicate they would leave.

Sofia	'What time did Phillip leave your room yesterday afternoon?'
Clarissa	'Before six. I invited him to come over last night but he declined. He obviously wanted to be with his family.'
Sofia	'Thank you, Ms Montgomery.'
Clarissa	'When can I leave this wretched place?'
Sofia	'Not yet I'm afraid. We may need to speak with you again.'
Clarissa	'Maybe you should take a closer look at his wife. Phillip stood to make a lot of money in the divorce. Now she gets to keep the lot.'

Clarissa had her back to the police and said no more. She walked over to the window and looked out across the island. She never saw herself as a vindictive person, but she was angry and in pain.

Sofia and Carl took their leave. Divorces could bring out the worst in people, Sofia knew that better than anyone, but money was often a motive for murder. It wasn't implausible that Geraldine had used her own phone and left it in the house after killing Phillip, claiming she was at the hospital all night.

Walking down the corridor, Carl said, 'Maybe Phillip had cold feet and wanted to call the whole thing off. We only have her word about his actions. A jilted lover without an alibi.'

Sofia agreed it was a motive; Clarissa was clearly rattled by Phillip's death. She appeared to love him, but was she jealous enough to kill?

'You were harsh on her back there? What's up with you?'

'Sorry. Nothing. It won't happen again.' Carl didn't want to talk about it. He was still reeling from the shock of his own parent's recent divorce. He had always thought they were a happy couple. Now his father was happy with someone else. His anger towards his father's behaviour was still raw. He didn't know how to comfort his mother, who was in pieces.

When Sofia and Carl re-entered the conference room, Harry was waiting for them.

'I'm off then,' Harry said.

'Already?' she sighed.

'Yes. Hopefully, tomorrow I'll have an idea of the type of weapon used on Phillip Locke. Then your team can begin a thorough search. All I can say right now was that it was smooth, small and curved.'

'Theresa's attack may have been spontaneous, but Phillip's was premeditated,' Sofia replied.

'That's if it was an assault,' Harry reminded Sofia. 'She may have simply fallen and hit her head.'

Sofia was still of two minds about Theresa's injuries. She walked Harry outside the hotel to where the minivan was waiting to take his team to the airport. They kissed tenderly before saying goodbye. Sofia felt guilty that her job had interrupted their holiday. But even if she wasn't in charge of this investigation, Harry knew his team would have been asked to head up the forensic investigation.

Harry put his arms around her and whispered, 'I'm not happy about you staying here alone. Are you sure you can't stay somewhere else tonight? You're potentially under the same roof as a murderer.'

'Don't worry. I'll be fine. Besides, Carl is here and we have police stationed at the hotel around the clock.'

'Just be careful.' Harry kissed Sofia softly again on the lips, not caring who saw.

'It's a small island, my suspects are limited,' Sofia chuckled. 'This has personal written all over it. I just need to know why. Then I'll know who.'

'Then I better get back and find you some evidence.'

Harry gave Sofia one last kiss and climbed onto the minibus. He promised Sofia the autopsy would be carried out first thing tomorrow morning.

When Sofia returned to the conference room, she asked Carl to head over to the annex and see if the Locke children were fit enough to be interviewed.

Carl escorted Andrew into the conference room, he knew there was no point asking Andrew any questions until his uncle, the lawyer, arrived. He simply offered Andrew a drink, which he politely declined. Carl felt for him; the weekend was supposed to be a happy family reunion.

Andrew tried to compose himself. He turned down the sergeant's offer to be interviewed tomorrow. He wanted to get it over with, he wanted to help find his father's killer.

When Callum finally entered the conference room, he announced they could begin.

Carl pulled out his notebook and pen, then turned on the tape recorder and stated who was present in the room and what the time and date was. Sofia asked the questions.

Andrew was calm and showed great composure. After stating his whereabouts last night, he answered all their questions as best he could.

Sunday, 3:35 pm
Interview with Andrew Locke

Andrew	'Like I said, I didn't know anything about Harriet until my mother told us last night, Inspector.'
Sofia	'Thank you, Andrew. Just a couple more questions, then you can go. When you arrived home from the hospital last night, did you leave the annex at any time?'
Andrew	'No.'
Sofia	'Do you know if it was locked?'
Andrew	'Um … I didn't check, sorry.'
Sofia	'Did you see your grandmother this weekend? Other than when she was put in the ambulance?'

Andrew was about to say no, then hesitated. Sofia caught his hesitation.

Sofia	'No matter how trivial or how long you met with her is important as we need to draw up a timeline of your grandmother's movements before her assault.'

Andrew	'I visited her in her room on Saturday afternoon. But it was a private matter.'
Sofia	'I'm sorry but we need to know what it was about.'

Andrew looked to his uncle for clarification, who nodded that he should answer.

Sofia had no doubt that Callum would have spoken to Andrew before the interview took place and knew what his nephew's meeting was about. If he was a half-decent lawyer that is. Sofia believed he was.

Andrew	'It was about Vivienne. Well about her boyfriend, anyway. She wanted access to her trust fund early, but Nan wanted me to find out why. She didn't believe Vivienne's story about needing it for school. I met her boyfriend once and disliked him on the spot. I told my Nan what I thought, and she asked me to look into him, so I did. He befriends women, students at the university who have money, he wines and dines them, then gets them to invest in his ill-gained schemes or ventures, if they even exist. Once he's squandered all their money he dumps them and moves on to someone else.'
Carl	'How do you know all this?'
Andrew	'I made enquiries around the university. I was told to look on a website that listed

scammers and con artists. I did, and he was on it. I contacted one woman who posted his picture and details on the site and she told me what he did to her. It wasn't the first time he's done it either.'

Sofia   'What did your grandmother say about that?'

Andrew   'She wasn't going to give Vivienne her trust fund. But Vivienne was with me and Hazel on Saturday and at the hospital most of the night.'

Carl   'What was Vivienne's boyfriend's name?'

Andrew   'Tommy Burke. He hangs around the university, but I doubt he studies anything.'

Carl   'Did you go into town at any time to confront Tommy Burke?'

Andrew   'No. I don't know where he's staying.'

Sofia   'A couple more questions, Andrew. They're delicate, but I have to ask. Do you know a Clarissa Montgomery?'

Andrew   'No.'

Sofia   'Did you know your father was having an affair?'

Callum   'Come on Inspector, that's out of line!'

Sofia   'I'm sorry, but I have to ask.'

Andrew was shocked by the directness of the question but nodded his head. He told them what Vivienne had seen when she visited their father's university a few months ago.

Sofia   'Thank you, you can go home now.'

She turned to Callum and asked if Vivienne and Hazel were ready to be interviewed or if they needed more time. Callum said that they were ready to be questioned.

Andrew stood up and left the room. He felt guilty, he had just lied to the police.

Carl   'Mr Cook, while we're waiting for Vivienne and Hazel to arrive, I'd like to ask you a few questions. Do you need a lawyer present?'

Callum   'Very funny, Sergeant. Ask away.'

Carl   'Where were you yesterday between 5:30 pm up to this morning?'

Callum   'I followed the ambulance to the hospital and stayed there with my sister until around midnight. Phillip, Khenan and the children left around 11 pm. I went straight to bed and came down to breakfast around 7 am as I wanted to go back to the hospital to check on my mother. Once these interviews are over, I'd like to go back to the hospital.'

Carl   'Can anyone corroborate your whereabouts from Saturday evening after you left the hospital?'

Callum paused for a moment.

> **Callum** 'Khenan Metcalfe was staying in my room, but he was asleep when I returned. I slept on the couch and was up early and headed back to the hospital.'

> **Sofia** 'Thank you. Did Mr Metcalfe arrive with you yesterday?'

> **Callum** 'No. Khenan arrived in the afternoon, he was invited by my mother. I only found out he was here when he knocked on my door yesterday afternoon.'

> **Sofia** 'Was his arrival a happy reunion?'

Callum paused.

> **Callum** 'It was a surprise, but not an unhappy one. My mother was trying to get us back together again.'

> **Carl** 'I see.'

Carl was meticulously making notes, as was Callum, even though the tape recorder was doing it for him.

> **Sofia** 'We'll talk to him once the family interviews are completed. I take it, you'd like to be present on that interview as well?'

> **Callum** 'Only if Khenan asks me to, he's also a lawyer.'

Carl could only smile.

Carl   'One more question if I may. Do you know a Clarissa Montgomery?'

Callum   'No? Who is she?'

Sofia   'That's all for now.'

Callum   'My family had nothing to do with Phillip's death or my mother's assault. It's absurd. Philip wasn't the greatest of husbands, but he loved his children and they loved him. They're still in shock, are you sure these interviews are necessary.'

Sofia   'You know we have to establish everyone's whereabouts as soon as possible, especially members of the victim's family. We'll be as quick and as delicate as we can, Mr Cook. They may have seen or heard something which could be important.'

Callum   'I appreciate that, but hand-on-heart my family didn't kill Phillip or assault my mother. If it even was an assault.'

Carl   'And I appreciate that too, Mr Cook, but as you know, most murders are committed by family members or close acquaintances of the victims.'

Callum conceded the point.

Sunday, 3:55 pm
Interview with Vivienne Locke

Sofia   'I'm very sorry for your loss, Vivienne.'

Vivienne's eyes were still puffy and her nose was red. She played and pulled at a tissue in her hands, trying to hold back more tears.

Sofia   'These questions are strictly routine and won't take too long. When did you arrive back on St Mary's?'

Vivienne 'I flew in with my brother yesterday around lunchtime.'

Sofia   'Had you met Harriet Smith or Ashley Lamb before yesterday?'

Vivienne 'No.'

Sofia   'Did you know anything about your mother's teenage pregnancy?'

Vivienne 'No.'

Sofia   'Do you recognise the name, Clarissa Montgomery?'

Vivienne 'No.'

Sofia   'I believe you knew about your father's affair, can you confirm that?'

This time Vivienne hesitated, she looked for guidance from her uncle.

Callum nodded at her that she should tell them what she knew.

Vivienne relayed the story of seeing her father, at his university, in the arms of another woman.

Sofia   'Thank you. Did you leave the annex at all last night after returning from the hospital, or early this morning?'

Vivienne   'No.'

Sofia   'Leading up to your grandmother's incident, did anything unusual happen yesterday or prior that may help with our inquiries? No matter how small, it could be important?'

Vivienne   'Um, no. I don't see her very often.'

Sofia   'What about yesterday, Vivienne? We know that you had a falling out with your boyfriend in the foyer of the hotel yesterday, because your grandmother refused to give you your trust fund. What happened when you spoke to her, did Tommy threaten her?'

Vivienne   'No.'

She sounded defensive. Vivienne looked over at her uncle, she was embarrassed and hurt that everyone knew her private business.

Carl   'We know about Tommy Burke. You both met with your grandmother yesterday. Vivienne, its best if you tell us the truth now.'

Callum   'Don't threaten her, Sergeant.'

Carl   'I'm not, but we will uncover the truth, if you lie or mislead us, that will be hindering our investigation. I'm sure you wouldn't want that.'

Vivienne looked at her uncle, who only nodded that she should answer.

Vivienne   'Yes … he's my boyfriend. Was my boyfriend.'

Carl   'Did he fly in with you, or arrive on the ferry?'

Vivienne   'He came by ferry, yesterday.'

Carl   'What did you speak to your grandmother about?'

Vivienne   'Nothing. I just wanted to introduce Tommy to her.'

Sofia   'But something caused you to have an argument with him in the lobby shortly after?'

Callum could see that his niece was getting agitated.

Callum   'Couldn't this wait until tomorrow, Sergeant?'

Carl   'Of course, if you wish, we'll stop. But we'll have to reinterview her tomorrow. We believe you and Tommy were two of the last people to see your grandmother before she went to the boathouse.'

Vivienne   'You're not suggesting he had something to do with it?'

Vivienne was becoming overwhelmed and started to cry again. Callum put his arm on her back and pleaded with Carl to end the interview. Sofia tried a softer approach.

Sofia   'Tommy Burke left the hotel in a stupor, why?'

Vivienne   'I wanted access to my trust fund, Nan said no. Someone told her lies about Tommy.'

Sofia   'How do you know they were lies?'

Vivienne glared at Sofia, her mouth was open, but she said nothing.

Carl   'Did Tommy head towards Hugh Town or did he hang around the hotel?'

Vivienne   'He just left, he was leaving the island.'

Vivienne finally broke down and Sofia knew it was time to stop.

As she left the room, Carl asked Vivienne one final question. He wanted to know where Tommy Burke was staying while on St Mary's. Vivienne gave Carl the name of the bed and breakfast in Hugh Town but categorically stated that he had nothing to do with her Nan's attack or her father's death for that matter.

Sofia sat down quietly at her desk and turned her computer on. She checked her emails and called Sergeant Ives to locate a Tommy Burke and detain him for questioning, if he hadn't already left the island.

Vivienne ran back to the annex and up to her room. She felt more terrified than when her mother broke the news of her father's death. Tommy hadn't returned her calls or text messages. Doubt washed over her like a gale-force wind. Did he hurt Nan? Did her father confront him? Did he kill her father? Was it all her fault? Vivienne buried her head in her pillow and cried and cried.

Hazel arrived with Geraldine, who insisted on sitting in on the interview. Sofia reassured her that it was perfectly fine, she was entitled to have a responsible adult present.

Sunday, 4:15 pm
Interview with Hazel Locke

Carl   'Hello, I'm Sergeant Carl Brooks. I'm sorry to meet under these terrible circumstances, but I would like to ask you some simple questions and I need you to answer them as honestly as you can.'

He spoke in his gentlest voice.

Hazel   'I'm not a kid, you know.'

Hazel put on a brave face, but she held tight to her mother's hand under the table.

Carl	'Of course not, and I'm sorry for what has happened to your father and grandmother.'

Hazel looked down at the table, then back up at her mum. She squeezed her mother's hand tighter.

Carl	'Could you please tell me when you got back home from the hospital last night and who you were with?'
Hazel	'My dad brought me back. It was late, about eleven.'
Carl	'Did you go out again after that?'
Hazel	'No.'
Carl	'Do you know if anyone else did?'
Hazel	'Um … my dad did. I couldn't sleep and I went into his room but he wasn't there. I went downstairs but he wasn't there either.'
Carl	'Did you tell anyone that he was missing?'
Hazel	'No. I just climbed into bed with Vivienne, as I didn't want to be alone.'
Carl	'We're going to find out who hurt your father. But we may need your help. Can you remember anything from yesterday that might be significant to our investigation? Something odd or unusual. Anything at all?'
Hazel	'Um, no.'

Sofia   'It doesn't matter how small. It could be important.'

Hazel   'Well. I heard the back door open and close last night, I thought it might be mum returning, I got up to check but no one was there. So I got back into bed with Vivienne. Then in the morning Andrew drove me to the hospital as dad wasn't there.'

Callum   'When did you hear this noise?'

Callum put his hand on Hazel's arm.

Hazel   'About an hour or two after we got home, I think. Sorry I don't know the exact time.'

Geraldine   'That's okay. You're doing great.'

Sofia   'Has anything else happened recently that you would like to tell me about, that concerns your grandmother or father?'

Hazel thought about what her sister said.

Hazel   'I think my dad was having an affair.'

Geraldine and Callum both looked at Hazel, simultaneously, surprised by her directness.

Geraldine asked Hazel how she knew something like that.

Hazel 'Only yesterday, Vivienne said she saw Dad with someone a few months ago when she visited him at his university.'

Carl made another note. So did Callum.

Carl 'Did Vivienne see the other woman?'

Hazel 'I think so.'

Carl 'You've been very helpful, Hazel.'

Carl thanked Hazel for her time and told her she could go home.

Sofia 'Thank you Mr Cook, I don't think we need to speak with your family again today.'

Callum nodded and left with his sister and niece.

'Have the police left yet?' Barbara asked Carrie at the reception desk.

'No, they're in the conference room. Why? Do you need to talk to them?'

'What about the forensic teams? Chef wants to know if they will be requiring anything to eat while they're here.'

'I believe they've already left for the airport. They're taking Mr Locke's body with them.'

'Oh, okay. I'll tell Chef that's a no then.' Barbara walked back to the kitchen.

Carrie looked on after her. She didn't care for Barbara at the best of times but she had been acting more distracted and distant lately than her usual grumpy demeanour.

Carrie was exhausted. She had spent most of the day trying to reassure guests. She had to reschedule flights and ferry tickets and assist the police with their queries. The mood in the hotel was solemn, and the weather was still windy and overcast. Not many guests had ventured out. Most were either in their rooms or in the games room, bar and lounge area. She hadn't been sure what to tell the guests. Should they leave, stay, rebook. A killer was on the loose, possibly staying at the hotel. Her guests were on edge. Geraldine had told her, if anyone wanted to leave early they could have a full refund, or the opportunity to rebook at a later date. A number of guests had already checked out. But a few regular guests had decided to stay.

For the remaining guests, Carrie had reassured them that the weather was going to improve tomorrow. She hoped, rather than believed, it would get people up and out of the hotel. She'd seen Geraldine walk past the reception desk early with Hazel looking withdrawn and dejected. *It could have been worse*, Carrie thought. She wondered if Theresa Cook would recover.

Geraldine sat by her mother's bedside at the hospital.

Callum had arrived half an hour ago. But it was getting late and Geraldine needed to get back to her family. She didn't want to leave her mother, but she had to think of her children. Her surprise weekend was a disaster. She was afraid Phillip had been killed because of her secret. But why kill Phillip?

'Do you think Phillip capable of attacking Mum? Then someone attacked him?' Callum asked.

'Don't be ridiculous, he couldn't hurt a fly. Why would anyone want to kill Phillip? He's harmless, so was Mum.'

'He's been keeping secrets from you. What else has he kept from you?'

'Oh come on. He's a university professor. Alright, he's been cheating on me, but I don't really care.'

'The police have been investigating Clarissa Montgomery. I looked her up, she works with Phillip, as a professor at the university. What if she followed him here to confront him, maybe killed him in a jealous rage?'

'Then the police will investigate her.'

Theresa stirred.

'Mum!' Geraldine leaned forward and stroked her mother's face. Callum ran out of the ward, calling for the nurse.

Theresa tried to open her eyes. She seemed dazed and confused by her surroundings. Then she turned her head and looked at her daughter. She murmured something unintelligible.

Callum returned with the nurse, who began checking Theresa's vitals.

'I'll get the doctor. This is good news, Mrs Locke.'

'Geraldine...'

'Yes, Mum.'

'Wesley ... you should know.' Theresa closed her eyes again.

'Know what, Mum? Mum!'

'Leave her, Geraldine. Don't push her,' Callum said.

Theresa fell back into a deep sleep.

Geraldine looked at her brother, thinking, *why would she say Wesley's name of all names? Why did he have to come to St Mary's?* She quickly put those negative thoughts out of her mind. Wesley would never hurt Theresa or Phillip. But fear was making Geraldine search for answers in places she didn't want to look.

Callum looked down at his mother. He leaned closer to Geraldine and whispered, 'I'm your brother as well as a lawyer. But you need to tell the police what she said. It's important.'

'No!'

'If Wesley is innocent, then he has nothing to hide.'

'He's not a killer. I was going to leave Phillip for him.'

'Then tell the police.'

'I can't.'

'Then I will. The killer is still out there.'

'I know that.'

'We should be grateful it isn't two murders instead of one, but Mum woke and said something. You owe it to her to tell the police what she said.'

Geraldine reluctantly agreed. But she knew in her heart, Wesley was not involved.

Callum put his hand on Geraldine's shoulder and said he would head back to the hotel and let the police officers know what Theresa said.

Geraldine could only nod at her brother. 'I'm going to stay a little longer in case she wakes again, then I'll head home. Hazel wants to come back this evening. Thank Khenan for me will you, he's been with the kids all day. I'm glad he came.' Geraldine held her brother's hand in a show of solidarity.

'So am I.'

Callum found the Chief Inspector in the conference room. He updated the police on his mother's condition and what she said.

'Thank you, Mr Cook. If she regains consciousness tomorrow, hopefully I can talk with her then.'

'That's fine, but I don't want her tired.'

'Of course not. But we both want to know who attacked her.'

Callum agreed, then headed to the door as Carl arrived. They exchanged a polite nod before Sofia updated him on what Callum just told her.

'That's unusual for a lawyer to offer up information like that, don't you think?' Carl said.

'True, but it leads us away from his family.'

'I can't picture it; Wesley's a commander in the navy. Cool heads and all that. I can't imagine him spontaneously lashing out at both of them, especially if Geraldine was going to leave Phillip anyway. And why assault Theresa, because of a twenty-five-year-old grudge? She can't hurt Wesley now; he has nothing to gain by attacking either of them.'

'True. My gut says it has to do with Harriet. I just don't know how.'

'I'm starving. Can we have dinner now?' Carl announced.

'Sure, let me get changed first,' Sofia said, realising that she was also hungry. 'I'll meet you in the dining room around six. Besides, I want an early night, as I want to read through the witness statements taken by the local police. More guests are leaving before lunch tomorrow; I want them ruled out of our investigation before they leave.'

'Will do, guv.'

Sofia looked at her watch. She was due to call Francesca soon and wanted to clear her head of murder and suspects before speaking to her.

There was a moment's pause.

'I spoke with Ronnie,' Carl said. 'They'll start background checks on everyone first thing in the morning.'

'I don't think Phillip's death was work related, he's a history professor for Christ sakes. Who would have motive, a disgruntled student with a bad exam mark? I'm inclined to stick with it being personal in nature. So, we can't rule out Clarissa or Geraldine for that matter. Or even Wesley Burrows, if he was jealous or still holding a grudge. I want the team to concentrate on them first. Find out how much this hotel is worth and what rights, if any, did Phillip have to it if they divorced.'

'Understood.'

Chapter Sixteen

The Windermere Hotel

Sunday, 7:35 pm

After a solemn dinner with her family, Geraldine checked in at reception to see how her guests were coping with the weekend's events. Carrie still hadn't retired for the night. Geraldine felt guilty, Carrie must have been swamped all day by frightened and frustrated guests and staff.

'Don't worry about the hotel, Geraldine. Everything is running smoothly, except for what happened, of course.'

'I'm sorry you got caught up in my family's business. I heard the police have spoken to all the guests staying at the hotel.'

'Yes, they did, about eight couples have checked out early.'

'Well, I don't blame them,' Geraldine said, demurely.

'Do you need me to book a flight for Harriet and Ashley? Will they be leaving soon?'

'I don't know. I'm about to talk to her now. It's understandable if she wants to leave.'

'Of course. Let me know if you need me to organise anything.'

'Thanks Carrie. I don't know what I'd do without you.' Geraldine managed a smile, then headed upstairs to speak with Harriet.

Geraldine tapped gently on the door of room 204. Harriet opened the door to see a dishevelled Geraldine standing in front of her. She had aged overnight. She quickly invited her in. Once inside, Harriet reached over and gave Geraldine a tight hug.

Geraldine's eyes began to water again. She looked so tired.

'I'm so very sorry,' Harriet said. 'For everything. How is Theresa?'

'She regained consciousness a little while ago but is still drowsy.'

'She's a strong woman, give her time, she'll pull through,' Harriet said. 'Hopefully she'll remember what happened.'

'I just can't believe it,' Geraldine began.

All three women sat down on the sofa.

'I'm sure you both want to leave, and I don't blame you. But please stay just a little while longer, I do want you to meet my children. I want something good to come out of all this. They wanted to meet you too, and I thought introducing you might help ease some of the pain of losing their father. A distraction, if that makes sense.'

'I understand.'

'Even if it's just to say hi. Then you can come back another time and really get to know them.'

Harriet nodded, but she was unsure about returning. She was afraid Phillip's death was down to her in some way. That she had caused some unrest. Even Theresa's accident appeared to involve her somehow. She so longed for this weekend, but all she felt was doom. She didn't quite know how to explain it to Geraldine.

Before Harriet could say anything, there was a knock at the door. Ashley jumped up to answer it. Wesley Burrows was standing in the corridor. He was about to speak, when he noticed Geraldine. His eyes were pleading to hold her, but he couldn't show his affection, not while Harriet and Ashley were in the room.

Ashley invited Wesley in. There was a moment of awkwardness before he addressed Harriet.

'I came to see if you're alright.'

'I'm fine, thanks. I'm just sorry for Geraldine and her family.'

Wesley approached Geraldine, but all he could manage was, 'I'm so sorry, Geri.'

Harriet looked at both her parents, she could see their eyes were locked onto each other's. They had a lot to talk about, but not while Ashley and herself were in the room.

'I think I'll take a walk,' she said, standing up and nodding at Ashley, who took a moment to register the request.

'I'll join you.'

When Wesley heard the door close, he sat down beside Geraldine on the sofa. He gently placed the palm of his hand on her cheek.

'I don't know what to say … I wanted us to be together, but not like this.'

'So did I. I keep feeling that I should be sadder than I am, but I'm not. I'm heartbroken for my children and I'll miss him, of course, but I stopped loving him long ago. And that makes me feel worse, guilty even. I had to break the news to Phillip's parents this afternoon. It was unbearable.'

'Don't beat yourself up over it, people fall in and out of love all the time. You said he found someone else to love.'

'I know, but who'd want to kill him?'

'I don't know. Do the police think your mother's assault was connected?'

'They're not sure yet, but they're not ruling it out either.'

'When this is all over, when you're ready, I'll apply for leave and I'll come back here to be with you. If that's what you still want?'

Tears ran down Geraldine's face. 'That's all I've ever wanted. I should have told you about Harriet all those years ago, maybe our lives would have been so different.'

'Forget the past. It's unchangeable. But our future isn't.'

'But will our children forgive us?' Geraldine asked.

'What's to forgive? We both would have been single. They'll want us to be happy, just give it time, your heart will heal.'

'Phillip's killer is still out there, somewhere. I'm afraid he or she may kill again. What if my children or Harriet become a target?'

'You mustn't believe that. Besides, I've seen the police stationed all around the hotel. Down by the boathouse, in the lobby and out the back. Give the police a chance to investigate. They'll find something, and when Theresa wakes, she'll remember what happened.'

'You're right.'

'Besides, the killer could have already fled the island.'

Wesley leant in and gently kissed Geraldine on the lips. He pressed against her as they leaned back into the sofa. Then he quickly pulled away and apologised. Geraldine was too emotional, and he knew he wouldn't be able to stop at just a kiss. Now was not the time.

Geraldine sat up and ran her hand through his hair, she looked longingly at Wesley.

'It'll keep.' She kissed him again gently on the lips.

Sofia was resting on her bed. She picked up Harry's pillows and smelt them. They still had his aftershave on them. She placed them behind her back as she read through today's witness statements. She was scribbling notes as she went along. She was interrupted by her mobile. It was Harry.

'Hi you,' she said.

'Missing me?'

'Of course.' Sofia looked at the empty bed next to her. 'You should be beside me right now in bed.'

'I wish I was. That could be a permanent thing. You only have to say yes…'

'I know. You'd be surprised how the sea air can clear one's mind. I'm lucky to have been given a second chance at love. More in love that I ever thought possible. But I don't want to dive in too quickly. I have to think about Francesca. I just need a little more time.'

There was a short pause before Harry answered. 'I'd marry you tomorrow if you'd let me. But being with you is enough for now. I love you.'

Sofia chuckled into her phone. 'I love you too.' She shouldn't feel this happy, not while she was surrounded by so much sadness.

Carl was dying for a beer but found the mood dismal at the hotel bar. There was only three other couples present in the lounge, who only had eyes for each other. It made him a little jealous. It had been a long day. He was about to head off when Carrie walked into the bar; she looked around and smiled at Carl before he said, 'looking for someone?'

'No, I'm just inspecting the rooms. Making sure everything is up to scratch before I clock off.'

'When do you get off? You don't work 24/7, do you?'

'No,' she smiled. 'But I'm in charge this weekend, and after everything that's happened, I'm just making sure everything is in its right place before turning in.'

'Would you like a drink?' he offered. Carrie was about to say no, but on second thought, said yes. She ordered a white wine and they walked over to the fire and sat down on one of the leather settees.

'How's your investigation going?'

'We've only just started, but don't worry we'll catch whoever killed Phillip Locke and assaulted Theresa Cook.'

'So, you believe Theresa was assaulted then?'

'Well, we aren't ruling it out yet.'

'I'm sure you'll catch whoever committed these crimes, Sergeant.'

'Please. It's Carl, I'm off duty now. How long have you been working at the hotel?'

'About five years. I'm finishing my degree in hotel management this year.'

'Congratulations! What will you do then?'

'What do you mean?'

'I mean, will you leave and work on the mainland, in a bigger hotel.'

'Oh, I don't know. I'm a local girl; St Mary's is my home.'

'It's a big world out there,' he replied, but Carrie only answered his question with another question.

'How long have you been a detective?'

'Going on nine years. I've worked with Chief Inspector Faraday for about five years. She's the best at the Yard.'

'Then we're lucky that she was on holiday here.'

'I don't think she'd see it that way,' he said, smiling.

They spent the next half an hour chatting about their lives. Carrie expressed a confidence and an honesty that he found attractive. Their conversation drifted towards family and Carl confided in Carrie about his parents' divorce. 'I'm still gobsmacked. I can't believe they're separated, I thought they would be together forever. What hope is there for plods like me if they can't make it?' Carrie was a good listener.

'How did your parents feel about you joining the police?'

'They were worried at first, especially when I was a bobby. But when I got into homicide, they were very proud of me. What about you? Your parents must be proud that you're running this hotel, even if it is only temporary.'

Carrie went a little solemn. 'Not really. They don't take much interest in what I do. I think I'm what you would call a mistake. My parents had me when they were in their mid-forties. Don't get me wrong, they love me, but they had to put things on hold while I was growing up. Now, they're always off seeing the world. But I like living on St Mary's.'

'Well, I'm proud of you and you should be proud of yourself.'

'I am.' Carrie smiled, with satisfaction.

Harriet and Ashley entered the bar and ordered some drinks. They nodded at Carrie and Carl, before they found a settee by the window.

Carrie looked at her watch and realised she'd stayed too long. 'Thanks for the drink, but I'm off to bed. I have another early start in the morning.'

Carrie rose and said goodnight once again. Carl watched her leave the room. He would have liked to have talked with her longer, but the vibe that emanated from her suggested she wasn't interested in him that way. *Never mind*, he thought, *there's always tomorrow*. His charms rarely let him down. He had a fleeting look over at Harriet and Ashley. He thought Ashley was quite attractive. Then he remembered they were potential suspects and quickly finished off his beer and left the room.

By midnight, the hotel was peaceful. The lobby and entertainment areas were silent as everyone had withdrawn to their guest bedrooms for the night. All that could be heard was the rain as the wind pushed it onto the giant windows that surrounded the old house. The night air echoed the sound of the waves, as they could be heard smashing into the shore.

Off in the distance, a fog horn reverberated across the island from one of the six lighthouses, warning sailors of the dangers lurking around the Scilly Isles.

Chapter Seventeen

Monday, 8.00 am

'Hi, everyone. Can you see us okay?' Sofia waved her hand in front of the laptop screen.

Sofia and Carl were in the conference room on a video call with their team in London. DS Shirley Smith, DC Devish Das, DC Ronnie O'Farrell, and DC Hillary Hubbard were all present at the other end of the call.

Sofia outlined what they knew so far and prioritised in what order the background checks should be carried out.

'We're liaising with the local constabulary and your contact will be Sergeant Oliver Ives. We need to find a connection between Theresa Cook and Phillip Locke, apart from the obvious. Start with Geraldine and her family. Carl has emailed you the transcripts of the interviews that were carried out yesterday and Sergeant Ives has received permission from the guests to check their mobile phone logs against the victims.'

'Yes, guv,' came the replies from her computer screen.

'Theresa Cook was meeting someone before she was attacked. Ashley Lamb thinks it had something to do with Harriet, so there may be another angle to explore, please look for any links there.'

'Will do, guv,' came more replies.

'Geraldine claims she only told her family about Harriet on Saturday, except her husband whom she told on Friday.'

Carl interrupted, 'Phillip Locke was having an affair, and his lover, Clarissa Montgomery is staying at the Windermere. Dig into her life also, as there could be the jilted lover angle.'

There were some chuckles from the London office. 'Did the wife know?'

'She had her suspicions, but didn't know exactly who with,' Carl replied.

'Okay, you have your assignments, I also want the manifests from all the flights in and out of St Mary's since Thursday and a passenger list from the daily ferry service.'

'Do you think the two attacks are by the same person?' Devish asked.

Sofia thought for a moment before answering.

'Something happened to initiate them. But my gut says yes. This is a quiet little isle, and for two serious assaults to happen a day apart, in the same location, is too coincidental for my liking. Theresa stirred last night, which is a good sign. Hopefully, once she's fully conscious, she'll be able to tell us what happened. Speak with Phillip's work colleagues and see if there's been any trouble at the university. Check his and Theresa's finances, see if there's been any unusual activity on their accounts.'

'Yes, guv.'

'This was supposed to be a happy weekend for the Locke family,' Sofia said. 'Geraldine was going to introduce her daughter to her family. But I can't see how that would warrant such violence. We should hear from the lab today. I've asked Dr Budd to video call us with the results. So I want you all in on that meeting.'

Sofia and Carl spent another ten minutes on the call with their team. Once they disconnected the call, Sofia wanted another word with Wesley Burrows. They headed upstairs to room 208.

Wesley opened the door and invited Sofia and Carl in.

'I would like to ask you a few more questions,' Sofia said.

'Of course,' he replied. 'Anything to help. I don't want to leave Harriet until you find who killed Phillip Locke.'

Sofia sat down at the small round dining table and had to move aside the uncleared breakfast plates.

Monday, 8:30 am
Interview with Wesley Burrows

Sofia	'How did you initially feel, when Geraldine told you about Harriet? That must have been a shock.'
Wesley	'Yes initially. But then I realised what she must have gone through back then and I forgave her.'
Sofia	'What about her parents?'

Wesley thought for a moment.

Wesley	'Well, her father's dead now. There's no point hating him. I admit I was angry with Theresa for lying to me for so long. I still don't think she likes me very much. But I didn't assault her, Inspector.'
Sofia	'I believe there's some animosity between your families.'
Wesley	'Oh, that! My parents detested Simon Hartnell, he's Geraldine's grandfather. Don't ask me why. Rivalry probably between him and my grandfather Christopher Burrows.'
Carl	'Do you know what started it?'
Wesley	'No. But my parents were glad when Geraldine left town. They said it was for the best. No one seemed to understand how much we loved each other back then. We were young so what did we know, right?'
Sofia	'Have you taken a DNA test in regard to Harriet?'
Wesley	'No, and I won't be.'
Sofia	'Has anyone else contacted you about Harriet, or questioned you about her parentage? I'm not implying anything by that, it's just that Theresa was meeting someone in the boathouse on Saturday evening, and it had to do with Harriet.'

Wesley   'I can't think of anything. Harriet holds no animosity towards Geraldine or myself, and I understand her adopted parents were okay with what she was doing.'

Sofia   'Thank you, that will be all for now.'

Monday 8.40 am

On a separate whiteboard, Carl had placed two photographs of their victims in the centre, then listed the suspects and close contacts of each victim and where they were during both attacks. He was joined shortly after by Sergeant Ives. They reviewed his guest witness statement notes and organised in what order they would interview the staff.

Harry had scheduled a video call for 11 am, so Sofia decided to head to the hospital again and check on Theresa Cook.

The weather had improved remarkably since yesterday. There was only a scattering of pillowy white clouds about St Mary's, and the sun was trying to break through and make up for yesterday's rainy disposition.

Sofia decided to walk to the hospital. She needed time to gather her thoughts. The crisp salty sea air smelt refreshing. It reminded her of her sailing trip with Harry on Saturday, stirring up an assortment of emotions. She missed him.

When she entered the hospital, she asked the nurse for an update on Theresa Cook. She was pleased to hear she had stirred a couple of times during the night. Her prognosis was good. When she arrived at Theresa's bedside, Geraldine was not there.

'When did Mrs Locke leave?' Sofia asked the nurse who followed her into the ward to check on her patients.

'About half an hour ago. She had fallen asleep, but she just went home to shower and change.'

'Thank you. If Mrs Cook wakes again, I want to know immediately.' Sofia handed the nurse her business card.

'Yes, of course.'

'And if she says anything at all, please write it down.'

'Will do.'

Sofia decided to sit down beside Theresa for a moment. She had time before her meeting and decided to keep her company. As Sofia looked at Theresa, she wondered how scared she'd be if it was her mother lying in the hospital bed with a head injury.

Sofia contemplated how much fate had played its part in Theresa's situation. If they had returned to the boathouse earlier the attack may not have happened. If they had returned later, Theresa would be dead now. Was murder simply a matter of timing? She stopped herself from feeling philosophical. It was life, pure and simple. Cause and effect dictated our destinies, she reminded herself.

Theresa stirred again. The nurse came over to check on her.

'I'll get the doctor.' The nurse walked quickly out of the ward.

Sofia wanted Theresa to wake up. She gently rubbed her arm, hoping the feeling would arouse her.

Theresa's eyes opened once again. She turned her head towards Sofia. *This woman isn't my daughter*, she thought.

'Geraldine…'

'I'll call her for you, Mrs Cook.'

'Who are you?'

'My name is Chief Inspector Sofia Faraday.'

'Warn Geraldine…'

'About what Mrs Cook?'

The nurse returned with the doctor.

Sofia gave them some space. She pulled out her mobile and rang Carl. Then she rang Geraldine, who said she would come straight back. Sofia decided to stay until Geraldine returned, hopefully Theresa would be a little more coherent.

The doctor was satisfied with Theresa's condition and said she was recovering well, however, there could be gaps in her memory for the foreseeable future. But he wouldn't elaborate for how long.

Sofia understood, Harry had already warned her about that. But as Theresa became more alert, she took in her surroundings.

'You're in the hospital, Mrs Cook. You sustained a blow to the side of your head in the boathouse. Do you remember?'

Theresa looked at Sofia.

'Where's my daughter?'

'She's on her way. She just went home to change.'

Theresa still seemed a little disorientated, the wait would give her more time to get to take in her surroundings. But it wasn't long before Geraldine returned with Callum. Sofia gave them a moment with their mother, but only a moment.

'I'm sorry. But I have to ask her some questions. I'll be as quick as I can.'

Geraldine looked at Callum, but he nodded his agreement.

'Mrs Cook, what can you remember about Saturday afternoon? Do you remember going into the boathouse?'

'No...'

'What do you remember?'

'Um ... I spoke with Callum and Khenan in his room.' Theresa looked at her son and smiled. 'Then I went back to my room.' Theresa was quiet for a moment. 'Ashley left me a voice message; she was worried about Harriet. I knocked on her door, but she wasn't there.' Theresa took a moment, then licked her lips as her mouth felt dry. Geraldine gave her a glass of water with a straw. Theresa took a slow, long sip before Sofia prompted her again.

'Do you remember what happened next?'

'I spoke with Andrew about Vivienne and her boyfriend. Then they came to see me. They weren't happy when they left.'

'What boyfriend?' Geraldine asked her mother.

'A waster by all accounts,' she said.

Geraldine looked at her brother.

'He's after her trust fund,' Callum said. 'But Mum sent him packing.'

Geraldine looked perplexed. Callum whispered that he'd fill her in later.

'Please continue Theresa, you're doing very well,' Sofia said.

'I got dressed for dinner. I remember feeling cold. Is Harriet all right?'

'Yes, she's fine, Mum. We're more concerned about you,' Callum said, rubbing his mother's arm.

Theresa was trying to think. 'I ... I ... what day is it?'

'It's Monday, Mum. You've been here since Saturday evening,' Callum said.

'What?' Theresa started to stress. She was unsure why, but she was afraid of something.

'It's okay Mrs Cook, you're quite safe here.'

Callum kept stroking his mother's hand. It seemed to calm her.

'I just have one more question Mrs Cook, yesterday when you woke, you said the name Wesley. Do you know why you mentioned him?'

Theresa looked towards Geraldine. *Too many lies and too many secrets.*

'I'm sorry Geraldine,' Theresa's eyes started to close. 'I'm truly sorry we should have told you from the start.'

'What are you talking about Mum? Mum?'

Theresa opened her eyes. 'William Burrows.'

'Wesley's dad? What about him, Mum?'

'He's my half-brother…'

Theresa Cook fell back to sleep. The interview was over.

Geraldine sat staring at her mother, unable to comprehend what she just said. She looked at Callum.

'Fucking bastard,' was all he could say.

Sofia knew it was time to leave. Geraldine jumped up and approached Sofia, she asked her not to say anything to Wesley. If it was true, that Wesley's father is the son of Simon Hartnell and not Christopher Burrows, she wanted to tell Wesley herself.

Sofia agreed and left the hospital. But she wondered if he already knew that. *Some secrets are best left buried*, she thought.

Sofia walked back to the hotel, all the while the seagulls were rudely squawking above her head, a fishing trawler was heading back to port. She allowed the smell of the ocean to unclog her thoughts once more. Was this latest news relevant to her investigation? Was Theresa confused? And what did it have to do with Phillip's death? Could this new revelation have pushed Wesley over the edge? Sofia pulled out her mobile and called Carl. She asked him to send a team member to Newquay to interview Wesley's parents and find out what they knew and who else might have known. They had already taken Wesley's fingerprints, but she wanted a DNA test done.

'I'm confident that neither Callum nor Geraldine knew about this,' Sofia said into her mobile as she arrived back at the hotel. Sofia hung up from Carl as she entered the hotel, she walked past the reception desk and nodded at Carrie. Carrie, who was busy booking more guests out of the hotel, stopped what she was doing and spoke to Sofia.

'I hope you have everything you need, Chief Inspector?'

Sofia stopped to thank her.

'How's Mrs Cook?' Carrie asked.

'Still no change,' lied Sofia.

Sofia entered the conference room to find Carl at his desk speaking with DS Shirley Smith via video link.

Shirley said she'd be in Newquay by early afternoon.

'What does that make Geraldine and Wesley, first or second half-cousins?' Carl asked, pulling a face. 'If Wesley's father is the son of Geraldine's grandfather.'

'Something like that,' Sofia replied.

'That isn't worth killing over!' he stated. 'Or is it?'

'To keep that secret buried. Possibly. People do desperate things when they're in love.'

'But if they didn't know, then there's no motive.'

'Everyone lies, Carl, you know that.'

'True, or they forget to tell us – same thing I guess.'

'But would Vivienne's boyfriend kill for her trust fund?' Sofia asked. 'How desperate was he for the money? It's a stretch, but have the police located him yet?'

'No. He checked out of his B&B. His name appeared on the ferry's manifest on the Sunday morning trip. I have the local police in Oxford checking to see if he's returned home. I've asked them to question him.'

'Great! I want the street cameras checked in and around Hugh Town and Old Town on Saturday night, they should be able to pick him up. I want his movements thoroughly checked.'

'Will do, guv.'

Chapter Eighteen

Monday, 11.00 am

'Can everyone hear me?' Harry asked, he was in his lab in London.

'Loud and clear,' Sofia said. They were on a three-way video link. All except Shirley who was on her way to Newquay to interview William and Joanna Burrows.

'Phillip was struck on the head by a small round smooth object,' Harry began. 'Nothing in the boatshed fits the bill, so the killer took the weapon with them. Now, I found minute traces of pine nuts and also chilli residue in the wound.'

This caused everyone to look at each other a little incredulously.

'Couldn't that have been in his hair already? Maybe from him running his hands through his hair after he's eaten?' Ronnie asked.

'No. It was in the wound, I'm confident it was transferred from the weapon.'

'Okay, well we're in a hotel, there's a kitchen, there's room service, we can assume the weapon came from the hotel, somewhere,' Carl said.

'Agreed,' Sofia replied. 'But it could have also come from the annex, where Geraldine and her family live. What about Theresa's injury?'

'Unfortunately, the ocean washed away any evidence where Theresa's body was found. I believe she was struck on the side of the head and knocked against the wall of the boathouse. We've dusted for fingerprints in the boathouse, but I'm afraid we've found quite a few. Before using the sailboat, I had to sign for it, so there should be a list of guests who have used the boathouse equipment. You can cross-reference those fingerprints first. But, in fact, anyone could go in there.'

Sofia blushed a little at the inference that they were out sailing together, but no one on the call seemed shocked or bothered. Nothing was kept private for long at the Yard.

'We'll cross-reference the fingerprints with the guests and staff. But can we assume now that Theresa's incident was an attack?'

'Theresa was reasonably healthy for her age, no drugs or alcohol in her system. Her toxicology tests were clean. Nothing there to report. I've had a look at her scans taken at the hospital and everything looks fine, there is no medical reason why she would just collapse in the boathouse. There is bruising on her left cheek, consistent with being struck, and there is a contusion on the right side of her head where she hit the wall. So I would agree it was an assault and not a medical episode that caused her injuries.'

'Thanks, Harry.'

Sofia disconnected him from the video call, then she addressed her team and asked them to continue investigating the Locke family and hotel staff, and anyone else who knew the victims personally.

'Bearing in mind, many guests used the boathouse, and our killer may have used gloves,' Carl said.

'Thanks for stating the obvious, Sherlock,' smirked Ronnie.

Sofia and Carl entered the kitchen and saw it was alive with activity in preparation for the lunch service.

'Please everyone, stop what you're doing,' Sofia announced. The bustle of the kitchen came to a halt.

'What is *da* meaning of *dis*?' Chef Allard demanded.

'Chef Allard, I don't wish to keep you and your staff from your work, but I need to speak with you all regarding the murder of Phillip Locke and the attack on Theresa Cook.'

'*C'est très gênant*,' Claude said, throwing the tea-towel down on the table.

Sofia's French was minimal but she understood the remark. 'I'm sorry for the inconvenience Chef Allard but it can't be helped, certain details have arisen that make this a priority.'

The kitchen drew silent, except for the sizzling of the food cooking on the stove tops. The kitchen staff looked back and forward between the inspector and chef, they weren't quite sure who outranked who in the kitchen. They clearly feared Chef Allard more than the police.

Claude finally nodded his consent.

'You will all need to be interviewed by the police again as we will need to re-establish your exact whereabouts from Friday afternoon until early Sunday,' Carl said.

'Chef Allard, if you don't mind, I'd like to start with you,' Sofia said. 'Can we go into your office?' It wasn't a request, as Sofia had already started walking towards his office.

'*Faites vite s'il vous plaît*,' he said, reverting to French.

Sofia didn't need it translated. 'I won't take too much of your time.'

While Sofia spoke with Chef Allard, Carl spoke with the kitchen staff. He started with Barbara Eyre, who said she was working on Friday night, but had no alibi once her shift was finished. The same could be said for Saturday.

Claude entered his office but stood by the door with his arms crossed.

Monday, 11:30 am
Interview with Claude Allard

Sofia	'Could you give me your whereabouts from Friday afternoon to Sunday morning?'
Claude	'*Oui*. I was in *da* kitchen Friday until nine then I went for *un* walk as I do each night to clear my '*ead*.'
Sofia	'Did you notice anyone hanging around that shouldn't be here?'

Claude was thoughtful for a moment.

Claude	'*Non*.'
Sofia	'What about Saturday?'

Claude '*Non.*'

Sofia 'Has anything stood out to you, or caused you to be suspicious of anyone in the last few days?'

Claude '*Desole.* Sorry inspector, I haven't noticed anything, just some minor thefts that I told Geraldine about. But that has been resolved. I'm not here to socialise, I prefer to keep my own company.'

Sofia 'Why?'

Claude '*Excuse-moi?*'

Claude looked perplexed.

Sofia 'Why do you feel you need to keep to yourself?'

Claude 'It's just a figure of speech, Inspector.'

There was a moment's pause.

Claude 'I like it here on St Mary's and the Windermere is a beautiful hotel. I'm grateful to Geraldine. I have no reason to cause her or her family harm.'

Sofia 'Thank you. I'll let you get back.'

Sofia re-joined Carl in the kitchen and helped him interview the remaining kitchen staff.

Later in the conference room, Sofia asked Carl to run a background check on Chef Allard, she sensed he was hiding something. As a guest at the hotel, Sofia had had the privilege of tasting some of Chef Allard's creations. He was obviously a culinary genius, which incited Sofia to wonder what he was doing on St Mary's and the Scilly Isles of all places.

Shirley enjoyed the drive to Newquay. When she pulled up in front of the Burrows home, she was famished and hoped Joanna Burrows would be a kind host and offer her a cuppa and biscuits.

Once Shirley was shown into the living room, Joanna excused herself as she went into the kitchen to make the tea.

Shirley took a stroll around the room while she waited for Joanna to return. There were family photos scattered on various countertops. Children of all ages. The house was as immaculate as its owner. Joanna was neatly dressed and wore her hair in a neat bun. She wore a turtleneck lavender top with white straight-legged trousers. She wore her age well. Shirley ran her finger along the mantle above the fireplace, knowing she wouldn't pick up any dust. She was embarrassed to think she couldn't do that in her own home. Shirley had never been one for cleaning, she put her shortcoming down to feminism. That seemed to justify most of her domestic failings.

Joanna Burrows re-entered with a tray. It was a full tea-service, Royal Albert bone china teapot, sugar and milk bowl with two teacups and saucers, along with two tea plates. One contained a selection of biscuits and slices of cake. *Thank God*, thought Shirley, as she sat down across from Joanna.

'I'm sorry my husband isn't here, Sergeant, but he's working. My son called me and told me what happened to Theresa. I hope she'll pull through. And I'm sorry to hear about Geraldine's husband. Ghastly business. But I don't know how I can help in this matter. I've never met Phillip Locke.'

'I'm here about another matter. It's a bit delicate I'm afraid. Theresa said something when she woke up in the hospital, it concerned Simon Hartnell and Stella Burrows. It's important I clarify and confirm what she said.'

Joanna lowered her head, she seemed to know what the policewoman was going to ask. 'I understand,' Joanna shook her head. 'But I don't want Wesley knowing about this, not from the police.'

'I believe Geraldine Locke is going to tell him. So it's true?'

'Thank you, Sergeant.'

Shirley pulled out her notepad and asked her to confirm the allegation about Simon Hartnell.

Monday, 1:00 pm
Interview with Joanna Burrows

Joanna   'Yes, of what my husband and his parents told me over the years, Simon Hartnell was a nasty piece of work. He took advantage of Stella's loneliness while Christopher was deployed overseas. He was stationed in Europe for some time. Simon was already married to Lucinda, but that didn't stop him playing around. He thought of himself as a ladies-man.'

Joanna scoffed the air to show her disdain.

Shirley   'So you can confirm that William, your husband, was the son of Simon Hartnell, not Christopher Burrows.'

Joanna   'Correct. Although Christopher stood by Stella. He loved her and, as he couldn't have children of his own, he decided to raise William as his own son. He told Simon he wasn't to make contact with William under any circumstances.'

Shirley   'Did you know Geraldine was pregnant with Harriet?'

Joanna   'No. We didn't know they were seeing each other, otherwise we would have put a stop to it. But they'd known each other since they were children. It was a small town, Sergeant.'

Shirley   'That would make them half-first cousins I believe.'

Joanna   'Correct. It was a scandalous affair at the time. Simon had his reputation to think about. He was a prominent lawyer. You didn't want to get on the wrong side of him.'

Shirley   'How did you feel about your son's relationship with Geraldine?'

Joanna   'I only found out about it when Theresa told me. They were just children, Sergeant. But Theresa and I agreed to keep them separated. Theresa told me she sent Geraldine away to school to finish her lower sixth before attending college. Wesley was heading to the military academy later that year, so we hoped their little romance would fizzle out once they were apart. We weren't proud of our part in all this, but we were protecting our son.'

Shirley   'Thank you, Mrs Burrows. I'm not here to judge, just record the facts.'

Joanna   'Thank you, Sergeant.'

Shirley   'Had Theresa said anything to you about Harriet recently?'

Joanna   'I spoke with Theresa after my son told me about her. She said it was a shock when Harriet contacted her, but she wasn't apologetic. Just surprised, but I think she was glad. I think she was a lonely woman until Harriet came into her life.'

Shirley   'Why would you say that. Did you know her well?'

Joanna   'We were on friendly terms, we moved in the same circles, Sergeant. But she had grown estranged from her children over the years. I felt sorry for her.'

Shirley   'How did your son feel when he told you about Harriet?'

Joanna   'He was excited. He has two sons, Sergeant. Who he's very proud of. But the way he spoke about his daughter, he sounded chuffed. Maybe not chuffed, but proud, excited about it. But I feel that may also have something to do with

	Geraldine. He said, "I hadn't realised how much I'd missed her". I'm not sure if Geraldine feels the same way. I guess only time will tell.'
Shirley	'Did Wesley tell you he was going to St Mary's?'
Joanna	'Yes.'
Shirley	'Did he say anything else about his daughter or Theresa Cook?'
Joanna	'Only that he was going to St Mary's to look out for Harriet as Geraldine had invited her to meet her children. I told him I didn't think it was a good idea, but he was protective of her. But I think deep down it was an excuse to see Geraldine again.'
Shirley	'Thank you, Mrs Burrows, you've been most helpful.'

Shirley helped herself to a piece of cake, she couldn't hold out any longer.

Joanna talked a little more about the family rivalry between Simon Hartnell and Christopher Burrows. Once Shirley was back in her car she called Carl and updated him on what she'd discovered.

She drove back to London on a full stomach, ready to continue the remaining background checks.

After lunch, Sofia and Carl walked to the annex to speak with Vivienne. Sofia made a courtesy call to Callum, informing him of their intentions to re-interview Vivienne.

He arrived by the time they knocked on the front door.

'How can we help you today, Inspector?'

'We would like to talk to you a little more about your boyfriend, Vivienne.'

Vivienne looked at her uncle for guidance. She had thought herself to be in love, now she only felt embarrassed and used. Callum indicated that she should talk to them, if only to help shift suspicion away from his family.

Monday, 1:30 pm
Interview with Vivienne Locke

Sofia	'Have you spoken to Tommy Burke since Saturday?'
Vivienne	'No. He left Sunday morning. He hasn't returned my calls or texts.'

Vivienne appeared deflated and wounded by Tommy's rejection.

'Good riddance,' Callum said, then added 'sorry,' raising his hands to Sofia and Carl, apologetically. He knew he shouldn't comment or offer personal opinions during the interview.

Vivienne	'He wouldn't hurt Nan, and he wouldn't have killed Dad.'
Sofia	'Your grandmother said he was a waster, why would she say that?'
Vivienne	'Andrew told me yesterday that he looked into Tommy and reported what

he found to Nan. He said I was a fool
for trusting him. I actually thought he
loved me, what a stupid idiot I've been.'

Vivienne began to cry again. Not just because of her father,
and grandmother, but because she'd laid her heart out on the
table and someone crushed it.

Carl	'Were you with him on Saturday night?'
Vivienne	'No. Once we came back from the hospital, I went to my room. I tried calling Tommy but he wouldn't answer. Hazel stayed with me as she was too upset to sleep alone.'
Carl	'So, you can't give him an alibi?'
Vivienne	'No.'

Vivienne lowered her head again, then leaned over to her
uncle, who took her in his arms. His look told Sofia that his
niece had had enough.

Sofia nodded her agreement and thanked them for their
time before they left the annex.

'There are cameras on every street, the local police should
have picked Tommy Bourke up on CCTV by now. Please
follow up with them.'

'Will do, guv.'

'I want this line of enquiry wrapped up pronto. I can't see him
killing Phillip, as he had no control over Vivienne's trust fund.
But Phillip could have warned him off and it got out of hand.'

'That sounds very feeble, guv, but I'll conclude that line of
enquiry.'

Carl conceded there were too many probabilities surrounding Phillip's death to rule anyone out, but he still didn't believe the two crimes were linked, as Sofia did. Maybe it was too personal for his Chief Inspector, considering it was her and Harry who saved Theresa.

Harriet and Ashley arrived back at the Windermere after taking a long walk around the island. Harriet appreciated the appeal of St Mary's. Ashley, on the other hand, was a London girl and was looking forward to getting back home.

They walked into the foyer and decided to have a drink before dinner. A young girl had followed them in. Harriet recognised Hazel from photos that Geraldine had shown her, but she wasn't sure if she should introduce herself, so she kept walking into the bar and ordered a drink.

Hazel watched Harriet enter the bar and followed her in. Her curiosity had gotten the better of her.

'Hi,' she said, cautiously introducing herself.

'Hello. You're Hazel, Geraldine's youngest. I'm so sorry about your father. And I'm sure Theresa will recover quickly.'

'Thank you. I hope so.'

'I wasn't sure if I'd get a chance to meet you this weekend. Geraldine has told me so much about you all. But I hope one day soon we can meet and get to know one another better.'

'I'd like that. I had to leave the house, it's sad and miserable in there. I needed some fresh air.'

'Well, there's no better place for that, than on St Mary's.'

'I agree. Are you leaving soon?'

'Do you want me to go?'

'No, no. I wanted to meet you,' Hazel said. She looked distraught. 'I just can't believe that Dad is dead! But I don't think it's registered in my brain yet. I keep expecting him to walk through the front door any minute, you know?'

'I do. It'll take time.'

'I probably shouldn't say this, but Mum and Dad were miserable together. I found out he was seeing someone else. I think they were going to separate.' Hazel kept fidgeting and was looking down at her feet.

Ashley quickly moved the conversation in a new direction. 'How's your Nan?'

'Better. I'm going to see her after dinner.'

'Say hi to her for me, won't you?' Harriet said.

'Will do.'

'Do you want me to walk you back home?' Harriet asked.

'No. It's just next door.'

At that moment, Carrie walked in and said to Hazel, 'There you are. Geraldine has been looking for you.'

Hazel rolled her eyes at Harriet and Ashley, then turned to Carrie and told her she was coming. She whispered to Harriet, 'she's *so* bossy, she acts like she owns this hotel half the time.' Then as she straightened up, 'I've gotta go. I hope I'll see you before you leave.'

Harriet smiled, 'I hope so too.'

Sofia sat on the beach with her legs up in front of her as she dipped her toes into the sand. The breeze was cold but refreshing. She raised her face to the sun and closed her eyes. She felt its gentle warmth. She wished Harry was beside her to share it.

This had been their first holiday together. Harry had asked Sofia to move in with him. But she had been hesitant, and on the few occasions when Harry broached the matter, Sofia managed to change the subject. She had to think about Francesca. She was only eleven. But Harry and Francesca got on like a house on fire. Francesca had taken to Harry instantly, especially after he bought her a dog – on Sofia's approval. Something she'd been asking for, for years. Sofia smiled as she remembered Franny's face when Harry brought the puppy home.

Sofia's ex was already re-married, and once a fortnight Francesca spent the weekend with him and his new wife. Living with her ex had been toxic for both her and Francesca. His heavy drinking brought on bouts of violent behaviour. In the end, she had to throw him out. But now, he appeared to have his drinking under control. If he hadn't, there was no way she would let Francesca anywhere near him.

Now, sitting on the beach she felt truly alone. She realised just how much she wanted Harry in her life. As she stood up and brushed the sand off her trousers, she promised herself that on her return to London, she would say yes to Harry's request. Life was too short for maybes. She wanted to live in the now, as often realised through her job, just how quickly it could all be taken away.

Sofia walked back to the hotel. As she looked up at the grand old house, she wondered why none of the guests had looked out of their windows on Saturday night and saw who followed Theresa into the boathouse. It would have made her job a lot easier having a witness. Was it simply down to luck that placed people in the right place at the right time, or the wrong place at the wrong time?

But murder was rarely that simple.

Sofia headed into the conference room. She had scheduled another video call with her team.

Carl was already present and making notes on the whiteboard. She asked him to start the video call and see what her team had uncovered.

Sofia made herself and Carl a coffee, while they waited for their team to come online.

'Hi, guv, Carl,' they said, as they appeared on Carl's laptop.

'Hi, everyone. Please tell me you have some news,' Carl asked.

Ronnie spoke first. 'We've eliminated most of the guests now. So, they can go home when they want. We couldn't find a single link between them and either victim. Most had alibis, which we've corroborated, thanks to DS Ives and his team.'

'What about the staff?' Sofia asked.

Devish was up next. 'Claude Allard, your head chef, I checked with the French police. They have a record on file against him for assault. It was against his ex-wife. But he wasn't charged, only cautioned.'

'Okay. We'll talk to him again about that. We'll also ask Geraldine Locke if she knew about his past. What else?'

'Junior chef Barbara Eyre,' said DC Hillary Hubbard, 'her record is clean, but she does have a child social services record. It wasn't easy to find as she had legally changed her surname. I've requested access. I checked with her previous employer, they didn't have much to say, except she was hard working and kept to herself. I finally spoke to her parents. She was adopted by the way. They said they haven't seen her in years. I didn't feel any affection from them towards her. They came across as cold and aloof. They said that when she came to them, she was troubled. But that wasn't unusual with adopted kids like Barbara, who were in and out of foster care for years.

Her mother said most children like Barbara develop a fear of abandonment, so they have trouble socialising and expressing their emotions.'

'Good work,' Sofia said. 'I want all the mobile phone numbers and email addresses for the staff scrutinised thoroughly, make a strict timeline, there must be a connection somewhere. I'm glad they all consented to provide this information, it shows how much they care about Geraldine.'

'Yes, guv,' came back the replies.

'How did you go with Joanna Burrows?' Sofia asked Shirley. She already had a rundown from Carl, but she liked to hear her team's input and opinions.

Shirley spoke up. 'Wesley has an exemplary military record, no criminal record and speaking to his mother today I couldn't find a motive for wanting to hurt either victim. He didn't need to kill Phillip Locke when Geraldine could just divorce him. Unless it was money related, as I'm sure the hotel is worth a fair bit. Wesley was happy about the Harriet situation. Joanne Burrows said that her son didn't know about his father's true parentage, but even if he did, she doubted it would have made a difference, as she thinks her son is still in love with Geraldine.'

'Did she mention Theresa Cook?' Sofia asked.

'Yes. She said that Wesley was angry with Theresa for the lies she told, but I just can't see him lashing out at her because of it. That would alienate Geraldine, which is the last thing he'd want. Joanna described Wesley as a disciplined, well restrained man, not the type to act out irrationally, especially not at an elderly woman. I can't see him attacking Theresa Cook. I personally don't think her attack fits his profile.'

'What about other staff members, Carrie Ford and Luke Myers, the night manager? They have access throughout the hotel. What have you found out about them?' Sofia asked.

'So far they're clean,' Hillary said. 'Nothing stands out in their mobile history. Carrie has worked for Geraldine for nearly five years. She's currently studying hotel management. No criminal record. She's lived on the island all her life. I haven't spoken to her parents yet, as they are away overseas.'

'And the night manager, Luke Myers?'

'He's worked at the hotel for two years, he's also a local man. His record is clean. But when I was checking the CCTV footage from the front of the hotel and reception area, Ashley had gone downstairs at around – hang on,' Hillary quickly checked her notes, '6:40 pm on Saturday evening and spoke to Carrie on reception for a few minutes.'

'Thanks, Hillary. We'll speak with Carrie later,' Geraldine replied.

Sofia brought up Phillip Locke next. 'His girlfriend's name was Clarissa Montgomery. What have you found out about her?'

'Again, she's clean,' Das said. 'We checked her phone records, and the only interesting call we found was to an obstetrician. I called them and they confirmed she's a patient, but said I needed a warrant if I wanted access to her medical records.'

'Well, I can simply go up and ask her before she leaves. But I'd say she's pregnant,' Sofia remarked.

'Man, he moves fast,' Carl said.

Sofia didn't believe Clarissa had a motive for attacking Theresa and, apart from the jilted lover scenario, even less motive for killing Phillip, especially if Phillip was leaving Geraldine for her.

Ronnie continued the dialogue, confirming he had spoken to Ashley and Harriet's parents. He read through his notes and confirmed that both were happy go lucky young women with no enemies that they knew of. He found nothing in their email correspondence or mobile records to indicate any previous contact with either victim until a month ago, when Harriet first made contact.

'Okay, then we have to work off the theory that Theresa's attack could have been spontaneous. Maybe Phillip found out something, and he was killed to keep him silent. But I want to know what Ashley meant when Theresa told her someone came to her room and said Harriet was a fraud. I want you to dissect Harriet's life and find something linking her to this accusation. We need to know who visited Theresa's room. Was it blackmail?'

'Yes, guv,' the officers replied from the laptop.

'Is Theresa still unable to say who it was?' Shirley asked.

'Yes. She can only remember up to when Vivienne and her boyfriend, Tommy Burke, came to her room. Then she struggles and gets confused, she needs more time. Which we don't have.'

Sofia said they'd video call again in the morning. Eight-thirty sharp. Once the link was disconnected, Sofia said she was going upstairs to talk to Clarissa Montgomery, then she would head over to the hospital.

Carl was going to continue the background checks when his mobile rang. It was Sergeant Ives.

'Alright, calm down and seal the room. We're coming down now.'

Sofia stopped in her tracks and waited for Carl to update her.

'Sergeant Ives has just found a small stone baton wrapped up in a tea towel in one of the staff bedrooms.'

'Whose bedroom?'

'In Carrie Ford's room. It was in her overnight bag.'

Sofia looked down at the object wrapped in a tea towel.

'It's a pestle,' she said.

'What the hell is a pestle?' Carl asked.

'A mortar and pestle are used in kitchens to grind nuts, garlic, herbs and so on into a paste to infuse flavours.'

'Of course you'd know that, wouldn't you,' Carl said, who had been lucky enough to taste Sofia's cooking on many occasions.

'Check with the kitchen staff again and find out when it was last used. Chef Allard said some items had been stolen from the kitchen. Find out if this was on his list of missing items.'

'Were you wearing gloves, Sergeant Ives?' Sofia asked.

'Yes, guv,' he replied.

Sofia could clearly see traces of blood on it.

'Are you going to arrest her?'

Sofia thought it odd. Carrie could have simply washed the pestle and put it back where she found it. Something didn't add up. She told Sergeant Ives to get it on the first flight out. She wanted it at the lab in London by this evening.

'Are you thinking what I'm thinking, guv?' Carl said, shaking his head.

'Very foolish,' Sofia replied.

'What?' Sergeant Ives asked, looking at each of them.

'It would be easy to implicate Carrie. She has access to the entire hotel. We can't dismiss this, but I think it's a crude attempt by the killer to divert attention towards someone else. Very crude and foolish, Sergeant.'

'Oh! Maybe the killer couldn't get back into the kitchen that night, for some reason. Not without being seen?'

'True, but we don't know when it was planted, and there are no security cameras below stairs.'

Sofia checked the staff bedroom lock and saw it was also a key card lock. Then said,

'Please ask Carrie to come into the conference room.'

'I'll do it now.'

Sergeant Ives placed the pestle and tea towel in an evidence bag and quickly left the room.

'You know, any member of staff or Geraldine's family, for that matter, could have obtained a skeleton key. They've all worked at the hotel at some point.'

'I know,' Sofia chastised herself. 'We need to know if the hotel's room key cards are logged each time they're used.'

'I'll get the IT guys to look into it,' Carl said.

'I want you to interview Chef Allard again and ask him about the assault charge back in France. Be discreet and find out when the pestle was last used.'

'Will do, guv.'

'Not many guests would go into the kitchen to steal a pestle,' she said. 'How would they know where to find it? There are plenty of other items inside a hotel they could use as a weapon.'

'Agreed,' Carl replied. 'Just like taking Geraldine's mobile from her kitchen table. It's very brazen and calculated.'

Sofia returned to the conference room and waited for Carrie to arrive.

Sergeant Ives gave the evidence bag to a constable to organise its transport off St Mary's. Then he headed into the kitchen to help Sergeant Brooks reinterview the kitchen staff.

When Carl entered the kitchen, he asked the staff when was the last time they had used the mortar and pestle, and if they had more than one.

Chef Allard confirmed they only had one in the kitchen.

'When did you last use it?'

'*Quoi?*' he replied. 'I do not know.' He looked to his staff, who all shrugged.

'We were looking for the pestle yesterday,' Barbara announced.

'Why is *dis* so important, Sergeant?' Chef asked, who was getting annoyed at yet another interruption.

'Because it may be our murder weapon.' This revelation caused a stirring of whispers around the room.

'I would have thought the killer would have thrown it away by now, Sergeant,' Barbara announced.

'Possibly, unless they were unable?'

Chef Allard thought that highly unlikely. But he asked his staff when they realised it was missing.

'Yesterday,' Barbara said. 'We couldn't find it to grind some herbs.'

'When did you last see it?'

'Um … I used it Friday around three o'clock,' said a junior chef. 'I was grinding some pine nuts for a pesto.'

'What did you do with it afterwards?'

'I left it on the table over there,' he pointed to the table against the far wall. 'I was going to clean it, but when I finally remembered, the mortar was there but not the pestle.'

The whole kitchen remained silent as they looked to one another, as if eyeing up who of them was now a suspect.

'You will all need to be reinterviewed by Sergeant Ives.'

Chef Allard swore again, but as it was in French, no one was offended by it.

Chapter Nineteen

'Thank you for talking with me, Carrie. I know you're busy. It shouldn't take long.'

'Anything I can do to help.'

Carrie sat down across from Sofia.

Sofia	'What did Ashley want on Saturday night?'
Carrie	'Excuse me?'
Sofia	'She came down to reception and spoke with you. What about?'
Carrie	'Oh … she just asked about Theresa Cook. I think she was waiting for her but she

hadn't heard or seen her. I told her about her accident.'

Sofia 'Did she say anything else to you?'

Carrie 'She wanted to speak with Geraldine, but I told her she had gone to the hospital with her mother. She wouldn't say what about.'

Sofia 'When was the last time you were in your staff bedroom?'

This change of direction caught Carrie off guard.

Carrie 'Why?'

Sofia 'Please just answer the question.'

Carrie 'Before breakfast. I've been on duty all day. Why?'

Sofia 'We believe we've found the weapon that killed Phillip Locke. It was discovered in your staff bedroom.'

Geraldine watched Carrie's expression carefully. She was surprised, then shocked at the allegation.

Carrie 'I ... I don't know what to say, other than I didn't put it there. I swear on my life I didn't hurt anyone. Why would I be silly enough to leave it where you'd find it? I knew the police have been searching the hotel, I was the one who gave them the skeleton key cards to search.'

Carrie shook her head in bewilderment.

Sofia agreed, wondering why anyone would hold on to a murder weapon.

Carrie	'It's always been safe here, on St Mary's. The staff rooms lock, but they are twin share. But in all the time I've worked here, we've never had any thefts.'
Sofia	'Did you know that Harriet Lamb was Geraldine's daughter?'
Carrie	'No. But when Harriet arrived on Saturday with her friend, I could see she was Geraldine's daughter.'
Sofia	'How do you get on with everyone at the hotel? Do you have any enemies?'

Carrie laughed at the idea.

Carrie	'Good lord, no. The staff here are really nice. There's always been a family atmosphere at the hotel. It's very homely, Geraldine made sure of that.'

Carrie looked down for a moment, as if she was having second thoughts about her last comment.

Sofia	'Anything small or trivial could be important.'
Carrie	'Well ... the only person I don't get on with, and I don't know why, is Barbara.

She's never taken to me. I thought maybe it was because of my close relationship with Geraldine. She can sometimes come across as jealous, snappy and even cagey at times. Which is silly, really.'

Sofia   'Why do you think that?'

Carrie   'I think Barbara is a lonely person. She snaps at me without reason. When I try to talk to her, she always brushes me off. I thought it might be shyness at first, but it's not. She's just rude. She keeps to herself mostly and I rarely see her socialise with the other staff.'

Sofia   'Did you run a background on Barbara before she started?'

Carrie   'Of course, Geraldine insists for every staff member. Her records checked out. I did ask her once about her family and life before moving here, as she hasn't taken any leave and gone to the mainland since she started working here. But she said there was nothing to tell, and that's all she said, so I didn't ask again. She's not into chit-chat.'

Sofia thanked Carrie and told her that was all for now. Sofia collected her mobile and headed up to room 201, before she planned to return to the hospital.

Sofia entered Clarissa's room, once Clarissa finally opened the door. Sofia promised Clarissa that her questions wouldn't take long. They sat down on the sofa together.

'Our investigation has led us to believe you may be pregnant. Can you please confirm this?'

'You do your homework, Chief Inspector. As it stands, yes, I am. About three months.'

'Did Phillip know?'

'Yes. I told him Saturday when he came up to my room. He was a little shocked by the news and left shortly after.'

'Do you think that would have altered his decision to leave his wife for you?'

'No. Phillip loved me, I knew that much. He would have come around to it.'

'What will you do now?'

'That's a personal question, and irrelevant to your investigation.'

'I'm sorry. I just meant it can be difficult raising a child on your own, I speak from experience. But it can also be very rewarding.'

'I'll manage.' Clarissa lowered her head; she wasn't entirely sure how she would cope on her own. She felt depressed and alone.

Sofia was relying on instinct in her assumption that Clarissa didn't kill Phillip or assault Theresa. She was far too calm and self-disciplined for such an aggressive and impulsive act. Her life had just been torn apart, her future had been ripped from under her, so she decided to leave the poor woman alone. Sofia thanked Clarissa and told her she could leave in the morning.

'Hi, Frannie. How're you getting on?' Sofia asked her daughter over the phone as she stepped out of the police car which had taken her to the hospital. It was only a short ride, but she didn't have the luxury of time to walk the few miles.

'Good. Nona and I took Archie to the park. You should have seen him run.'

'That's great. But make sure you teach him to obey. Remember what the trainer said, you don't want him running off.'

'I will. He sits when I tell him to now, and Granddad is teaching me a whistle so that he'll recognise it and come to me.'

Sofia laughed. 'That's great. I'm not sure when I'll be home, but hopefully I'll see you in a day or so. Harry is back in London now, so he may stop by to say hello.'

'Alright. What about your holiday?'

'We'll just have to reschedule for another time. Is your Nona there? Can I talk to her, please?'

Sofia heard her daughter yell out for her grandmother.

'How's the investigation going?' her mother asked.

'It's very tragic, but it's coming along. Is Archie behaving himself?'

'Argh, yes. Those two are inseparable.'

'Please tell me you haven't let him sleep on Francesca's bed?'

There was a slight pause on the other end of the line. Sofia knew she had.

'Mum!'

'I couldn't help it. They both pleaded with me with their big brown eyes. How could I say no?'

Sofia rolled her eyes as she walked into the hospital, 'quite easily, Mum.' Sofia had agreed to let Archie stay in the house at night, but under the condition he wouldn't sleep on Francesca's bed. *So much for rules*, Sofia thought. She said her goodbyes as she entered the ward.

Watching the kitchen staff hard at work preparing the evening's dinner menu had made Carl hungry.

He walked over to Claude and asked if he could have another word. Claude brushed him off and told him to come back later, he was busy.

Carl leaned in towards Claude and said quietly, 'I can speak with you informally in your office, or officially in an interview. It won't take long. I know you're busy, but this is a murder investigation.'

Claude could see the officer was not to be trifled with and realised he must have done his due diligence and checked with the French police. His shoulders dropped into submission and, after nodding at Carl, he removed his hat and walked into his office. His team watched on silently – not daring to comment. Barbara took the lead and told everyone to get back to work.

'How can I help you, Sergeant?'

'I'm sure you can appreciate that we had to do background checks on everyone working at the hotel.'

On y va, Claude thought. He had expected it.

Monday, 5:20 pm
Interview with Claude Allard

Carl   'I need to ask you about the assault on your wife that took place fourteen months ago in Paris.'

Claude	'I wondered when you would bring that up.'
Carl	'Can you please tell me what happened?'

Carl could see Claude was embarrassed and ashamed and would rather not recount his story.

Claude	'I loved my wife, Sergeant.'
Carl	'Then why did you hit her?'
Claude	'It's not as black and white as that. We were arguing and things got out of control.'
Carl	'Is that why you ended up here?'
Claude	'*Oui.* I worked in one of my father-in-law's restaurants. He owns a number of *dem* in France and Belgium. I love being a chef, but it means I work long hours. My wife was having an affair. *Contraire* to what you may think about the French, Sergeant, I believe in fidelity and *da* oath I took. I was faithful to Constance and I deserved *da* same respect. *Da* affair had been going on for some time. I came home early from work one night. I was unwell. I found them together in my bed. I grabbed him and threw him out of my house. My wife was so embarrassed and angry with me, she started throwing things at me. Finally, she threw a plate at me, but I deflected it and it rebounded back at her and hit her in *da* head. She sustained a cut to her head. There was a lot of blood. I was ashamed at

what I did because our fighting had woken our children. They saw what happened.'

Carl   'I see. Who called the police?'

Claude   'Francois, her lover, he heard us arguing from outside and called *da* police. I wasn't charged but cautioned. I lost my job and my home and I'm fighting for custody of my two children. My father-in-law made it clear I would never work in France again. He's tried and succeeded, in the past, to undermine any position I applied for.'

Carl   'That must have made you very angry.'

Claude   '*Bein sur,* of course, wouldn't you be? But I'm not a violent man. This is why I left France and came to work here.'

Carl   'Does Geraldine Locke know about your past?'

Claude   '*Oui.* I told her everything during my interview for head chef. She asked me to cook for her and I did. She offered me *da* job *dare* and *den*. I don't think she had many candidates, not of my calibre. St Mary's isn't for everyone. But I like *da* serenity of the Scilly Isles. I fly home once a month to see my children. Hopefully next year I can return to Paris and open my own restaurant and see my children more often. Geraldine has been good to me. I would never wish her harm or any of her family.'

'Thank you, Claude.' Carl believed him, he seemed beaten down but not out. He noticed two pictures on his desk of a young boy and girl.

Carl	'Has anything changed recently in the kitchen? Any tension, arguments or anything personal that has happened between your staff?'
Claude	'Do you suspect one of my kitchen staff, Sergeant?'
Carl	'We believe a pestle was used to kill Phillip Locke. It was missing on Sunday. I'm not accusing anyone, but we find it hard to believe a guest would come into the kitchen and take it.'

Claude was thoughtful for a moment.

Claude	'My two junior chefs are apprentices. I don't know them very well, but they seem to be *'appy* enough. They work hard and follow instructions. I'm *'appy* with *dare* work. They haven't said anything to me about their personal lives, neither have *da* waiters. My sous chef, Holly Burnett is very gifted, we're lucky to have her. She was born here on St Mary's. I suggested she should spread her wings and get more experience working in a Michelin star restaurant on *da* mainland, but *dat* idea intimidated her. She's comfortable here on St Mary's so I didn't push *da* issue.'

Carl   'What about Barbara Eyre?'

Claude   'Hard worker. She arrived about six months ago. She has a room in *da* staff quarters downstairs. She keeps to herself, but I think she suffers bouts of depression. I recognise the signs. But she gets over it and I have no complaints about her work. She's a fast learner.'

Carl   'I believe there has been a problem with thefts recently? Can you elaborate on that?'

Claude   '*Oui*, fish.'

Carl   'Fish?'

Claude   '*Oui*. But I have resolved that little issue.'

Carl   'Thank you, Claude. I appreciate you sparing the time to talk to me.'

Carl stood up to leave. He turned around at the door and said, sincerely, 'I hope you get to go home soon.' He nodded and left.

Carl called Shirley and asked if Barbara's child social services record had arrived yet. Shirley said they hadn't, so Carl printed a copy of the final witness statements taken and had them ready for Sofia to read when she returned from the hospital.

Geraldine and Callum were sitting across from each other beside their mother's bed in the hospital. Hazel was sitting by her mother's side. She had been crying again. Sofia wanted to update them on the investigation, the discovery of the murder weapon would spread fast through the hotel.

'Hello, Mrs Cook,' she said. Callum stood up to offer Sofia his chair.

'Thank you,' she said, but raised her hands to gesture there was no need.

'It's alright. I'm leaving shortly,' he insisted. Sofia thanked him and sat down. She was pleased Theresa was sitting up in bed. She had a nasty wound on the side of her head but she appeared coherent.

Sofia didn't want to talk about the case while Hazel was present. She looked up at Callum and nodded towards Hazel that he should take her home.

Geraldine kissed her daughter and gave her a long, tight hug. 'Go home with your uncle, sweet pea. I'll be home soon.'

Hazel reluctantly left. Sofia could now speak directly with Theresa and Geraldine.

'We found the murder weapon. It was a pestle, which was taken from the kitchen sometime late Friday evening.'

'You think it was a staff member?' Geraldine asked.

'Possibly, but I'm not ruling anyone out, yet. But I just can't see a guest stealing it.'

'So, you believe it was premeditated then? What about my mother's attack?'

'It's possible, Theresa, that you knew something and confronted your attacker, not realising the danger you were in.'

'Do you think it was someone who knows my family well?' asked Geraldine.

'I think so. We've checked the location of your phone that night through the cell towers and it wasn't anywhere near the hospital. Not until Hazel brought it to you.'

'Then someone came into my home and used it.'

Sofia nodded that they had, then she turned her attention to Theresa. 'I was hoping to ask you a few more questions, Mrs Cook. If you're feeling up to it?'

'I'll do anything to help, Chief Inspector. Poor Phillip, my grandchildren are very distraught. God, I wish I could remember who I agreed to meet. It's still hazy, it's more a feeling of dread than an actual memory.'

'Don't distress yourself, your memory will return. Just give it time but trust your instinct.'

Sofia asked Theresa about her father's affair with Stella Burrows.

'My mother told me about my father's affair and the child they had, William. She told me my father had numerous affairs, but they never lasted long. He would never leave my mother, he would've lost half his fortune, not to mention his reputation.' Theresa turned her attention to her daughter. 'Neither I nor your grandmother stood up to him when you were pregnant, Geraldine. We should have. But knowing what we knew we thought it was for the best that we kept you and Wesley apart.'

'It's alright, Mum,' Geraldine leaned forward and put her hand on her mother's. 'The past is the past, let's just think about the future.'

'When you first told us you were pregnant, I thought, we'll make it work. I could help raise the child while you continued at school. But when you told me who the father was, I panicked.'

'I told your father about your pregnancy and he confided in your grandfather, who was furious, to say the least. He wanted you to terminate it. But it was too late by then. We told William and Joanna Burrows about the two of you, but not that you were pregnant. It was all decided, you would head off to college the following year, while Wesley joined the navy.'

'Why didn't you simply tell Geraldine and Wesley the truth?' Sofia asked.

'We thought it best they never know.' Theresa started to cry, her years of built-up guilt and emotion was too overwhelming for her to control any longer. 'I was afraid of losing you. My father was adamant that you have nothing to do with Wesley. He was more concerned about his own reputation. When you met Harriet, you were so happy, I didn't want to see you get hurt again. But it was obvious you still loved Wesley.'

'Oh, Mum.'

'Christopher Burrows was a better man than my father ever was, and a war hero. He was a great father to William. My father's hatred only grew over the years as Christopher had the son he always wanted.'

'Serves the bastard right,' Geraldine spat.

Theresa put her hand out for her daughter's and said, 'Family is everything to me. I won't let anything come between that again.' On saying that, she paused and looked deep in thought. 'Something ... something's wrong.'

'With what, Mrs Cook?' Sofia asked.

'With Harriet. Something is wrong. God ... Why can't I remember? It's a feeling I have. Something is wrong. Her name? It's on the tip of my tongue. Why can't I remember?'

'What about her name?' Sofia urged.

'There's something ... the name is the same. But that can't be?'

'It's alright, Theresa, give it time. Your memory will return.'

'I think my mother needs to rest now, Chief Inspector.' Geraldine didn't want to hear anymore. What was her mother trying to say about Harriet? Whatever it was, she didn't want to hear.

'Thank you, Theresa. I'll let you rest now.'

Sofia said goodbye and reassured Geraldine that the police were still patrolling the hospital.

When Sofia arrived back at the hotel, Callum was waiting for her outside. He asked what transpired at the hospital. Sofia knew he was asking in a professional capacity and so she told him what was said. But as they continued to stroll along the path, Callum opened up about his family and himself on a more personal level.

'I always knew what I was, Inspector. I was never embarrassed about it as it was who I really was. But I was scared to tell my family because I knew how my grandfather and in turn, my father would react. They would make me feel less of a man. My grandfather fired Khenan in front of the junior partners at the firm, I was so disgusted with him. I quit there and then. That's why Andrew had no intention of working for the family firm, either. That hatefulness is gone now from our family. We're a grieving family. Phillip was a fool at times, and we were never that close, but he was a fool in love, that's all. For what that's worth.'

'I understand, I do. But in my profession I've met many ordinary people, who've lashed out on impulse, or in a moment of anger and regret. Sometimes good people do bad things.'

Callum only nodded his understanding. She knew he was only trying to protect his family. Sofia headed to the conference room, while Callum headed into the bar where he knew Khenan was waiting for him. He was heading back to the mainland the next morning.

'Anything else come in while I was away?' Sofia asked Carl when she entered the room.

'No. But I've printed all the witness statements and background checks on the staff and guests, which is now complete.'

Carl filled Sofia in on his conversation with Chef Allard.

'How did he come across? Did you believe him?'

Carl thought for a moment, but replied, 'Yes. I did. He misses his children and can't go home until he can find another job or open his own restaurant. He had no reason to kill Phillip that I could fathom, and less reason to attack Theresa Cook. He's grateful to Geraldine, I can't see him hurting her family. I checked his employee record and the assault charge is noted on it. Geraldine hired him anyway. I've pretty much ruled him out as a suspect.'

'She obviously believes in giving people a second chance,' Sofia said, almost to herself.

Sofia updated Carl on what took place at the hospital. 'I want the team to look deeper into Harriet's past. Check on her adoption and cross reference anything you find. Theresa Cook mentioned Harriet's name again. I don't know in what context she was referring to but check back as far as the adoption agency.'

'Will do. I'll get Shirley to do it, as she's looking into Barbara's child social services record as well. If there's something there, Shirley will find it.'

'Let's call it a night. I'm starving and I want to read through these witness statements. Do you want to eat together in the dining room? Or do you want your own space?'

'No. Dining room's fine. I saw what the chef was preparing tonight,' Carl said, licking his lips.

Sofia chuckled, 'Okay, I'm going upstairs to freshen up and I'll see you in the dining room at 7 pm.'

Sofia took the folder containing the witness statements upstairs to her room. She walked into the bathroom and ran a bath. She took a bottle of red wine out of the minibar and poured herself a drink.

The atmosphere in the hotel had shifted in the last few days, this was evident when Sofia walked into the dining room that evening. Each pair of eyes were upon her, and she knew why. She was no longer a guest on a romantic holiday, but a Chief Inspector investigating a brutal murder.

She nodded at a couple of guests who recognised her and who politely nodded back.

'How's the investigation going, Inspector?' Joan Herbert asked, as they were finishing off their desserts. 'Or can't you tell us?'

'It's coming along, thank you, Joan.' Sofia was pleased she remembered the woman's name. Harry and Sofia had joined the Herberts on a walk on the Thursday morning. They were good enough to show them the best walking tracks around the island that afforded the most splendid views.

Lorna and Hugh Grisham also nodded at Sofia. This had been their honeymoon. Lorna had wanted to leave once the police had confirmed they were free to go, but Hugh had talked her into staying, citing it would be a holiday they'd never soon forget. Although she didn't see it that way.

There was no sign of Wesley Burrows, Harriet Smith or Ashley Lamb. It wasn't surprising as they would only have been gawped at all night.

Even though the dining room was sombre, the meal was delicious. Sofia only wished Harry was sitting across from her instead of Carl. There was so much she wanted to say to him.

At 9 pm, Clarissa Montgomery sat alone in her room contemplating her future. Her bags were packed; she was leaving on a morning flight. She was grasping a half-empty glass of water and sitting on a small window seat.

She had planned it all; their wedding, their home, even how much time she would take off after the baby was born. Now, she sat alone in her room, looking out the window, wondering how she was going to manage without Phillip.

Clarissa rested back against wall and tried to remember Phillip's smell. His touch on her. She was going to miss more than just his physical presence – the security and companionship she had grown to love. She started to run her hand down her cashmere sweater, lightly over her breasts and resting her hand on her stomach.

Her confidence was waning, could she really go it alone? What choice did she have now?

'God damn you, Phillip,' she yelled to an empty room, throwing the glass across the room, then she started to cry.

Chapter Twenty

Tuesday, 8.00 am

Once again, all eyes were on Sofia and Carl as they quietly ate their breakfast in the sunroom. The light poured in through the windows, illuminating the conservatory. It was obvious to everyone that it was going to be a beautiful day on the Scilly Isles.

Their morning briefing was scheduled for 8:30 am. Shirley confirmed she had Harriet's adoption records, while Devish and Ronnie had spent yesterday cross referencing all the witness statements and phone records in the hope of finding a link. They had finally finished interviewing Phillip's work colleagues, but no one had a bad word to say about him, although they did know about his affair with Clarissa Montgomery.

PC Hubbard had put together a timeline of Phillip's movements for the last month in the hope of finding a link with anyone staying at the hotel or visiting the university that had arrived within the last week. So far, she had no luck.

'I'm sorry, guv,' announced Ronnie, 'but we couldn't find anyone who had a grudge against either Theresa or Phillip. If they had a dispute with someone, it must be recent and with someone on St Mary's. I think we need to concentrate on Harriet. Our motive must lie with her. We drew a blank with Harriet's friends, also. She was well-liked. Brought up in a happy home. Devish and I spoke with her parents yesterday. They're dead cut up about what's happened, Harriet had been so excited to meet Geraldine's children.'

'How did they feel about Harriet finding her biological parents?' Sofia asked Ronnie.

'They kept no secrets from Harriet. Susan Smith said they told Harriet that she was adopted at age seven. They didn't want her to find out later in life, as they felt it would be a betrayal of trust. Harriet had always been okay with it. She loved them, so they weren't intimidated when she announced she wanted to meet her biological parents. She wanted to know where she came from. Curious more than anything so they supported her in that.'

'Okay, thanks.'

'There's one more thing. Don't know how significant it is, but her parents said that when Harriet contacted the General Register Office, she had to fill in a form to obtain her original birth certificate. One question on the form asked if she wanted to speak with a counsellor before they handed her the information. It isn't compulsory, as she was born after 1975, but she said yes. When she went in for her interview, they said she had already requested this information. Harriet told them she hadn't. They were surprised, because their records showed they had been accessed recently. She asked her parents if it was them, they said no.'

'What if someone was impersonating her?' Hillary offered up.

'For what purpose?' Sofia replied.

Hillary couldn't offer an explanation.

'Harriet would have to provide her personal details before the General Register Office could hand over any details. Besides, why would anyone want to do that?' Sofia asked, pleased that Hillary was thinking outside the box.

'I'll check it out when I go there today,' Shirley said. 'You asked me to check out Barbara and Harriet's lives going back to their adoption.'

'Thanks, Shirley. Take Hillary with you.'

'Will do.'

'Do you have all the contact details from the witness statements?' Sofia asked her team.

'Yes. We're going through the last of them this morning,' Devish said.

Sofia thanked Devish and asked to be informed the moment they found a match.

'The murder weapon was a pestle,' Carl said, changing the subject, 'which I now know is used to crush herbs and spices. Some staff members have no alibi for Phillip's murder as they were asleep in bed at the time. I want you to prioritise them. I've flagged them on the email I sent you.'

'I'll get on that,' Devish said.

Ronnie announced, 'We can now eliminate Tommy Burke from our enquiries. CCTV shows him going into a pub in Hugh Town and not leaving until closing. The publican has confirmed that. Plus, the owner of the B&B confirmed his return early Sunday morning and confirmed he didn't leave until the next morning after breakfast.'

'Thanks,' Sofia said.

'One more thing you should know, while we were reviewing the CCTV cameras, we caught Tommy having an argument with a young man, on Sunday morning, near the ferry terminal. We've identified his as Andrew Locke.'

Sofia and Carl exchanged looks, disappointed more than anything else at being lied to. 'Okay, Carl and I will address that issue. You all have your assignments, please update us as soon as you have anything. Theresa Cook is starting to remember things. It won't be long before she remembers who attacked her.'

The team all said 'yes, guv' and the call was disconnected.

'What now? Do you want to talk to Andrew again?' Carl asked.

'I most certainly do.'

This time Geraldine didn't contact Callum, she wanted to confront Andrew on his own. Unless he specifically asked for his uncle, he was over eighteen, so legally there was no issue of an appropriate adult. Sofia decided to forego the courtesy.

'How can I help you, Inspector?' he said, when they entered the sitting room.

Tuesday, 9:00 am
Interview with Andrew Locke

Sofia	'You lied to us in your interview on Sunday.'
Andrew	'Excuse me?'
Sofia	'Please don't play games, this is a murder investigation. You were seen on CCTV

in Hugh Town on Sunday morning in a confrontation with Tommy Burke.'

Andrew instantly realised his mistake. He was embarrassed and ashamed that he lied because he had acted impulsively.

Andrew 'I … yes … I went into town on Sunday morning before I went to the hospital, to confront Tommy. I had a terrible feeling it was him who hurt my gran. I thought it was all my fault for exposing him as a fraud.'

Carl 'What happened between you?'

Andrew 'I did grab him because he turned away from me. He said he was in the pub all night. He said he had witnesses. He got angry that I accused him. He pushed me, I pushed back. I told him to stay away from Vivienne. I said I'd be looking out for him around Oxford, and that if I caught him with another woman, I'd expose him to the police.'

Sofia 'What did he do then?'

Andrew 'He just laughed at me, then threatened me, and so I pushed back. Then he walked to the ferry. I followed him to make sure he was leaving the island. I jogged home, I wasn't in for very long before Hazel came downstairs looking for dad. Once Mum told us about Dad, I wondered if Dad confronted him too.

Could he have killed Dad? But if he was in the pub all night, he would have had plenty of witnesses. Then you said, someone used Mum's phone to lure Dad to the boatshed, well how could he have done that? I panicked, I thought I'd made a terrible mistake.'

Carl 'You should have told us. We could have detained him before he boarded the ferry.'

Andrew 'I'm sorry, I was trying to protect Vivienne, and I messed up.'

Carl 'Is there anything else you've omitted to tell us?'

Andrew 'No. I swear.'

Sofia and Carl left the annex and headed back to the hotel to speak with Harriet and Ashley, but there was no answer at their room. When they returned downstairs, they asked Carrie if she'd seen them.

Carrie confirmed she saw them leave the hotel with Mr Burrows about half an hour ago. But unfortunately, she didn't know where they went.

Sofia and Carl walked towards the beach hoping to spot them. They had no luck, so Sofia told Carl to head south along the beach while she headed north.

'Call me if you find them.'

The sky was crystal blue as Sofia walked along the beach. Her mind drifted to happy times with Harry. She felt the sun's rays warm against her face. She almost forgot she was investigating a murder. People were out strolling along the beach and enjoying the many water sports on offer, taking advantage of the beautiful weather. There were sailboats circumnavigating the island. It made Sofia think of Harry. He had planned to take Sofia to watch the seals near Pelistry. He had pointed it out to her when they sailed past the bay last Saturday. She ached for Harry. She felt alone and wished Harry was with her, so they could stroll hand in hand together along the beach. Her thoughts drifted back to their sailing trip. Harry had found a small, secluded cove on the north eastern side of the island. They had gone ashore and picnicked for lunch. After finishing a bottle of white wine, they made love on a blanket, which had nestled down snugly to the curves and dips of their bodies in the sand. As first, Sofia was embarrassed, on guard in case someone came past. But before long she was lost in the moment in Harry's embrace. Nothing could touch her except pure happiness. They fell asleep in each other's arms, which was why they were late returning.

'Morning, Chief Inspector!'

Sofia was plucked away from her thoughts by James Herbert. He and his wife, Joan were walking in the opposite direction. They had their customary backpacks on and were on an extended walk around the island. He was holding his giant hiking stick.

'Morning, Mr Herbert.'

'Taking the morning off? I don't blame you. It's beautiful, isn't it?' Joan said, indicating the ocean with her outstretched arm.

'It is, isn't it?' Sofia said.

'But I expect you'd prefer to see it with your beau Harry?' she said.

'Yes…' Sofia smiled at Joan.

'Make sure you come back and finish what you started,' Joan said, pointing her finger at Sofia.

'We will.'

'Nicked anyone yet?' James asked.

Sofia chuckled, 'No. But we're making progress.'

Before they continued walking, Sofia asked them a question. 'You've been coming here for many years. What's your opinion of the Locke family?'

The Herberts looked at each other before Joan answered for the both of them.

'Geraldine has always been a gracious host. Which is why we love coming back each year. It's like our second home. Her children have always been polite and well-mannered. They sometimes work in the hotel during the holidays. So we've seen them grow up. Good kids. But we don't know them personally.'

'What about her husband, Phillip?'

The Herberts looked at each other again before answering.

'He was a bit of a shit if you ask me,' Joan said. 'He's got a bit on the side, you know.'

'Yes, so I've been told. How did you know?'

'She's here. I saw him going into her room the other night,' James announced. 'Told the police officer as much too.'

Sofia smiled, 'Yes. Thank you.'

'Look! The Scilly Isles isn't for everyone, it's quiet and isolated,' Joan declared. 'You either love it, or you don't. But the mainland isn't far away if you want the hustle and bustle of city life. I don't think Phillip ever took to it. He was an academic. Could have told you it wouldn't last.'

Sofia thanked them and continued on her walk. She didn't go far when her mobile rang. It was Carl telling her he'd found Wesley, Harriet and Ashley.

They agreed to meet at a café at Porthmellon Beach.

By the time Sofia arrived, they were all on their second coffee.

Sofia ordered a macchiato and a tall glass of water, before asking her first question.

'Could you take me through what happened when you went to the General Register Office to get your original birth certificate before adoption?'

'Ashley came with me. I was nervous but Ashley found the whole thing exciting. I filled in the forms, date of birth and so on. Mum helped me with the date of adoption. I submitted the form, then went in for an interview.'

'Your mother told one of my officers that they said you had already requested the adoption details several months prior.'

'Yeah, that was weird. I didn't. I just assumed it was a mix up.'

'Do you think Theresa's attack had something to do with that, Inspector?' Ashley asked.

'I can't say for sure yet, but we must investigate all connections, no matter how small. I would like our forensic team to run your DNA, Harriet, I need to confirm it's a match for Geraldine and Wesley,' Sofia quickly put up her hands. 'I'm just dotting the i's, you understand.'

'Yes, fine,' Harriet said.

'What are you thinking, Chief Inspector?' Wesley said.

'I'm not sure. But if Harriet didn't request the file at the General Register Office, I need to find out who did and why? We need to be thorough.'

'Harriet, did you get any indication from anyone that they weren't happy that you came?' Carl asked.

There was a moment's pause, 'No. We met Hazel last night in the lounge. She's sad about her dad but was keen to approach me and introduce herself.'

Ashley shook her head. 'What if it was a scammer? Someone obtaining Harriet's original birth certificate to commit fraud. Get a passport and so on.'

'It's a possibility,' Sofia said. 'Harriet's current passport would be in her adoptive name, if someone obtained her original birth certificate, then they could use her birth name.'

'That was what was niggling at me the other night. The mix up at the Register Office,' Ashley said, shaking her head.

'But what does all this have to do with Phillip?' Wesley asked.

'I don't know yet,' Sofia said honestly. 'But that's it for now. Thank you for your time.'

'Are Geraldine and Harriet safe?' Wesley asked.

'I think so. But just don't go anywhere on your own, Harriet.'

Harriet nodded, looking at Ashley.

'Please find out who killed Phillip,' he said.

'I will.'

Sofia and Carl headed back to the hotel.

Chapter Twenty-One

Sergeant Shirley Smith and Constable Hillary Hubbard arrived in Southport a little after 1 pm. They had a meeting booked with the same counsellor who interviewed Harriet at the General Register Office.

Showing their warrant cards, they didn't need to wait very long.

'I'm Alyson Burbridge, please come this way.' The counsellor escorted them into her office. 'I have her file here,' she said, tapping a file on her desk as she sat down.

'Thank you,' replied Shirley, as both police officers made themselves comfortable across from Alyson. 'Did anything stand out at all during your interview with Harriet? What was Harriet's demeanour like during the interview?'

'It was a standard interview. She said she'd always known she was adopted and just wanted to know who her birth parents were. When I showed her the original birth certificate, it only showed her mother's details. She was disappointed, but her friend said they could easily find out from the mother who her father was.'

'Do you remember the friend's name?'

'Yes. I've got it in my notes.' Alyson searched through her paperwork. 'Ashley Lamb. I remember Harriet being nervous, but her friend was very enthusiastic.'

'Harriet said that you believed she'd been here before to enquire about her adoption. Can you confirm that?'

'Yes. Our records showed that her file had been accessed about seven months prior. But she knew nothing about it.'

'Do you have the details of who enquired? Did they come in? I'll also need to see the original application form that this person filled in, also.'

'I'll dig it out for you.'

Alyson stood to leave the room.

'If we obtain the other application form, will it show us who requested it?' Hillary asked before she left.

'Correct. You can't just ask for someone else's adoption information. They would need to provide identification and other relevant details. The application form will show who asked for it, then we can ask them why.' Alyson left the room to seek out the paperwork.

Alyson returned within ten minutes with another file. She opened it and read through the contents.

'This is strange,' she said, at the completion of her review. 'I'm not sure what happened here. The surname of the adopted parents and the child's date of birth are the same. But the adoptee's name is different.' She handed Shirley the application form so she could compare both names and signatures. Shirley could see that Harriet's application form was filled in more concisely but the second one, signed by Anne Richardson, had not been filled out in full. She pointed this out to Alyson.

'Well, not all children know every particular detail of their adoption. They might not know their adoption date. But they should have a birth certificate with their date of birth on it, which doesn't change on either birth certificate. All this applicant knew,' Alyson pointed to the second application, 'was the surname of their adopted parents and her birth date. The other one,' Alyson pointed to Harriet's application form, 'knew quite a lot more.'

'So, we have two applicants asking for the same information. This second applicant, Anne Richardson, she must have made a mistake.'

'Well, I don't see how. See here,' Alyson said pointing to the application form, 'she's put the correct surname of Smith and her date of birth.'

'Are you able to do searches on your database, based on surnames, birthdates, and their sex?'

'Yes.'

'Could you run a search using the birthdate and see if we get any other matches? We only need female adoptees. There shouldn't be that many.'

Alyson agreed and started typing. Within a minute she brought up a short list of names and printed them. Alyson handed the list to Shirley.

Shirley scanned down the meagre names. Nothing caught her eye until she came down to the name Smith. Then below it was another adopted child with the surname Smythe.

'Here.' She showed Alyson the two surnames. 'Harriet wrote the name Smith and had attached her birth certificate, after adoption. But what if this applicant,' pointing to Anne Richardson, 'spelt the surname incorrectly. Maybe she didn't know the correct spelling and simply spelt it, Smith. The counsellor searched the database just like you have done now using the surname and date of birth written on the form. A match appeared so it wasn't scrutinised.'

'Oh my goodness. We must have given the first woman the original birth certificate of Geraldine Cook's child.'

'But she's signed it Anne Richardson,' asked P.C. Hubbard.

Alyson reviewed her file. 'That's because Anne Richardson was originally adopted by the Smythes. But she was put back into care at the age of four after they were killed in an accident. She was then moved around to various foster families until she was seven. Then she was adopted again by the Richardsons. The woman obviously didn't remember much of the first adoption as she was so young, other than the surname which she spelt incorrectly.'

'So, to clarify, this Anne Richardson was given the original birth certificate of Geraldine Cook's child in error. Instead of her own original birth certificate.'

Alyson was speechless for a long moment. 'Um, yes, I think she was.'

'I need a copy of this file, plus I need all records of Anne Smythe/Richardson adoption records. I also need a copy of Anne's original birth certificate.'

'Right away.' Alyson scurried out of the interview room, thoroughly embarrassed about her department's error.

'What a stuff up,' Hillary said to Shirley when they were outside the building.

'I want you to read through the file while I drive back to London. Make notes as you go along. Then we'll need to trace Anne Richardson.'

'Will do, Shirley.'

Shirley placed a call to Sofia, who was finally relieved they had a new lead to track down.

'Get that file copied and sent to me as soon as you return to the Yard. I'll speak to you once you're back in London. Have Ronnie run a background check on Anne Richardson, find out where she lives and if she's local, tell him to get over there. See if she's tried to make contact with Geraldine.'

'Yes, guv.'

'I'll speak with Geraldine and see if anyone else has contacted her, but I doubt it, otherwise she would have said.'

'Yes, guv.'

'We need to find Anne Richardson. If nothing else, she needs to know the truth. Have Devish cross-reference her name against the flight manifests and ferry service schedules.'

'Yes, guv.'

'That poor child. In and out of foster homes wouldn't have been ideal. Then to be re-adopted, that couldn't have been easy.'

'Hilary's going through the file now.'

'Good work. We need to know if Anne Richardson is on St Mary's. She may be unstable or simply looking for her birth mother. Finding her is now a priority, especially if she's realised Harriet is here.'

'Yes, guv.'

DC Ronnie O'Farrell kept knocking at the door of a ground floor apartment in a quiet street in Watford, north of London. But no one answered. He went next door and knocked on a neighbour's door.

An elderly gentleman answered. Ronnie showed him his warrant card and asked him if he knew his neighbour, Anne Richardson.

'Yes, I did. But she don't live there anymore. She just up and left one day.'

'When was this?'

'Oh … about six months past.'

'Did she say where she was going?'

'No, sorry. She rented the ground floor flat next door. She kept herself to herself, we only chatted about this and that. I'd say allo to her when I was out in me garden.'

'Do you know where she worked?'

'No. Oh … hang on. She said once about working the late shift at a hotel. But I don't know which one.'

'Did she ever talk about her family or where she was from, that sort of thing?'

The old man thought for a moment. 'No. Sorry. She was a quiet one. But I guess she just wanted her privacy. Why? Has something happened to her?'

'No. We just need to find her. We'll try her family.'

'Oh. I don't think she had any. I asked once whether she was going home for Christmas, but she said she was working through Christmas. I said that was a shame, but she only said she had no family. Sad, really.'

'I see. Thank you for your time.'

'I hope she's alright.'

Carl cross-referenced the name Anne Richardson against the guest list and staff employment records at the Windermere without any luck.

'If someone out there thinks that Geraldine Locke is her mother that could be a problem,' Sofia said. 'Especially now that Harriet's turned up. But would it warrant attacking Theresa Cook and killing Phillip Locke? The first attack may have been spontaneous, but the second was premeditated. Double check that there is a constable stationed at the hospital at all times until this is resolved.'

'Sergeant Ives is in charge of the police patrols, here and at the hospital, but wouldn't it be better to remove Harriet and Theresa from the island altogether?'

'Normally I would say yes. But Harriet said she wanted to stay. She said it would give off a callous impression if she just fled back to the mainland. She wants to stay for Geraldine and her grandmother, and I want to keep Theresa close in case her memory returns. I think she's safe enough at the hospital. Besides, Harriet has Ashley and her father with her now. If she goes home, the killer could simply follow her.'

'I'll call Sergeant Ives and update him on this latest revelation. Make sure his team's vigilant,' Carl said, before opening his mobile to make another call.

'Thanks, Carl. I'm going back to the hospital now. See if I can help jog Theresa's memory a little further into Saturday evening.'

'For my two pence worth, I still don't think Theresa's assault is linked to Phillip's murder,' Carl said, before his call went through.

Sofia conceded that Carl could be right, she still hadn't found any credible links between the two attacks. Sofia cursed under her breath how easily she'd jumped to conclusions, simply because she didn't like coincidences. She gathered her coat and bag as Carl disconnected his call.

Carl had to consider that their killer was staying at the hotel, so he couldn't rule anyone out, not even Carrie and the rest of the hotel's staff. Everyone was a suspect until proven innocent. But they either had motive, but had an alibi, or they had no alibi, but had no motive.

'It was a pathetic attempt to implicate someone,' he reminded Sofia. 'But someone at the hotel might hold a grudge against Carrie as well as Geraldine.' Carl felt a connection with Carrie from the moment he arrived, she was easy on the eyes, and easy to talk to. 'I did think for a moment that Carrie might believe she's Geraldine's daughter, she's the same age as Harriet. But Ronnie confirmed she wasn't adopted.'

Sofia told him to keep digging as she put her coat on and walked out of the conference room and through the foyer of the hotel. She found Carrie at reception assisting a guest. She only nodded as she passed her. Sofia accepted a lift in the police car, so it wasn't long before she was walking through the small hospital again.

Word had spread fast around St Mary's. People were uncomfortable, murder wasn't something they were accustomed to in the Scilly Isles. The hotel had become front page news in the local paper. Not the type of publicity Geraldine would welcome.

Carl knocked on the door of room 204. Wesley Burrows opened the door. He stood aside to let Carl enter.

Monday, 4:00 pm
Interview with Harriet Smith and Ashley Lamb

Carl   'I just needed to ask you a couple more questions, Harriet.'

Harriet 'Sure, anything to help.'

Carl 'Have you ever been approached by someone asking you about your adoption?'

Harriet appeared puzzled.

Harriet 'No. No one knew except my parents and Ashley.'

Carl 'What about you, Ashley?'

Ashley 'No. Only what I told you about Theresa, that someone approached her and said Harriet was a fraud.'

Wesley 'Why are you asking her these questions, Sergeant?'

Carl 'You were correct, someone did access your original birth records, but we believe it was an oversight at the General Register Office. Someone was given the wrong birth certificate.'

Wesley 'So, you're saying someone out there thinks Geraldine might be her mother?'

Carl 'Yes. It's a possibility. We're not ruling anything out yet.'

Wesley 'Should I take Harriet and Ashley home, Sergeant?'

Carl had to think for a moment; he didn't believe that was necessary, unless Harriet was having second thoughts about staying.

Carl   'She's safe enough with you and Ashley. But just don't go anywhere alone until we've made an arrest.'

Wesley   'She's not going anywhere without me, Sergeant,'

Wesley shifted his stance. Defiantly protective.

Harriet   'Are you any closer in finding out who killed Phillip Locke?'

Carl   'We've found a link, but I'll need you to be patient a little while longer.'

Harriet simply nodded.

Carl had no doubt her father would protect her. He left the room and headed back downstairs, when his mobile rang. It was Ronnie, he updated Carl on his conversation with Anne Richardson's neighbour. Carl immediately rang Sofia.

'Has my mum come back yet?' Hazel asked Carrie.

'Sorry, Hazel. She's still at the hospital.'

'Do I need to work in the dining room tonight?'

'I shouldn't think so, I've called in reinforcements. Why don't you go back home and stay with your brother and sister?'

'It's depressing being there. I'm hungry and I don't know when my mum's returning.'

'Well, I'm sure Chef will fix you something.'

Hazel made her way through the dining room and into the kitchen. She said hello to everyone as she was on a first-name basis with all the kitchen staff. They all offered their condolences. She looked a little forlorn when she asked if she could have a bite to eat before the dinner service began.

'*Bien sûr, petite,*' Claude said, only too happy to help Hazel. He could see she was miserable. It made him think of his own daughter.

'*S'il te plaît,* Barbara, make Hazel some pasta. We'll have you fed in no time, *ma cherie.*'

'Thanks, Chef.'

Hazel sat on the opposite side of the bench and watched Barbara put some pasta into a boiling pan on the stove. Then she returned to the counter and continued to prepare the vegetables for tonight's dinner service.

'How is your mum holding up, Hazel?' she asked.

'She's tougher than she looks. She's worried about Nan. But she's out of danger now.'

'Thank goodness for that,' she said, without looking up from her chopping board.

'Guess what! I have a new sister, and she didn't take nine months to arrive, either,' Hazel tried to chuckle.

'Really!'

'I met her yesterday. She's really nice, and you know, I can see Mum in her.'

Barbara carried on preparing the vegetables. She was using a sharp knife, which made fast work of the carrots.

'You should meet her, you'd like her.'

'I dare say, Hazel.' Barbara started to chop the celery.

'It must have been hard for my mum to give her up when she did. But she was adopted by nice people. So that's good.'

Barbara didn't answer but continued to chop more vegetables.

'Hopefully, she'll come back soon.'

Barbara stopped chopping and stared at Hazel.

She held the knife tightly in her left hand. 'That would be nice for your mum,' she said.

'Yeah, I'm going back to the hospital tonight. Nan has woken up, soon she'll be able to tell the police who hit her.'

Barbara put the knife down and walked over to the stove and removed the ravioli from the pan. She then added some pasta sauce, which she had made earlier, and handed the bowl to Hazel. She forewent the garnish and parmesan cheese as she knew Hazel didn't like it.

Chapter Twenty-Two

Tuesday, 5.00 pm

Sofia entered the ward to find Theresa sitting up and eating. Geraldine was diligently sitting beside her bed. Sofia asked Theresa how she was feeling this evening. Theresa could only say that she'd been better, but at least she had her appetite back. Especially, since Chef Allard had made her a mouth-watering stew that Geraldine had brought with her. She smiled all the same and asked Sofia to thank Harry for saving her life.

'How's the investigation going, Chief Inspector?' Geraldine asked.

'That's why I'm here. Has anyone approached you, other than Harriet, in relation to your daughter's adoption?'

Geraldine thought that a strange question, but said no.

'Does the name Anne Richardson or Anne Smythe mean anything to you, possibly in an email or phone call, or maybe a job application within the last several months?'

Again, Geraldine said no.

Sofia went on to explain what they discovered at the General Register Office. Geraldine was surprised by the revelation.

'Do you really think this person may be on the island, believing she's my daughter?' Geraldine asked.

'It's possible. We're trying to trace her now, but I was hoping we could retrace your steps on Saturday afternoon again, Theresa. It might help jog your memory a little more. Try to remember smaller details this time.'

Theresa moved her tray away and closed her eyes as she tried to focus her thoughts. She began by recounting her time in the bar and lounge, talking to a pregnant woman. Then headed to Callum's room once Khenan arrived. Theresa remembered that she was in good spirits.

'It was going to be a new beginning for all of us. Then I went back to my room to have a lie down before dinner.'

'What happened next?' Sofia urged.

'I remembered Ashley's text message, so I knocked on Harriet's door, but there was no answer, so I returned to my room, I was a little tired. Then Vivienne and her new boyfriend arrived, and we had an argument about her trust fund. They didn't stay long, not once he knew my answer.'

'Oh, Mum! You should have told me about Vivienne when she first approached you. I would have spoken to her about it. She falls in love too easily, and gets her heart broken each time.'

'I'm sorry, but you already had a lot to think about with Harriet. I thought I could handle it myself.'

'Go on, Theresa,' Sofia prompted.

'I laid back down on the bed for a rest, then there was a knock on my door sometime later, it woke me up.' Theresa started to get confused and closed her eyes again, but then opened them quickly. 'I remember now, she looked vaguely familiar.'

'Who?' Geraldine prompted.

'I don't know her name, but her face, I've seen it before in the hotel. She wanted to talk to me.'

'About what, Mrs Cook?'

'I can't remember. Why can't I remember? Think Theresa,' she admonished herself.

Theresa looked down at her hands. She turned them over, palms up, as if she was reading something on them.

'She showed me something. A piece of paper. God ... Why can't I remember what it was?'

'It's okay, Theresa,' Sofia reassured her. 'Do you remember anything else that night? Take your time. Do you remember if you took your mobile with you to the boathouse or did you leave it in your room?'

Theresa tried hard to remember.

'Yes, I did. I was told to keep it with me. Who told me to do that? Oh, come on Theresa,' she said, tapping the side of her head with her hand. Then she stopped and looked at Sofia, 'Ashley told me to take it with me and call her back as soon as I learned the truth.'

'Truth about what Mum?'

'I ... I ... It was about Harriet.'

Sofia decided to put some selective words in the mix. 'If I said the words, birth certificate or adoption to you, does that stir up a memory in relation to your meeting in the boathouse?'

Theresa started to panic. Something was wrong, flashbacks were surfacing. 'Oh God! I remember saying to her she was mistaken. I felt sorry for her. But she was adamant, she showed me a document. It's frustrating.'

'It's okay, Mum. Don't force it. It'll come when you're ready.'

Geraldine sat patiently beside her mother hoping she'd remember Saturday afternoon's events. But Sofia wasn't as patient and really needed Theresa to remember.

'Um … my scarf. I wrapped my scarf around my shoulders because I was cold. The wind was whipping across my face, and I remember thinking this was a bad place to meet, my hair was going to get wind-swept.'

Geraldine chuckled at her mother's selective memory.

'No. That's good, touch, smell, sounds, sensory images. It's coming back bit by bit,' Sofia reassured her.

Sofia called Carl and asked him to organise photos of all the female staff members. Then Sofia's mobile rang, it was Shirley with an update.

'Go ahead, Shirley.'

'I think we've found her, guv. Anne Richardson's original name was Barbara Anne Smythe. She was put back into care after her adopted parents died in a car crash. She was in and out of foster homes until around seven, when she was finally adopted by the Richardson's. She went by Anne Richardson after that. I've read her reports from child services. There were numerous accounts of disruptive behaviour at school. But nothing violent. However, there was a police report of an assault by Barbara – nee Anne – against her adopted father, Barry Richardson. The report states she hit him over the head with a statue. Cracked his skull open apparently. He received six stitches. She was twelve at the time. Her adoptive parents stated in their interview that their daughter had always been a difficult child, that she was a liar and liked to provoke confrontation. However, the psychologist's report doesn't say anything about behavioural problems, in fact the opposite. He said Barbara was an intelligent girl and believed her behavioural problems could possibly be down to the trauma she suffered as a child from losing both parents in the crash. She was also in the car but sustained minor injuries. Unfortunately, the Richardson family couldn't cope with her and put her back into care at thirteen. But she's had a clean record ever since.'

'That's great Shirley. Do you have a picture of her?'

'Yes. But it's old. It's at age thirteen. I'm scanning them now and I'll email them to you shortly.'

'Thanks, Shirley.'

Sofia waited for the email to arrive. But she already knew who Shirley was referring to. She just needed confirmation before she showed Theresa the photos. When the email arrived, Sofia opened the attachments and read through the reports. Sofia viewed the photo of Anne Richardson taken at the time of her arrest; there was no doubt that she was looking at Barbara Eyre.

Sofia walked over to Theresa's bed and showed her the photo. Fear gripped Theresa instantly, on recognition of the girl in the photo. She made a fist and held her nightgown tight as a flurry of memories started to surface.

'Why?' said Geraldine. 'Why would Barbara attack my mother?'

'Did you ever sense anything indigent about Barbara that gave you cause for concern?' Sofia asked Geraldine.

'No. Nothing. I knew Barbara had family issues, she gets maudlin at times, but she seemed to really like working at the hotel. She's a great chef.'

'I think Barbara believes that you are her biological mother.'

'The poor girl!' Theresa said, shaking her head.

Geraldine could only feel pity for her. She understood Barbara's desire to know her original birth parents. With numerous surnames and adopted parents, at such as young age, it would have been traumatic not having her own identity. She felt pity for Barbara; she obviously needed to belong to someone.

'I think there's been a terrible error made,' Sofia said. 'Barbara came here looking for you. But you said she's never approached you about it.'

'No. She must have been too scared. I remember during her interview she said she was here on a holiday and noticed the position vacant advertised in town, so she applied. I had no reason to say no as her previous employment was excellent. Christ! So you're saying she just changed her name and applied for a job at my hotel to be near me.'

'She changed her surname some time ago, obviously looking for a new start and wanted nothing to do with the Richardson family. Her record stated she changed it to Eyre, over five years ago.'

'What was she waiting for?' asked Geraldine. 'Why not simply approach me and tell me what she believed.'

'She's had a lot of tragedy in her life,' Sofia replied. 'Maybe she was afraid of rejection. Then when Harriet arrived, her hopes were dashed in an instant. It must have caused her to act out irrationally and violently.'

'Are you saying she's unhinged?' Theresa asked.

'I can't answer that. But that doesn't explain her motive for killing Phillip?'

Geraldine couldn't believe Barbara would attack her family.

Sofia was interrupted when her mobile rang again, it was Carl. He'd just received Shirley's email confirming that Barbara Eyre was Anne Richardson.

'I'm on my way back to the hotel. Put out a warrant for her arrest for Theresa's assault. She can't have gone far. Notify the airport and the ferry terminal.'

'Will do, guv. I'll head back into the kitchen now in case she's returned. The kitchen staff said she walked out for a cigarette break about ten minutes ago and never came back.'

Sofia grabbed her bag to leave, but Geraldine asked to accompany her.

'Please, Inspector, Barbara must be devastated. I can't condone what she's done to my mother, but I just can't believe she killed Phillip.'

Sofia agreed, but before leaving the ward she instructed the local constable to stay in the ward with Theresa.

Carl raced back into the kitchen but Barbara had not returned. The local police had started a search in and around the hotel for Barbara.

Hazel was finishing off her dinner and asked Carl why he was looking for her.

'We need to talk to her again about her movements on Saturday evening,' was all he could say.

The kitchen staff all looked at each other in bewilderment. Hazel didn't know whether to be angry or shocked by the revelation. Why did they believe it was Barbara? Barbara wouldn't hurt anyone, especially her grandmother or father, she barely knew them.

Claude stopped what he was doing and asked Carl if he thought she killed Phillip Locke.

'I can't comment on that, Claude. But I need to find her now.' Carl was about to head out towards the beach when Claude asked him to wait a moment.

Claude contemplated his next move, he knew Barbara had issues, but then didn't everyone. He always thought he was a good judge of character. She was an artist, like himself. Artists lived to create not destroy. That was his heartfelt belief. But he remembered the thefts that had taken place over the last few months and remembered what measures he took to catch the culprit. He asked Carl to follow him into his office. Carl hesitated but seeing that Claude had already turned his back on him, he thought it best to follow him.

Sofia asked Geraldine if there was any place on the island that she knew of, that Barbara liked to go to, to think or be alone.

Geraldine thought for a moment. 'Yes, there's a small bay north of the hotel, it's secluded, she likes to go there and have a cigarette, especially after her shift.'

When Carl left the kitchen, he received a text from the Chief Inspector advising where to look for Barbara.

Barbara looked out across the beautiful blue ocean, possibly for the last time. She decided to forego her cigarette this time and just breathe in the fresh air. Tears ran down her face. *How could she have got it so wrong*, she thought. She'd done a terrible thing.

She only wanted to find her birth mother. But Harriet claimed to be Geraldine's daughter now, not her.

It was time to turn herself in. It was only a matter of time before Theresa remembered what happened. She opened her phone and started to flick through photos of Geraldine. She reminisced at what could have been – as Geraldine's daughter. She felt morose, she didn't deserve any kind of happiness, not after what she'd done.

Barbara tapped her mobile phone until she was back at the home page, but something caught her eye in the reflection on the screen. She half turned around to see someone standing over her, but before she could acknowledge who it was, something hard clipped her on the side of her head. She fell down into the sand, dazed and in pain.

Carl raced out of the hotel. He was on his mobile yelling at Sergeant Ives to meet him down at the beach, in a small bay, north of the hotel.

Barbara could feel herself being dragged along the sand. Blood ran down her face, she could taste it as it entered her mouth. Then she felt the frigid water. It shocked her into consciousness; she tried to struggle free as she was dragged deeper into the ocean. Someone was forcing her head down into the salty water. Barbara couldn't comprehend what was happening. *Do I deserve this? No past deeds go unpunished*, she thought. But as she swallowed the cold salty water it brought her to her senses and she started to fight back. She wanted to live.

She used all her might to force her attacker off her. She was running out of time. She tried to open her eyes but the salt water stung her eyes. Finally, she dug her feet into the sandy bed and forced her legs up and tossed her attacker backwards into the water. Barbara quickly pulled herself up and gasped for air before opening her eyes to see who and where her attacker was.

Barbara regained her footing and stood up; she quickly gathered her senses but didn't know whether to heave herself back into shore or swim away from her attacker. She couldn't fight off a man, she wasn't strong enough and her head ached and she felt dizzy. Barbara spun around and saw Carrie lift herself up out of the water. She was momentarily relieved that it wasn't a man who attacked her, she'd have a fighting chance now, but when she saw the cold viciousness in Carrie's eyes, she knew she was in trouble. She never did like her.

Carrie came at her again, she was ferocious. Carrie grabbed at Barbara's hair and tried to force her head back down into the water. Barbara struggled to stay on her feet but Carrie was stronger, more determined. More enraged. Barbara lost her footing and went down under the waves again. She panicked as she tried to regain her footing. She couldn't get a foothold as Carrie had her arm around her neck and was forcing Barbara down with her knee pressed against her back. She started to swallow the salty water once again. Her breath had finally escaped her. This was it! She knew she was going to die.

Suddenly, Carrie let go, Barbara scrambled quickly to the surface and managed to take in a deep gulp of fresh air. She was disorientated and started coughing up salty water as she tried to find her bearings. Once she reached the shoreline she fell onto the sand in exhaustion. Still coughing, she looked across to see

Carrie lying on the sand, Sergeant Brooks was handcuffing her. Carrie looked feral as she struggled to free herself.

'I swear, I didn't kill your husband,' Barbara pleaded to Geraldine. 'Please believe me.'

Sofia and Geraldine had arrived back at the hotel and entered the conference room to find Carl, Barbara and Carrie wrapped in blankets. The kettle had just stopped boiling and a PC was making everyone a hot drink. Geraldine sat down across from Barbara, leering at her, waiting for her to deny what she'd done. Carrie sat on a separate table by herself, still handcuffed. Sergeant Ives was standing behind her. They had both been read their rights, and both had declined a solicitor. Carl and Sofia were pacing the room talking quietly between themselves when Callum arrived. He walked quickly up to this sister and sat down beside her.

Geraldine slammed her hand down on the table, defiantly, and said to Barbara, 'But you did hit my mother. Why?'

Barbara bowed her head, 'I'm sorry, Geraldine. I didn't mean to.' Tears were freely running down her face. 'I'm not a monster.'

'Why didn't you simply approach me? If you were angry with me, you should have taken your frustration out on me?'

'I would never do that,' Barbara said, wrapping the blanket around her, more tightly for protection and slowly rocking herself for comfort. 'I was afraid. I wanted to every day, then I heard that another woman arrived, stating to be your daughter and my head started to spin, I was confounded. I approached your mother to find out if it was true, but she just laughed and said I was mistaken. I showed her my birth certificate, but I had the adoption papers in my room. We agreed to meet so

I could show her. Then in the boathouse when I gave her the documents, she just shook her head and said I was wrong. She thought I was delusional. Your mother destroyed all my hopes and dreams in a single moment, without a second thought of how I felt. I felt so inconsequential.'

Geraldine kept shaking her head in disbelief. 'Barbara, I'm sure that wasn't her intention. But there has been a terrible mistake made.'

'If you hit her in a moment of anger, why did you then proceed to move Theresa down the ramp so she would drown when the tide came in?' Sofia asked her.

Barbara looked up at her, shocked by the revelation. 'I … I didn't put her in the water.' She kept looking around the room at each person, they were all judging her. 'I was angry, yes, I lashed out at her and hit her. I panicked and ran out of the boathouse. I expected to be arrested, lose my job, but when I heard she nearly drowned, I grew frightened. I didn't know how that could have happened. I knew I would be blamed for it all the same.'

At that moment, the door to the conference room opened and Theresa Cook was wheeled in by the local constable who had been assigned to guard her.

'Mother, what the hell are you doing here? You should be in the hospital,' Callum said.

'I'm fine, the doctor said I could recuperate here at the hotel. I've remembered what happened in the boathouse,' she said in Carrie's direction. Then Theresa looked at Barbara, who lowered her head in shame.

Geraldine made room for her mother's wheelchair beside her.

'Barbara, my team spoke to the General Register Office, we uncovered a terrible mistake. They gave you the wrong original birth certificate.'

'What?' Barbara couldn't comprehend what Sofia had said.

Sofia took a step towards Barbara and handed her a copy of her birth certificate – after adoption, and of her adoption papers. 'Barbara, you were born on the same day as Harriet, and both of you were put up for adoption. But your adopted parents, the Smythes, were killed in a car crash a few years later.'

'Yes.' Barbara was looking from Sofia to Geraldine not fully understanding what Sofia was saying.

Sofia continued, 'You were put back into care until you were seven then adopted again by the Richardson's but your time with them wasn't ideal and for that I'm truly sorry. You were then put back into care until you left school and started your apprenticeship.'

'So … you've read my file. That doesn't make me a killer. I just wanted to find my mother, my birth mother.'

'I know,' Sofia continued, 'but your adopted family surname was Smythe. Spelt S-M-Y-T-H-E but on the application form you filled in at the General Register Office, you wrote S-M-I-T-H and the case worker found the file with that spelling of the surname. It just so happened that it had the same sounding surname and date of birth as yours. But it was the wrong family name.'

'Oh, Barbara, I'm so sorry,' Geraldine said. 'All this time you thought that I was your mother. I wished you had said something earlier.'

Barbara just shook her head. 'I was afraid you'd reject me.' Barbara couldn't hold back the tears any longer, she no longer had the strength to be resilient.

Sofia continued, 'Tell me about your adopted parents, Beverley and William Smythe?'

Barbara kept shaking her head – not wanting to remember.

'It must have been hard for you, after the accident, being put back into care.'

'My parents were kind and loving, they were there one day and gone the next.'

'Then the Richardson's adopted you.'

'I don't want to talk about them,' snivelled Barbara, still trying to forget the ordeal.

'I'm sorry if they treated you badly, Barbara, they had no right,' Sofia said, kindly.

Barbara was looking down at the table. All her spent anger, rage, and regret were finally released in a flood of sobs which she couldn't hold back. She was deflated.

'I changed my surname to Eyre because I wanted nothing to do with the Richardson's. I was going to change it back to Smythe but the memory of their deaths was still painful so I changed it to someone who was always close to my heart. Another orphan, Jane Eyre. It was the last book my mother bought me before she died.' Barbara started to rock back and forth. Then she stopped and looked up at Sofia.

'The Richardsons wouldn't even let me keep my first name,' she said. 'I had to be called Anne. They didn't like Barbara. It didn't matter that it was my name. I could never please them, no matter how hard I tried. They were never satisfied. I was a disappointment to them from the beginning. Then I stopped trying. Fuck them, I thought.'

Geraldine moved her chair closer to Barbara and put her arm around her to calm her. 'I would have been proud to have called you my daughter. But you have to put the past behind you, otherwise it will consume your life. I know better than most how regret can eat away at you. You must only think about your future.'

Barbara slowly pulled away from Geraldine. 'What future? I don't even have a home anymore. All I have is prison, which is what I deserve.'

Geraldine was thoughtful for a moment, then spoke softly to Barbara. 'Yes, you do. You have a home at the Windermere. I know you didn't mean to hurt my mother and I'm not sure what will happen to you, but once the dust settles, your job will still be here for you, if you choose to return.'

Barbara looked kindly at Geraldine, she was overwhelmed and couldn't believe what Geraldine had just said. She didn't deserve it.

'Why would you do that?'

'Because I understand your pain.' Geraldine touched Barbara's face with the palm of her hand. The intimacy was too much for Barbara, who quickly flinched backwards.

'Barbara, you're going to be charged with the assault on Theresa Cook,' Sofia announced.

Barbara nodded that she understood what she had done. But reiterated that she didn't kill Phillip Locke. 'I swear on my life, Geraldine, I didn't.'

Carrie had sat quietly while these revelations had been revealed, pleased that Barbara had admitted to Theresa's assault. She had protested her innocence all the way from the beach, but Carl had refused to listen to her.

'You keep telling yourself that, Barbara,' Carrie said. 'I told you she was deranged. It was probably her who tried to frame me for Phillip's murder. I only went down to the beach looking for her because she was needed in the kitchen. Then she just attacked me and tried to drown me. I had to fight back otherwise I would have drowned.'

'You keep telling yourself that, Carrie,' Carl said, distastefully.

'Chief Inspector,' Theresa spoke up. 'What if I don't wish to press charges against Barbara?'

Barbara looked dumbfounded at Theresa after her startling remark.

'Unfortunately, that will be up to the CPS to decide, not you Mrs Cook, but under the circumstances they may be lenient. But I can't guarantee anything. A constable will take your full statement Theresa, now that you've remembered everything.'

'Of course, Inspector.'

Sofia and Carl often had a suspect with motive but lacking evidence. But this time they had evidence but lacked the motive for Phillip Locke's murder. Sofia wanted to chastise herself, she had led the investigation under the assumption that Theresa's assault and Phillip's death were committed by the same perpetrator. She chastised herself for allowing this case to become too personal.

'We will be charging Barbara with common assault. But we're going to charge you, Carrie, with the murder of Phillip Locke and possibly the attempted murder of Theresa Cook.' Sofia read Carrie her rights again but added the murder of Phillip Locke to the charges.

Sofia watched Carrie's reaction, but she remained stony faced, as if what was just said hadn't registered. She simply rubbed her hands across her trousers, as if brushing lint of them. She had a hotel blanket wrapped around her to keep warm, as did Barbara, but she didn't appear to be shivering, even though her demeanour was ice cold.

'Why would I want to kill Geraldine's husband? I barely knew him.'

'True, but you're close to Geraldine and cared about her very much. Was it jealousy towards Harriet that threatened your position here?'

Carrie scoffed at the thought. Sofia turned her attention to Theresa, and continued her summation, 'Theresa, do you remember how you ended up down the ramp and submerged in the water? Did Barbara drag you down into the water?'

Theresa looked at Barbara, then shook her head. 'I remember arguing with Barbara, then she hit me and I fell against the wall of the boathouse. Barbara ran off and I couldn't get up. I was very dizzy. But after a while someone came in. I remember seeing Carrie look down at me. I was relieved. I thought she was going to help me but instead I felt myself being dragged. Then I became very cold and wet, and I couldn't get up. That's all I remember.'

Sofia turned back to Carrie. 'You saw Barbara and Theresa go into the boathouse and then see Barbara run out shortly after. You then went down to the boathouse to investigate. You saw Theresa lying on the ground barely conscious and saw an opportunity.'

'That's ridiculous! Why would I?'

'It was you who went into the annex and used Geraldine's phone to lure Phillip to his death. You knew Geraldine was at the hospital so she had an alibi. You knew her family would all be there, so they all had alibis.'

'Why would I kill someone I barely knew?' She opened the palms of her hands to indicate the emptiness of her summation.

'That's what I want to know. We know you stole the pestle from the kitchen and used it to kill Phillip Locke. We have video footage of you entering the kitchen and taking the pestle from the mortar on Saturday night.'

'That's a lie. There aren't any security cameras in the kitchen.'

Sofia looked over to Carl and nodded at him. He opened his laptop and brought it over to the interview table. Geraldine and Callum came around to look at the video footage. No one spoke as they watched the video. He opened a video file and pressed play. The video footage showed Carrie walking into the kitchen late Saturday evening and taking the pestle from the mortar and putting it in her pocket.

Carl took the lead. 'Chef Allard had been concerned about the amount of fish being stolen from the kitchen so he attached a small camera on the wall of the kitchen to see who was taking his stock. He'd uncovered the culprit on the Friday morning, it was Hazel. She was taking fish to feed a baby seal she'd found over on Pelistry Bay. She was concerned it didn't have a mother to care for it. She owned up to Chef Allard when he confronted her on Friday afternoon before her shift started. But the camera was a motion sensor camera and only came on when there was movement in the kitchen. He hadn't removed it on Saturday. The only person to enter the kitchen after 11 pm was you, Carrie. Clearly taking the pestle from the kitchen table.'

'Why?' Geraldine shouted. 'I've only ever supported you.'

Carrie looked down at the table to compose herself. She hadn't expected to be captured on camera. This was an unexpected setback. She thought she'd planned for every contingency. Carrie gave herself a minute to compose herself before she continued. There was no point denying it, not now, it was there for everyone to see.

'I overheard you talking about divorcing Phillip. He'd want half the hotel. I couldn't allow that.'

Geraldine took a step back, stunned by Carrie's coldness and presumption, 'You ... couldn't allow it?'

Carl asked Carrie why she crudely planted the pestle in her own room.

'Why? Because this is my home! I was going to run this hotel for Geraldine one day and her pathetic cheating husband was going to take half of it. I've seen the hotel's books; she couldn't have afforded to buy him out. Her only option would be to sell the hotel. Which I couldn't let happen. I did it for you, Geraldine. For us.'

Geraldine gripped her fists over the top of the chair and squeezed them tightly to stem the rage that was building up inside her.

'Why would you presume to think it would be you that would run this hotel one day, Carrie? Geraldine would more likely pass the running of the hotel on to one of her children,' Sofia said.

Carrie scoffed at the idea. 'They don't want to stay here. This island is beneath them. They think they're too good for this place. I'm the best person to run this hotel and Geraldine knows it. You've said so, many times.'

Geraldine's face had turned to stone.

'How did you know Phillip was going to divorce Geraldine, and claim half the hotel?' Carl asked.

'I heard him talking to someone on his mobile on Saturday. His lover apparently. That's how I knew about Harriet before she arrived. He wasn't going to leave with nothing.'

'That was my concern, not yours. My business, not yours!' Geraldine shouted.

'I did you a favour!' Carrie shouted back. 'You'll see that in the long run.'

Geraldine uncharacteristically lunged at Carrie and slapped her across the face. Carl quickly pulled her away. Callum took hold of Geraldine and tried to calm her.

Carrie tried to compose herself. She rubbed her cheek, then turned from Geraldine and looked squarely at Carl, defiantly.

Carl closed the laptop, and said, 'did you see Barbara go into the boathouse?'

'Yes, everything was going fine until Geraldine's mother interfered. Why the hell couldn't she leave well alone? I overheard her talking to Geraldine on the phone about Harriet, her long lost love child,' Carrie scoffed at the thought.

'Were you jealous of Harriet?' Carl asked.

'In a way, yes. But as long as she kept her paws off the hotel, I had no quarrel with her. Then I heard Geraldine and Theresa talking about new beginnings and how she had to think hard about the hotel's future. Making up for lost time with Harriet. Blah, blah, blah. Theresa suggested Geraldine sell up.'

'Why would that make you angry? You're just an employee, you could've worked anywhere in England, or Europe for that matter, with your credentials,' Theresa interrupted, shocked by Carrie's brazenness.

'As I've said before, this is my home,' she yelled, leaning forward. 'Why the fuck should I leave? Geraldine has been more like a mother to me, than my own pathetic mother has. She saw potential in me. She admires me. I know this hotel inside and out. I'm the one who should take over from Geraldine, not Andrew, Vivienne, or Hazel or bloody Harriet. I wasn't going to be pushed aside and forced to leave my home.'

'Tell us what happened on Saturday afternoon?'

Carrie looked up at the ceiling, then around her, thinking how much she was going to miss the hotel. Then her shoulders dropped and she looked across at Sofia.

'I saw Theresa enter the boathouse, followed shortly after by Barbara. Then Barbara ran out, and no Theresa, so I walked down there and saw her lying on the top of the ramp. Her head was bleeding. Stupid old fool. I moved her down the ramp and left her there. Too many people have hurt Geraldine over the years, her mother being one of them and her husband being the other. I thought, everything would get back to normal if they weren't around anymore to cause her any more pain.'

'Did you take her mobile?' Carl asked, still in shock that he had actually cared for this cold-blooded killer.

'Yes, I saw it on the floor by the door. I was going to put it in her pocket but when I pressed the screen there was a message on it from Ashley asking her about her meeting. I had to assume Ashley knew she was meeting Barbara, so I saw an opportunity to kill two birds with one stone. I could lay all the blame on Barbara.'

Carrie confirmed it was her who took Geraldine's phone from her kitchen counter and texted Phillip. Luring him to his death. She had disabled the security cameras and confronted him in the boathouse.

Everyone remained silent for a minute until Sofia spoke up.

'Thank you, Carrie. Sergeant, please place Ms Ford under arrest for the murder of Phillip Locke and the attempted murder of Theresa Cook.'

'You cold bloodedly killed an innocent man for nothing, you spiteful bitch,' spat Geraldine.

Everyone stopped what they were doing and looked at Geraldine.

'Phillip would not have gotten half this hotel,' Geraldine said. 'It was given to me as a gift from my grandmother. He would only have been entitled to ten percent, which was half the proceeds of our house, and a percentage of profit earnings. I was going to divorce him and keep the hotel.'

Carrie's face went blank. She had prided herself on knowing everything that went on in her hotel, but she hadn't known that.

Sofia watched as Sergeant Ives escorted Carrie from the room. She instructed the other local constable to keep the two women separate at all times when they were held at the police station.

'Good work, Carl. The video was our smoking gun,' Sofia said to her sergeant quietly.

'Thank the paranoid head chef, Claude for that,' he smiled.

Sofia could see how distraught Geraldine was, she was still in disbelief.

'It's often the case in life that we don't always know the true worth of a person,' Sofia said. 'Carrie was obviously obsessed with you and the Windermere. She interpreted your kindness and interest in her for something other than professionalism and probably preferred you to her own mother, so she killed to preserve what she had.'

'Do you think she would have killed Harriet?'

'I can't say. If Harriet had shown any interest in the hotel in the future, she may have done something about it. It's in her nature to protect what she sees as hers. Similarly, as to why Barbara lashed out at your mother, when she thought she'd lost what she'd only just found … you. Only, Barbara acted on impulse, it wasn't premeditated. She so desperately wanted you to be her mother.'

'These poor girls. So insecure. Will Carrie get life?' Theresa asked.

'Quiet possibly, she's shown no remorse.'

'I need to go to my children, Chief Inspector. I need to tell them what's happened.'

'Please do. We have reports to write up but we've finished here now. We'll head home tomorrow.'

'Thank you for everything, Sofia.'

'You're welcome, Geraldine.'

Both women shook hands before Geraldine picked up her coat and wheeled her mother out of the room, alongside her brother, Callum. He nodded towards Sofia and Carl, indicating his gratitude. Sofia unlocked her mobile and rang Wesley to update him and Harriet on the arrests, she didn't envy Geraldine having to tell her children who killed their father.

Sofia sat down and took a deep breath, then she called Francesca. She needed to hear her voice.

'Hi, sweetheart, how's everything going at home?'

'Everything is fine, mum. Harry's here, he's having dinner with us tonight. Nona has made his favourite, steak and kidney pie, yuck.'

Sofia laughed into the phone. 'Just pick out the kidney pieces, you'll be fine. I'll be home tomorrow.'

'That's great. Do you want to speak with Harry?'

'Yes, please.' Sofia waited a minute until she heard his warm and reassuring voice on the other end.

'Have you solved the murder, Chief Inspector? Who dunnit?'

'Carrie, the assistant manager.'

'What? She was so nice. I guess you never can tell.'

'I've missed you. I'll be home tomorrow.'

'Don't worry about the holiday. We'll organise another one. What about Santorini or Mykonos?'

'I don't care, as long as it's with you and there's no murder to solve.'

Harry chuckled, 'I love you.'

'Love you too.'

'Let's go home, Carl,' Sofia sighed, after disconnecting the call.

'Only if we fly, I've just seen the weather report.'

Sofia smiled at her fearless sergeant.

Chapter twenty three

Two months later

Geraldine walked into the hotel's kitchen and found Barbara preparing a sauce for one of the night's dishes.

'Barb, can I have a word? Someone's here to talk to you.'

Barbara looked to Chef Allard, who nodded, before she asked one of the junior chefs to take over. She followed Geraldine through the hotel and into her office.

Barbara had pleaded guilty to the assault, but after Theresa and Geraldine both stood up and spoke on her behalf at her sentencing hearing, the judge gave her a suspended sentence and community service. Geraldine had kept her word and allowed Barbara to keep her job at the Windermere.

When she entered Geraldine's office, she was introduced to a case worker from the General Register Office.

'Please take a seat, Barbara.'

'My name is Alyson Burbridge, I want to sincerely apologise for the error we made in giving you the wrong birth certificate nine months ago.'

'It was as much my fault, for giving you the wrong information.'

'I'm here because I have reviewed your original birth certificate and took the liberty to investigate your birth parents with the help of Chief Inspector Faraday. I have their details here with me if you still want to know who they are. If you no longer wish to know, I'll hold them in my office in case you change your mind. But I thought I would come in person to offer my apologies.'

Barbara looked at Geraldine for guidance, she did and didn't want to know. She couldn't cope with any more disappointment and heartache.

'It's up to you,' Geraldine said. 'But it's better to know than not know in my opinion. I lived without knowing Harriet all those years, and it was an ache that doesn't go away.'

Barbara trusted Geraldine's opinion; she nodded at the case worker and took a deep breath and said, 'alright.'

'Would you like me to leave the room?' Geraldine asked.

'No. Please stay.'

Alyson continued, 'Barbara, your mother's name was Nola Donnelly, she was thirty-two when she had you. Unfortunately, she was a long-time drug user and succumbed to her condition over fifteen years ago. She's buried in a cemetery in Somerset. I have the details here.' Alyson handed over the paperwork of the cemetery's location and the plot number. 'I'm so very sorry. However, your father was listed on the original birth certificate. He's still alive and living in Hereford. He's married with two grown children. I have his contact details with me. If you wish,

I'm happy to contact him on your behalf and see if he would like to meet you.'

Barbara took the paperwork and read his name on the birth certificate.

'I ... I don't know. What if he doesn't want to know? Or maybe he's no better than the Richardson's.'

'From the Inspector's investigation, your mother met him while she was at a clinic, getting over her addiction. He was a patient at the same clinic, after a work-related injury he had grown addicted to painkillers.'

'But what if he's kind and would jump at the chance to know you?' Geraldine asked. 'Just like Wesley was with Harriet. Do you want to deny yourself a father?'

Barbara knew Geraldine was being kind, but she wasn't so sure this time.

'I'd like to think about it for a while.'

'That's fine, Barbara,' Alyson said. 'Take as much time as you need.'

'I'm happy in the here and now.' She looked at Geraldine, who nodded she understood.

'Small steps. Barb.'

Barbara thanked Alyson and Geraldine before she left Geraldine's office. Instead of going back to the kitchen, she walked out the hotel and down towards the beach.

It was a beautiful day. Summer had arrived in all its glory. Barbara sat down in the sand and as she raised her face to the sun, she closed her eyes and felt its warmth infuse into her skin. She finally knew who she was, and where she belonged. It felt as penetrating as the sun's rays through her body.

Barbara could now let go of her past because she was finally in control of her future. She could steer her life in any direction she wanted. She heard the seagulls squawking overhead as she weighed up the possibility of yet another rejection. She sat with her feet in the sand for a full half-hour until she made up her mind.

Geraldine escorted Alyson Burbridge out of the hotel. But she didn't re-enter straight away. She headed down to the beach. The last month had been a whirlwind of emotion for her family. But they had gotten through it, together, as a family.

Geraldine had only seen Wesley once since that awful weekend, at Phillip's funeral with Harriet. They had agreed to keep a respectful distance apart. Yesterday, she finally asked him to return to St Mary's as she had something important to discuss with him. She needed to be honest with him and expected the same in return. Geraldine didn't want their relationship to end up like two ships that pass in the night. That kind of relationship would never last. Her life was The Windermere; she didn't want to live on the mainland. But she couldn't ask him to give everything up for her, he had his career to think about. Geraldine had hardened herself for their final goodbye.

She found Wesley sitting on a sand dune looking out across the ocean. His arrival coincided with Barbara's visitor; they had arrived on the same flight. Geraldine asked him to wait, as she wanted to be present to support Barbara. Wesley had taken himself off for a walk along the beach.

Geraldine walked up to Wesley and sat down next to him. She took a deep breath and said what she needed to say. Then she held her breath, waiting for his reply. To her surprise, he simply wrapped his arm around her and spoke softly to her.

'I've decided to retire from the navy at the end of the year,' he said. 'I'll still do reservist work, but I thought I would buy myself a boat and start a charter service, take people fishing and sightseeing, so why not do it around the Scilly Isles. What do you think? I was hoping that there'd be a place for me here, too?'

Geraldine's smile erupted across her face, tears of happiness overwhelmed her, 'Would my guests at the Windermere get a discount?' she asked, snuggling into his chest.

Wesley chuckled. 'Absolutely. But I'm going to marry you Geraldine, as soon as you say yes. I'm not losing you a second time.'

Geraldine snuggled deeper into his embrace, feeling a sense of serenity. They sat on the sand dune and watched the sun begin to set.

THE END